F   Block, Lawrence   HC
BLO   A ticket to the
           boneyard

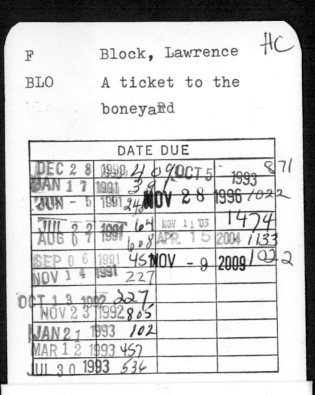

A
TICKET
TO THE
BONEYARD

Mathew Scudder Books by Lawrence Block

Lawrence Block

A TICKET TO THE BONEYARD

A Matthew Scudder Novel

WILLIAM MORROW AND COMPANY, INC.
NEW YORK

Library of Congress Cataloging-in-Publication Data

Block, Lawrence.
    A ticket to the boneyard : a Matthew Scudder novel / by Lawrence
Block.
      p.   cm.
    ISBN 0-688-09070-2
    I. Title.
PS3552.L63T44   1990
813'.54—dc20   90-5710
                                                                              CIP

Printed in the United States of America

          4   5   6   7   8   9   10

BOOK DESIGN BY KATHRYN PARISE

For Lenore Nathan Block Rosenberg

Hi, Mom!

Several of nature's people
I know, and they know me;
I feel for them a transport
Of cordiality;

But never met this fellow,
Attended or alone,
Without a tighter breathing,
And zero at the bone.
          —EMILY DICKINSON,
            "The Snake"

A bloody and a sudden end,
          Gunshot or a noose,
For Death who takes what man would keep,
          Leaves what man would lose.
He might have had my sister,
          My cousins by the score,
But nothing satisfied the fool
          But my dear Mary Moore;
None other knows what pleasures man
          At table or in bed.
What shall I do for pretty girls
          Now my old bawd is dead?
          —WILLIAM BUTLER YEATS,
            "John Kinsella's Lament for Mrs. Mary Moore"

A
TICKET
TO THE
BONEYARD

ONE

New York had a cold snap that year right around the time of the World Series. Oakland and the Dodgers were in it, so our weather didn't affect the outcome. The Dodgers surprised everybody and won it in five, with Kirk Gibson and Hershiser providing the heroics. The Mets, who'd led their division since Opening Day, were in it through seven playoff games. They had the power and the pitching, but the Dodgers had something more. Whatever it was, it carried them all the way.

I watched one of the games at a friend's apartment and another at a saloon called Grogan's Open House and the rest in my hotel room. The weather stayed cold through the end of October and there were speculative stories in the papers about long hard winters. On the local news shows, reporters took camera crews to farms in Ulster County and got rustics to point out the thick coats on the livestock and the woolly fur on the caterpillars. Then the first week of November Indian summer came along and people were out on the streets ·in their shirtsleeves.

It was football season, but the New York teams weren't

showing much. Cincinnati and Buffalo and the Bears were shaping up as the power in the NFL, and the best Giants linebacker since Sam Huff drew a thirty-day suspension for substance abuse, which was the current euphemism for cocaine. The first time this had happened he'd told reporters that he had learned a valuable lesson. This time he declined all interviews.

I kept busy and enjoyed the warm weather. I was doing some per diem work for a detective agency, an outfit called Reliable Investigations with offices in the Flatiron Building at Twenty-third and Broadway. Their clients ran heavily to attorneys representing plaintiffs in negligence suits, and my work consisted largely of tracing potential witnesses and getting preliminary statements from them. I didn't like it much, but it would look good on paper if I decided to get myself properly credentialed as a licensed private investigator. I wasn't sure that I wanted to do this, but I wasn't sure that I didn't, and in the meantime I could keep busy and earn a hundred dollars a day.

I was between relationships. I guess that's what they call it. I had been keeping company for a while with a woman named Jan Keane, and that had ended some time ago. I wasn't certain it was done forever, but it was done for now, and the little dating I'd done since had led nowhere. Most evenings I went to AA meetings, and afterward I generally hung out with friends from the program until it was time to go home and to bed. Sometimes, perversely, I went and hung out in a saloon instead, drinking Coke or coffee or soda water. That's not recommended, and I knew that, but I did it anyway.

Then, on a Tuesday night about ten days into the warm weather, the god who plays pinball with my world turned a shoulder to the machine and lurched into it. And the Tilt sign came on, bright and clear.

*   *   *

I had spent most of the day finding and interviewing a ferret-faced little man named Neudorf, who had presumably witnessed a collision involving a Radio Shack delivery van and a bicycle. Reliable had been retained by the bicyclist's attorney, and Neudorf was supposed to be able to testify that the van's driver had thrown open the door of his vehicle in such a manner that the bicyclist could not avoid running right into it.

Our client was one of those ambulance chasers who advertise on television, and he made his money on volume. His case looked solid enough, with or without Neudorf's testimony, and it figured to be settled out of court, but in the meantime everybody had to go through the motions. I was getting a hundred dollars a day for my part in the dance, and Neudorf was trying to find out what he could get for his. "I dunno," he kept saying. "You spend a couple days in court, you got your expenses, you got your loss of income, and you wanna do the right thing but how can you afford to do it, you know what I mean?"

I knew what he meant. I knew, too, that his testimony was worth nothing if we paid him for it and not much more than that if he wasn't well motivated to supply it. I let him think he'd get paid off under the table when he testified in court, and meanwhile I got his signature on a strong preliminary statement that might help our client get the case settled.

I didn't really care how the case was resolved. Both parties looked to be at fault. Neither one had been paying sufficient attention. It cost the van a door, and it cost the girl on the bicycle a broken arm and two broken teeth. She deserved to get something out of it, if not the three million dollars her lawyer was asking for. As far as that went, maybe Neudorf deserved something, too. Expert witnesses in civil and criminal proceedings get paid all the time—psychiatrists and forensics experts, lining up on one side or the other and contradicting the experts on the other side. Why not pay eye-witnesses, too? Why not pay everybody?

I wrapped up Neudorf around three, went back to Reliable's offices and typed up my report. AA Intergroup has its offices in the Flatiron Building, so I stopped on my way out and answered phones for an hour. People call there all the time, out-of-town visitors looking for a meeting, drunks who are beginning to suspect that something may not be working for them, and people coming off a bender and looking for help to get into a detox or rehab. There are callers, too, who are just trying to stay sober a day at a time and need someone to talk to. Volunteers work the phones. It's not dramatic, like the 911 command center at Police Plaza or the hotline at Suicide Prevention League, but it's service and it keeps you sober. I don't think anybody ever got drunk while he was doing it.

I ate dinner at a Thai place on Broadway, and at six-thirty I met a fellow named Richie Gelman at a Columbus Circle coffee shop. We sat over cups of coffee for ten minutes before a woman named Toni rushed in, apologizing for having lost track of the time. We went down into the subway and took a couple of trains, the second one a BMT line that let us off at Jamaica Avenue and 121st Street. That's a good ways out in Queens, in a neighborhood called Richmond Hill. We asked directions at a drugstore and walked half a dozen blocks to a Lutheran church. In the large basement room there were forty or fifty chairs set up, and some tables, and a lectern for the speaker. There were two large urns, one with coffee and the other with hot water for tea or instant decaf. There was a plate of oatmeal cookies with raisins, and there was a table of literature.

There are two basic types of AA meetings in the New York area. At the discussion meetings, a single speaker talks for twenty minutes or so, and then the meeting is open for general discussion. At speaker meetings, two or three speakers tell their stories, and that takes the entire hour. This particular group in Richmond Hill held speaker meetings on Tuesday nights, and this particular Tuesday we were the speakers. Groups all over the city send members to speak at other groups; otherwise we'd hear the same people telling the same stories all the time, and the whole thing would be even more boring than it already is.

Actually it's pretty interesting a fair percentage of the time, and sometimes it's better than a night out at a comedy club. When you speak at an AA meeting you're supposed to tell what your life used to be like, what happened, and what it's like now. Not surprisingly, a lot of the stories are pretty grim—people don't generally decide to quit drinking because they've been hurting their sides laughing all the time. Still, the grimmest stories come out funny some of the time, and that's how it went that night in Richmond Hill.

Toni went first. She'd been married for a time to a compulsive gambler, and she told how he had lost her in a poker game and won her back several months later. It was a story I'd heard before, but it was especially funny the way she told it this time. She got laughs all through her talk, and I guess her mood was infectious, because I followed her and found myself telling stories from my days on the job, first as a patrolman and then as a detective. I was coming up with things I hadn't even thought of in years, and they were coming out funny.

Then Richie finished out the hour. He'd run his own public-relations firm through years of blackout drinking, and some of his stories were wonderful. For years he had his first drink of the day every morning in a Chinese luncheonette on Bayard Street. "I got off the subway, put a five-dollar bill on the counter, drank a double scotch neat, got back on the subway and rode to my office. I never said a word to them and they never said a word to me. I knew I was safe there, because what the hell did they know? And, more important, who could they tell?"

17

We had coffee and cookies afterward and one of the members gave us a lift to the subway. We rode back into Manhattan and uptown to Columbus Circle. It was past eleven by the time we got there, and Toni said she was hungry and asked if anybody wanted to get something to eat.

Richie begged off, saying he was tired and wanted to make an early night of it. I suggested the Flame, a coffee shop where a lot of the crowd from our home group generally winds up after a meeting.

"I think I'd like something a little more upscale," she said. "And more substantial. I missed dinner. I had a couple of cookies at the meeting, but aside from that I haven't eaten anything since lunch. Do you know a place called Armstrong's?"

I had to laugh, and she asked me what was so funny. "I used to live there," I said. "Before I got sober. The place used to be on Ninth Avenue between Fifty-seventh and Fifty-eighth, which put it right around the corner from my hotel. I ate there, I drank there, I cashed checks there, I ran a tab there, I met clients there, Jesus, I did everything but sleep there. I probably did that too, come to think of it."

"And now you don't go there anymore."

"I've tended to avoid it."

"Well, we can go someplace else. I didn't live around here when I was drinking so I just think of the place as a restaurant."

"We can go there."

"Are you sure?"

"Why not?"

The new Armstrong's is a block west, at Fifty-seventh and Tenth. We took a table along the wall and I looked around while Toni made a pilgrimage to the ladies' room. Jimmy wasn't around, and there was no one in the joint I recognized, neither employees nor customers. The menu was more elaborate than it used to be, but the same sort of dishes were featured, and I recognized some of the photos and artwork on the walls. The general feel of the place had been upgraded and yuppified a notch, and the overall effect was more fern bar than saloon, but it wasn't all that different.

I said as much to Toni when she came back. She asked if they'd played classical music in the old days. "All the time," I told her. "When he first opened up Jimmy had a jukebox, but he ripped it out and brought in Mozart and Vivaldi. It kept the kids out, and that made everybody happy."

"So you used to get drunk to *Eine Kleine Nachtmusik?*"

"It did the job."

She was a pleasant woman, a couple of years younger than I, sober about the same length of time. She managed a showroom for a Seventh Avenue manufacturer of women's wear, and she'd been having an affair for a year or two with one of her bosses. He was married, and for months now she'd been speaking up at meetings and saying she had to end the relationship, but her voice never carried much conviction and the affair survived.

She was a tall leggy woman, with black hair that I suspect she dyed and a squareness to her jawline and her shoulders. I liked her and thought her good-looking, but I wasn't attracted to her. Or she to me—her lovers were always married and balding and Jewish, and I was none of the above, so that left us free to be friends.

We were there well past midnight. She had a small salad and a plate of the black-bean chili. I had a cheeseburger, and we both drank a lot of coffee. Jimmy had always given you a good cup of coffee. I used to drink it laced with bourbon, but it was even good all by itself.

Toni lived at Forty-ninth and Eighth. I walked her home and dropped her at the lobby of her high rise, then started back to my hotel. Something stopped me before I'd gone more than a block. Maybe I was wired from speaking in Richmond Hill, or stirred up some from returning to Armstrong's after such a long absence. Maybe it was the coffee, maybe it was the weather, maybe it was the phase of the moon. Whatever it was, I was restless. I didn't want to go back to my little room and its four walls.

I walked two blocks west and went to Grogan's.

I had no business there. Unlike Armstrong's, Grogan's is a pure ginmill. There's no food served, there's no classical music, and there are no potted Boston ferns hanging from the ceiling. There's a jukebox, with selections by the Clancy Brothers and Bing Crosby and the Wolfe Tones, but it doesn't get much play. There's a television set and a dart board, and a couple of mounted fish, and dark wood walls and a tile floor and a stamped-tin ceiling. There's neon in the window advertising Guinness stout and Harp lager. The Guinness is on draft.

Mick Ballou owns Grogan's, although someone else has his name on the license and ownership papers. Ballou is a big man, a hard drinker, a career criminal, a brooding man of cold dark rage and sudden violence. Circumstance had thrown us together not too long ago, and some curious chemistry kept drawing me back. I hadn't figured it out yet.

The crowd was sparse, and Ballou himself wasn't there. I ordered a glass of club soda and sat at the bar with it. There was a movie playing on one of the cable stations, a colorized version of an old Warner Bros. gangster movie. Edward G. Robinson was in it, and half a dozen others I recognized but couldn't name. Five minutes into the movie the bartender went over to the set and turned down the color-level knob, and the film was magically restored to its original black-and-white.

"Some things should be fucking left alone," he said.

I watched about half of the movie. When my club soda was gone I had a Coke, and when that was gone I put a couple of dollars on the bar and went home.

Jacob was on the hotel desk. He's a mulatto, with freckles on his face and the backs of his hands, and curly red hair that's starting to go thin on top. He buys books of difficult crossword puzzles and Double-Crostics and works them in pen-and-ink, staying slightly buzzed all the while on terpin hydrate and codeine. The management has fired him a couple of times over the years for unspecified reasons, but they always hire him back.

He said, "Your cousin called."

"My cousin?"

"Been calling all night. Four, five calls, must of been." He plucked a sheaf of message slips from my pigeonhole, leaving the letters behind. "One, two, three, four, five," he counted. "Says call her whenever you come in."

Someone must have died, and I wondered who. I wasn't even sure who was left. What family there was had long since scattered far and wide. Sometimes I got a card or two at Christmas, once in a great while a phone call if an uncle or cousin was in town and at loose ends. But what cousin did I have who would call more than once to make sure a message got to me?

Her, he'd said. *Call her.*

I reached for the handful of slips, scanned the top one. *Cousin called,* it read. Nothing else, and the time of the call was left blank.

"There's no number," I said.

"She said you'd know it."

"I don't even know who she is. Which cousin?"

He shook himself, straightened up in his chair. "Sorry," he said. "Getting a little too relaxed here. I wrote her name on one of them slips. I didn't write it each time. It was the same person over and over again."

I sorted the slips. Actually he'd written it twice, on what seemed to be the first two slips. *Please call your cousin Frances,* I read. And, on the other: *Call cousin Frances.*

"Frances," I said.

"That's it. That's the name."

Except I couldn't recall a Cousin Frances. Had one of my male cousins married a woman named Frances? Or was Frances some cousin's child, a new cousin whose name I'd never managed to learn?

"You're sure it was a woman?"

"'Course I'm sure."

"Because sometimes Francis is a man's name, and—"

"Oh, please. Don't you think I know that? It was a woman, said her name was Frances. Don't you know your own cousin?"

Evidently I didn't. "She asked for me by name?"

"Said Matthew Scudder."

"And I was to call her as soon as I came in."

"That's right. Last time or two she called, it was already late, and that was when she stressed it. No matter how late, call her right away."

"And she didn't leave a number."

"Said you knew it."

I stood there, frowning, trying to think straight, and in a wink the years fell away and I was a cop, a detective attached to the Sixth Precinct. "Call for you, Scudder," someone was saying. "It's your cousin Frances."

"Oh, for God's sake," I said now.

"Something?"

"It's all right," I told Jacob. "I suppose it would have to be her. It couldn't be anybody else."

"She said—"

"I know what she said. It's all right, you got it straight. It just took me a minute, that's all."

He nodded. "Sometimes," he said, "it'll do that."

I didn't know the number. I had known it, of course. I had known it well for many years, but I hadn't called it in a while and couldn't summon it up from my memory. It was in my address book, though. I had recopied my address books several times since I'd last had occasion to call that number, but I must have known I'd want to call it again, because each time I'd chosen to preserve it.

Elaine Mardell, I had written. And an address on East Fifty-first Street. And a phone number that was familiar to me once I saw it.

I have a phone in my room, but I didn't go upstairs to use it. Instead I crossed the lobby to the pay phone, dropped a quarter in the slot, and made the call.

TWO

An answering machine picked up on the second ring, and Elaine's recorded voice repeated the phone number's final four digits and advised me to leave a message at the sound of the tone. I waited for it and said, "This is your cousin returning your call. I'm home now, and you have the number, so—"

"Matt? Let me turn this thing off. There. Thank God you called."

"I was out late, I just got your message. And for a minute or two there I couldn't remember who my cousin Frances was supposed to be."

"I guess it's been a while."

"I guess it has."

"I need to see you."

"All right," I said. "I'm working tomorrow, but it's not something I can't find a free hour in. What's good for you? Sometime in the morning?"

"Matt, I really need to see you now."

"What's the problem, Elaine?"

"Come on over and I'll tell you."

25

"Don't tell me history's repeating itself. Did someone go and blow a main fuse?"

"God. No, it's worse than that."

"You sound shaky."

"I'm scared to death."

She had never been a woman who scared easy. I asked if she was still living in the same place. She said she was.

I said I'd be right over.

As I left the hotel an empty cab was cruising by on the other side of the street, heading east. I yelled at him and he stopped with a squeal of brakes and I trotted across and got in. I gave him Elaine's address and settled back in my seat, but I couldn't stay settled back. I rolled down the window and sat on the edge of the seat and looked out at the passing landscape.

Elaine was a hooker, a classy young prostitute who worked out of her own apartment and got along just fine without a pimp or a mob connection. We got to know each other back when I was a cop. I met her for the first time a couple of weeks after I made detective. I was at an after-hours in the Village, feeling very good about the new gold shield in my pocket, and she was at a table with three European manufacturers and two other working girls. At the time I noted that she looked a good deal less whorish than her sisters, and a lot more attractive.

A week or so after that I met her in a bar on West Seventy-second Street called Poogan's Pub. I don't know who she was with, but she was at Danny Boy Bell's table, and I went over to say hello to Danny Boy. He introduced me to everyone there, Elaine included. I saw her once or twice after that around town, and then one night I went to the Brasserie for a late bite and she was at a table with another girl. I joined the two of them. Somewhere down the line the other girl went off on her own, and I went home with Elaine.

For the next several years I don't suppose there was a week when I didn't see her at least once, unless one or the other of us was out of town. We had an interesting relationship, and one which seemed to serve us both. I was a sort of protector for her, usefully supplied with cop skills and cop connections, someone she could lean on, someone who could push back hard if anybody tried to lean on her. I was, too, the closest thing she had or wanted to a boyfriend, and she was as much of a girlfriend or mistress as I could have handled. Sometimes we went out—for a meal, to a fight at the Garden, to a bar or an after-hours. Sometimes I dropped in on her for a quick drink and a quick bounce. I didn't have to send flowers or remember her birthdays, and neither of us had to pretend we were in love.

I was married then, of course. The marriage was a mess, but I'm not sure I realized it at the time. I had a wife and two young sons living in a mortgaged house out on Long Island, and I more or less assumed the marriage would last, just as I assumed I would stay on with the NYPD until departmental regulations forced me to retire. I was drinking with both hands in those days, and while it didn't seem to get in my way any it was having a subtler effect all along, making it remarkably easy for me to turn a blind eye on the things in my life I didn't want to look at.

Ah, well. What Elaine and I had was a nonmarriage of convenience, I suppose, and we were hardly the first cop and hooker to have found this particular way to do each other some good. Still, I doubt it would have lasted so long or suited us so well if we hadn't liked each other.

She had become my cousin Frances so that she could leave messages for me without arousing suspicion. We didn't use the code often because there wasn't much need for it; our relationship was such that it was usually I who called her, and I could leave whatever message I wanted. When she called me, it was generally either to break a date or because of an emergency.

One such emergency had come to mind while I was talking to her, and I'd alluded to it, recalling when someone had blown a main fuse. The someone in question had been a client, an overweight patent attorney with offices way downtown on Maiden Lane and a home up in Riverdale. He'd been a regular john of Elaine's, showing up two or three times a month, never giving her any grief until the afternoon he picked her bed as the site for what a medical examiner later called a massive myocardial infarction. It's high on every call girl's list of nightmares, and most of them have given a little thought to what they'll do if it happens. What Elaine did was call me at the station house, and when they said I was out she told them to get word to me, that it was a family emergency, that I should call my cousin Frances.

They couldn't reach me, but I called in myself within the half hour and they gave me the message. After I spoke with her I found an officer I could trust and we rode up to her apartment. With Elaine's help, we got the poor bastard into his clothes. He'd been wearing a three-piece suit, and we dressed him up all right, knotting his tie, tying his shoes, hooking his cuff links. My buddy and I each looped one of his arms over our shoulders, and we walked him out to the freight elevator, where one of the building's porters had the car waiting. We told him our friend had had too much to drink. I doubt that he bought it—the guy we were dragging looked a lot more like a stiff than a drunk—but he knew we were cops and he remembered the kind of tips Miss Mardell passed out at Christmas, so if he had any reservations he kept them to himself.

I was driving a department vehicle, an unmarked Plymouth sedan. I brought it around to the service entrance and we wrestled the dead lawyer into it. By the time we had him in the car it was past five o'clock, and by the time we fought our way down to the Wall Street area the offices were closed and most of the workers on their way home. We parked across the entrance to a narrow alley off Gold Street, maybe three blocks from the man's office, and we left him in the alley.

His appointment book had the notation "E.M.—3:30" under that day's date. That seemed cryptic enough, so I returned the book to his breast pocket. I checked his address book, and she wasn't listed under the M's, but he had her number and address with the E's, listed by her first name only. I was going to tear out the page, but I noticed other female first names listed here and there, and I couldn't see any reason to inflict all of that on the widow, so I stuck the address book in my pocket and ditched it later on.

He had a lot of cash in his wallet, close to five hundred dollars. I took all of it and split it with the cop who was helping me out. I figured it was just as well to let it look as though someone had rolled our friend. Besides, if we didn't take it the first cops on the scene would, and look at all we'd done to earn it.

We got out of there without attracting any attention. I drove us up to the Village and bought my buddy a couple of drinks, and then we called it in to Headquarters anonymously and let them route it to the local precinct. The ME didn't miss noticing that the deceased had died elsewhere, but death itself was clearly a result of natural causes, so nobody had any reason to make waves. The old whoremaster died with his reputation unbesmirched, Elaine stayed out of trouble, and I got to be a hero.

I've told that story a couple of times at AA meetings. Sometimes it comes out funny, and other times it's anything but that. It depends, I guess, on how it's told, or how you listen.

Elaine lived on Fifty-first between First and Second, on the sixteenth floor of one of those white brick apartment buildings that went up all over town in the early sixties. Her doorman was a West Indian black, very dark-skinned, with perfect posture and the build of a wide receiver. I gave him her name and mine and waited while he spoke on the intercom. He listened, looked at me, said something, listened again, and handed me the phone. "She wants to talk to you," he said.

I said, "I'm here. What's up?"

"Say something."

"What do you want me to say?"

"You just mentioned a man who blew a fuse. What was his name?"

"What is this, a test? Can't you recognize my voice?"

"This thing distorts voices. Look, humor me. What was the fuse man's name?"

"I don't remember his name. He was a patent lawyer."

"Okay. Let me talk to Derek."

I handed the thing to the doorman. He listened for a moment while she assured him I was okay, then motioned me to the elevator. I rode up to her floor and rang her bell. Even after the ritual over the intercom, she checked the judas peephole before opening the door for me.

"Come in," she said. "I apologize for the dramatics. I'm probably being silly, but maybe not. I don't know."

"What's the matter, Elaine?"

"In a minute. I feel a lot better now that you're here, but I'm still a little shaky. Let me look at you. You look terrific."

"You look pretty good yourself."

"Do I? That's hard to believe. I've had some night. I couldn't stop calling you. I must have called half a dozen times."

"There were five messages."

"Is that all? I don't know why I thought five messages would be more forceful than one, but I kept picking up the phone and dialing your number."

"Five messages may have been better," I said. "They made it a little harder to ignore. What's the problem?"

"The problem is I'm scared. I feel better now, though. I'm sorry for the inquisition before but it's impossible to recognize a voice over my intercom. Just for your information, the patent attorney's name was Roger Stuhldreher."

"How could I ever have forgotten it?"

"What a day that was." She shook her head at the memory. "But I'm being a terrible hostess. What can I get you to drink?"

"Coffee, if you've got some."

"I'll make some."

"It's too much trouble."

"It's no trouble at all. You still like it with bourbon in it?"

"No, just black."

She looked at me. "You stopped drinking," she said.

"Uh-huh."

"I remember you were having some trouble with it the last time I saw you. Is that when you stopped?"

"Around then, yes."

"That's great," she said. "That's really great. Give me a minute and I'll get some coffee made."

The living room was as I remembered it, done in black-and-white with a white shag rug and a chrome-and-black leather couch and some matte black mica shelving. A couple of abstract paintings provided the room's only color. I think they were the same paintings she'd had before, but I couldn't swear to it.

I went over to the window. There was a gap between two buildings that afforded a view of the East River, and the borough of Queens on the other side of it. I'd been over there a matter of hours earlier, telling funny stories to a bunch of drunks in Richmond Hill. It seemed ages ago now.

I stayed at the window for a few minutes. I was in front of one of the paintings when she came back with two cups of black coffee. "I think I remember this one," I said. "Or did you just get it last week?"

"I've had it for years. I bought it on impulse at a gallery

31

on Madison Avenue. I paid twelve hundred dollars for it. I couldn't believe I was paying that kind of money for something to hang on the wall. You know me, Matt. I'm not extravagant. I always bought nice things, but I always saved my money."

"And bought real estate," I said, remembering.

"You bet I did. When you're not handing it to a pimp or sucking it up your nose, you can buy a lot of houses. But I thought I was crazy, paying all that money for a painting."

"Look at the pleasure it's brought you."

"More than pleasure, honey. You know what it's worth now?"

"A lot, evidently."

"Forty thousand, minimum. Probably more like fifty. I ought to sell it. Sometimes it makes me nervous, having fifty grand hanging on the wall. For Christ's sake, when I first hung it I got nervous having twelve hundred dollars on my wall. How's the coffee?"

"It's fine."

"Is it strong enough?"

"It's fine, Elaine."

"You really look great, you know that?"

"So do you."

"How long has it been? I think the last time we saw each other must have been about three years ago, but we haven't really seen anything much of each other since you left the police department, and that must be close to ten years."

"Something like that."

"You still look the same."

"Well, I've still got all my hair. But there's a little gray there if you look closely."

"There's a lot of gray in mine, but you can look as close as you like and you won't see it. Thanks to modern science." She drew a breath. "The rest of the package hasn't changed too much, though."

"It hasn't changed at all."

"Well, I've kept my figure. And my skin's still good. I'll tell you, though, I never thought I'd have to put so much work into it. I'm at the gym three mornings a week, sometimes four. And I watch what I eat and drink."

"You were never a drinker."

"No, but I used to drink Tab by the gallon, Tab and then Diet Coke. I cut out all of that. Now it's pure fruit juice or plain water. I have one cup of coffee a day, first thing in the morning. This cup's a concession to special circumstances."

"Maybe you should tell me what they are."

"I'm getting there. I have to sort of ease into it. What else do I do? I walk a lot. I watch what I eat. I've been a vegetarian for almost three years now."

"You used to love steak."

"I know. I didn't think it was a meal unless there was meat in it."

"And what was it you used to have at the Brasserie?"

"Tripes à la mode de Caen."

"Right. A dish I never liked to think about, but I had to admit it was tasty."

"I couldn't guess when I had it last. I haven't had any meat in close to three years. I ate fish for the first year, but then I dropped that, too."

"Ms. Natural."

"C'est moi."

"Well, it agrees with you."

"And not drinking agrees with you. Here we are, telling each other how good we look. That's how you know you're old, isn't that what they say? Matt, I was thirty-eight on my last birthday."

"That's not so bad."

"That's what you think. My last birthday was three years ago. I'm forty-one."

"That's not so bad either. And you don't look it."

"I know I don't. Or maybe I do. That's what somebody told Gloria Steinem when she turned forty, that she didn't look it. And she said, 'Yes I do. This is what forty looks like now.'"

"Pretty good line."

"That's what I thought. Sweetie, you know what I've been doing? I've been stalling."

"I know."

"To keep it from being real. But it's real. This came in today's mail."

She handed me a newspaper clipping and I unfolded it. There was a photograph, a head shot of a middle-aged gentleman. He was wearing glasses and his hair was neatly combed, and he looked confident and optimistic, an expression that seemed out of keeping with the headline. It ran across three columns, and it said, AREA BUSINESSMAN SLAYS WIFE, CHILDREN, SELF. Ten or twelve column inches of text elaborated on the headline. Philip Sturdevant, proprietor of Sturdevant Furniture with four retail outlets in Canton and Massillon, had apparently gone berserk in his home in suburban Walnut Hills. After using a kitchen knife to kill his wife and three small children, Sturdevant had called the police and told them what he had done. By the time a police cruiser arrived on the scene, Sturdevant was dead of a self-inflicted shotgun wound to the head.

I looked up from the clipping. "Terrible thing," I said.

"Yes."

"Did you know him?"

"No."

"Then—"

"I knew her."

"The wife?"

"We both knew her."

I studied the clipping again. The wife's name was Cornelia, and her age was given as thirty-seven. The children were Andrew, six; Kevin, four; and Delcey, two. Cornelia Sturdevant, I thought, and no bells rang. I looked at her, puzzled.

"Connie," she said.

"Connie?"

"Connie Cooperman. You remember her."

"Connie Cooperman," I said, and then I remembered a bouncy blond cheerleader of a girl. "Jesus," I said. "How in hell did she wind up in—where was this, anyway? Canton, Massillon, Walnut Hills. Where are all these places?"

"Ohio. Northern Ohio, not far from Akron."

"How did she get there?"

"By marrying Philip Sturdevant. She met him, I don't know, seven or eight years ago."

"How? Was he a john?"

"No, nothing like that. She was on vacation, she was up at Stowe on a ski weekend. He was there, he was divorced and unattached, and he fell for her. I don't know that he was rich but he was comfortably well off, he owned furniture stores and made a good living from them. And he was crazy about Connie and he wanted to marry her and have babies with her."

"And that's what they did."

"That's what they did. She thought he was wonderful, and she was ready to get out of the life and out of New York. She was sweet and cute and guys liked her, but she was hardly what you'd call a born whore."

"Is that what you are?"

"No, I'm not. I was a lot like Connie actually, we were both a couple of NJGs who drifted into it. I turned out to be good at it, that's all."

"What's an NJG?"

"A neurotic Jewish girl. It's not just that I turned out to be good at it. I turned out to be capable of living the life without getting eaten up by it. It grinds down an awful lot of girls, it erodes what little self-esteem they started out with. But it hasn't hurt me that way."

"No."

"At least that's what I think most of the time." She gave

35

me a brave smile. "Except on the occasional bad night, and everybody has a few of those."

"Sure."

"It may have been good for Connie early on. She was fat and unpopular in high school, and it did her good to find out that men wanted her and found her attractive. But then it stopped being good for her, and then she got lucky and met Philip Sturdevant, and he fell for her and she was crazy about him, and they went out to Ohio to make babies."

"And then he found out about her past and went nuts and killed her."

"No."

"No?"

She shook her head. "He knew all along. She told him from the jump. It was very brave of her, and it turned out to be the absolute right thing to do, because it didn't bother him and otherwise there would have been that secret between them. He was a pretty worldly guy, as it turned out. He was fifteen or twenty years older than Connie, and he'd been married twice, and while he'd lived all his life in Massillon he'd traveled a lot. He didn't mind that she'd spent a few years in the life. If anything I think he got a kick out of it, especially since he was taking her away from all that."

"And they lived happily ever after."

She ignored that. "I had a couple of letters from her over the years," she said. "Only a couple, because I never get around to answering letters, and when you don't write back people stop writing to you. Most of the time I would get a card from her at Christmas. You know those cards people have made up with pictures of their children? I got a few of those from her. Beautiful children, but you would expect that. He was a good-looking man, you can see that from the newspaper photo, and you remember how pretty Connie was."

"Yes."

"I wish I had the last card she sent. I'm not the kind of

person who keeps things. By the tenth of January all my Christmas cards are out with the garbage. So I don't have one to show you, and I won't be getting a new one next month because—"

She wept silently, her shoulders drawn in and shaking, her hands clasped. After a moment or two she caught hold of herself, drew in a deep breath, let it out.

I said, "I wonder what made him do it."

"He didn't do it. He wasn't the type."

"People surprise you."

"He didn't do it."

I looked at her.

"I don't know a soul in Canton or Massillon," she said. "The only person I ever knew there was Connie, and the only person who could have known she knew me was Philip Sturdevant, and they're both dead."

"So?"

"So who sent me the clipping?"

"Anybody could have sent it."

"Oh?"

"She could have mentioned you to a friend or neighbor there. Then, after the murder and suicide, the friend goes through Connie's things, finds her address book, and wants to let her out-of-town friends know what happened."

"So this friend clips the story out of the paper and sends it all by itself? Without a word of explanation?"

"There was no note in the envelope?"

"Nothing."

"Maybe she wrote a note and forgot to put it in the envelope. People do that sort of thing all the time."

"And she forgot to put her return address on the envelope?"

"You have the envelope?"

"In the other room. It's a plain white envelope with my name and address hand-printed."

"Can I see it?"

She nodded. I sat in my chair and looked at the picture that was supposed to be worth fifty thousand dollars. Once I'd come very close to emptying a gun into it. I hadn't thought about that incident in a long time. It looked as though I'd be thinking of it a lot now.

The envelope was as she'd described it, five-and-dime stuff, cheap and untraceable. Her name and address had been block-printed in ballpoint. No return address in the upper-left corner or on the back flap.

"New York postmark," I said.

"I know."

"So if it was a friend of hers—"

"The friend carried the clipping all the way to New York and put it in the mail."

I stood up and walked over to the window. I looked through it without seeing anything, then turned to face her. "The alternative," I said, "is that someone else killed her. And her kids. And her husband."

"Yes."

"And faked it to look like murder and suicide. Faked a call to the cops while he was at it. And then waited until the story was printed in the local paper, and clipped it, and brought it back to New York and put it in the mail."

"Yes."

"I guess we're thinking of the same person."

"He swore he'd kill Connie," she said. "And me. And you."

"He did, didn't he."

"'You and all your women, Scudder.' That's what he said to you."

"A lot of bad guys say a lot of things over the years. You can't take all that crap seriously." I went over and picked up the envelope again, as if I could read its psychic vibrations. If it held any, they were too subtle for me.

I said, "Why now, for God's sake? What's it been, twelve years?"

"Just about."

"You really think it's him, don't you?"

"I know it is."

"Motley."

"Yes."

"James Leo Motley," I said. "Jesus."

THREE

James Leo Motley. I'd first heard the name in that same apartment, but not in the black-and-white living room. I'd called Elaine one afternoon, dropped by shortly thereafter. She fixed bourbon for me and a diet cola for herself, and a few minutes later we were in her bedroom. Afterward I touched the tip of one finger to a discolored area alongside her rib cage and asked her what happened.

"I almost called you," she said. "I had a visitor yesterday afternoon."

"Oh?"

"Someone new. He'd called, said he was a friend of Connie's. That's Connie Cooperman. You met her, remember?"

"Sure."

"He said she gave him my number. So we talked, and he sounded all right, and he came over. I didn't like him."

"What was wrong with him?"

"I don't know exactly. There was something weird about him. Something about his eyes."

"His eyes?"

"The way he looks at you. What is it Superman's got? X-

41

ray vision? I felt as though he could look at me and see clear through to the bone."

I ran a hand over her. "You'd miss a lot of nice skin that way," I said.

"And there was something very cold about it. Reptilian, like a lizard watching flies. Or like a snake. Coiled, ready to strike without warning."

"What's he look like?"

"That may have been part of it. He's kind of strange-looking. A very long narrow face. Mouse-colored hair, and a lousy haircut, one of those soup-bowl jobs. It made him look like a monk. Very pale skin. Unhealthy, or at least that's how it looked."

"Sounds charming."

"His body was strange, too. He was completely hard."

"Isn't that something you strive for in your line of work?"

"Not his cock, his whole body. Like every muscle was tense all the time, like he never relaxed. He's thin, but he's very muscular. What you call wiry."

"What happened?"

"We went to bed. I wanted to get him into bed because I wanted to get him out of here as soon as possible. Also, I figured once I got him off he'd be calmer and I wouldn't be as nervous. I already knew I wasn't going to see him again. In fact I would have asked him to leave without taking him to bed, but I was afraid of what he might do. He didn't exactly do anything, but he was an unpleasant trick."

"Was he rough?"

"Not exactly. It was the way he touched me. You can tell a lot from the way a man touches you. He touched me like he hated me. I mean, who needs that shit, you know?"

"How'd you get the bruise?"

"That was after. He got dressed, he wasn't interested in taking a shower and I didn't suggest it because I wanted him O-U-T. And he gave me this look, and he said we'd probably be seeing a lot of each other from now on. *That's what you think,* I thought, but I didn't say anything. He was on his way out, and he hadn't given me any money, or left anything on the dresser."

"You didn't get money in front?"

"No, I never do. I don't discuss it ahead of time, not unless the man brings it up, and most of the time they don't. A lot of men like to pretend to themselves that the sex is free and the money they give me is a present, and that's fine. Anyway, he was ready to walk out without giving me anything, and I came this close to letting him go."

"But you didn't."

"No, because I was angry, and if I was going to have to trick a shitheel like that I was at least going to get paid for it. So I gave him a smile and said, 'You know, you're forgetting something.'

"He said, 'What am I forgetting?' 'I'm a working girl,' I said. He said he knew that, that he could tell a whore when he saw one."

"Nice."

"I didn't react to it, but I did say I got paid for what I did. Something like that, I forget how I put it. And he gave me this very cold look, and he said, 'I don't pay.'

"And then I was stupid. I could have let it go, but I thought maybe it was just an ego thing, a matter of terms, and I said I didn't expect him to pay, but maybe he'd like to give me a present."

"And he hit you."

"No. He walked toward me, and I backed off, and he kept coming until I was backed up against the wall there. He put his hand on me. I was dressed, I had a blouse on. He put his hand right here and he just pressed with two fingers, and there must be a nerve there or some kind of pressure point, because it hurt like fury. There was no mark then. That didn't show up until this morning."

"It'll probably be worse tomorrow."

"Great. It's sore now, but it's not terrible. While he was

doing it, though, the pain was incredibly intense. I went weak in the knees and I swear I couldn't see. I thought I was going to black out."

"He did that pressing with two fingers."

"Yes. Then he let go of me and I was holding on to the wall for support and he fucking grinned at me. 'We'll see a lot of each other,' he said, 'and you'll do whatever I tell you to do.' And then he left."

"Did you call Connie?"

"I haven't been able to reach her."

"If this clown calls again—"

"I'll tell him to shit in his hat. Don't worry, Matt, he's never getting in the door again."

"You remember his name?"

"Motley. James Leo Motley."

"He gave you his middle name?"

She nodded. "And he didn't ask me to call him Jimmy, either. James Leo Motley. What are you doing?"

"Writing it down. Maybe I can find out where he lives."

"In Central Park, under a flat rock."

"And I might as well see if we've got a sheet on him. From your description, it wouldn't surprise me."

"James Leo Motley," she said. "If you lose your memo book, just call me. It's a name I'm not likely to forget."

I couldn't find an address for him, but I did pull his yellow sheet. He had a string of six or seven arrests, most of them for assaults upon women. In each case the victim withdrew the complaint and charges were dropped. Once he'd been in a traffic accident, a fender-bender on the Van Wyck Expressway, and he'd given the driver of the other vehicle a serious beating. That case got to court, with Motley charged with first-degree assault, but eyewitness testimony suggested that the other driver may have started the fight, and that he'd been armed with a tire iron while Motley had defended himself with his bare hands. If so, he'd been good enough with those hands to put the other man in the hospital.

Six or seven arrests, no convictions. All of the charges involving violence. I didn't like it, and I was going to call Elaine and let her know what I'd found out, but I didn't get around to it.

A week or so later she called me. I was in the squad room when she called, so she didn't have to identify herself as Cousin Frances.

"He was just here," she said. "He hurt me."

"I'll be right over."

She had reached Connie. Connie had been reluctant to talk at first, finally admitting that she'd been seeing James Leo Motley for the past several weeks. He'd gotten her number from someone, she wasn't sure who, and his first visit had been not unlike the first visit he paid to Elaine. He told her he wasn't going to pay her, and that she'd be seeing a lot of him. And he hurt her—not badly, but enough to get her attention.

Since then he'd been turning up a couple of times a week. He'd started asking her for money, and he'd continued to brutalize her, hurting her both during and after the sex act. He told her repeatedly that he knew what she liked, that she was a cheap whore and she needed to be treated like what she was. "I'm your man now," he told her. "You belong to me. I own you, body and soul."

The conversation upset Elaine, understandably enough, and she'd been meaning to tell me about it, just as I'd intended to let her know about Motley's record. She'd let it go, waiting until she saw me, knowing that she wasn't in any danger because she wasn't going to see the son of a bitch again. When he did call, the day after her conversation with Connie, she told him that she was busy.

"Make time for me," he said.

"No," she said. "I don't want to see you again, Mr. Motley."

"What makes you think you have any choice?"

"You asshole," she said. "Look, do us both a favor, will you? Lose my number."

Two days later he called again. "I thought I'd give you a chance to change your mind," he said. She told him to drop dead and hung up on him.

She told all three doormen not to send anyone up without calling first. That was standard policy anyway, but she impressed them with the need for extra security. She turned down a couple of dates with new clients, wary that they might be fronting for Motley. When she left her apartment she had the feeling that she was being followed, or at least observed. It was an uncomfortable feeling, and she didn't go out unless she had to.

Then a few days passed and she didn't hear further from him, and she started to relax. She meant to call me, and she meant to call Connie again, but she didn't call either of us.

That afternoon she got a call. A man she knew was in town from the Coast, a studio executive she'd see every few months. She got in a cab and spent an easy hour and a half in his suite at the Sherry-Netherland. He told her all sorts of movie-biz gossip, made love to her twice, and gave her a hundred or two hundred dollars, whatever it was. More than enough to cover the cabs.

When she got back to her apartment Motley was sitting on the leather couch, not quite smiling at her. She tried to get out the door but she'd locked it and put the chain on the minute she came in, before she saw him, and he had hold of her before she could get the door open. Even if she hadn't had to screw around with the locks, she figured he would have caught her. "At the elevator," she said, "or I'd have tripped on the hall carpet, or something. I wasn't going to get away. He wasn't going to let me get away."

*   *   *

He hauled her into the bedroom, ripped her clothes getting them off of her. He hurt her with his hands. The bruise he'd inflicted the first time was faded now, but his fingers went right to the spot and the pain was like a knife. There was another spot he found, on the inside of her thigh, that produced a pain so intense she honestly thought she was going to die from it.

He went on hurting her with the simple pressure of his fingers until all her will was gone, all her capacity to resist. Then he flung her facedown on the bed, dropped his pants, and forced himself into her anal passage.

"I don't do that," she said. "It's painful, and I think it's disgusting anyway, and I never liked it. So I don't do it. I haven't done it in years. But it actually wasn't that bad this time because the pain was nothing compared to what he'd been doing to me with his fingertips. And anyway by this time I was sort of detached from it all. I was afraid he was going to kill me, and I was detached from that, too."

While he sodomized her, he talked to her. He told her she was weak and stupid and filthy. He told her she was only getting what she deserved, and what she secretly wanted. He told her she liked it.

He told her he always gave his women what they wanted. Most of them wanted to be hurt, he told her. Some of them wanted to be killed.

"He said he wouldn't mind killing me. He said he'd killed a girl a while ago who'd looked a lot like me. He killed her first, he said, and then he fucked her. He said a dead girl was as good a fuck as a living one, maybe even better. If you got her while she was still warm, he said. And before she started to stink."

Afterward he went through her purse and took all her cash, including the money she'd just earned at the Sherry.

47

She was one of his women now, he told her. She'd have to pull her weight. That meant he expected her to have money for him when he came to see her. And it meant she would never again refuse to see him, and she would certainly never again mouth off at him, or call him bad names. Did she understand that? Yes, she said. She understood. Was she sure she understood? Yes, she said. She was sure.

He half smiled at her, and ran a hand over that funny cap of hair, then stroked his long chin. "I want to make sure you understand," he said, and he clapped one hand over her mouth and used the other to find the spot on her rib cage. This time she did pass out, and when she came to he was gone.

The first thing I did was take her over to the Eighteenth Precinct. The two of us sat down with a cop named Klaiber and she filed a complaint, charging Motley with assault and battery and forcible sodomy. "There'll be more charges after he's picked up," I said. "He took money from her purse, so that's robbery or extortion or both. And he got into her apartment in her absence."

"Any signs of forced entry?"

"Not that I could spot, but it's still illegal entry."

"You already got forcible sodomy," Klaiber said.

"So?"

"Forcible sodomy and illegal entry, you put them both down and you get a jury confused. They figure it's two ways of saying the same thing." When Elaine excused herself to go to the bathroom he leaned forward and said, "She a girlfriend or something, Matt?"

"Let's say she's been the source of a lot of useful leads over the past few years."

"Fine, we'll call her a snitch. She's on the game, right?"

"So?"

"So I don't have to tell you how hard it is to make an

48

assault charge stand up when the complainant is a prostitute. Let alone rape or sodomy. Far as your juror's concerned, all she did was give away what she usually sold."

"I know that."

"I figured you did."

"I don't expect a pickup order's going to accomplish anything, anyway. His last known address is a Times Square hotel, and he hasn't lived there in a year and a half."

"Oh, you've been looking for him."

"A little bit. He's probably in another midtown flophouse or living with a woman, and either way he'll be hard to find. I just want her complaint on file. It can't hurt further on down the line."

"Got it," he said. "Well, no problem, then. And we'll put out a pickup order just in case he happens to walk into our arms."

I called Anita and told her I'd be staying in the city around the clock for the next few days. I told her I was on a case I couldn't break away from. I'd done this before, sometimes legitimately, sometimes because I hadn't felt like going out to Long Island. As always, she believed me, or pretended to. Then I cleared all of my own cases, dropping some and shunting others off on other people. I didn't want anything else on my plate. I wanted to get James Leo Motley, and I wanted to get him right.

I told Elaine we'd have to trap Motley and she'd have to be the bait. She wasn't crazy about the idea, didn't really ever want to be in the same room with him again, but she had a nice tough core to her and she was willing to do what had to be done.

I moved in with Elaine and we waited. She canceled all her bookings and told everyone who called that she had the flu and wouldn't be available for a week. "This is costing me a fortune," she complained. "Some of these guys may never call back."

"You're just playing hard to get. They'll want you all the more."

"Yeah, look how well that worked with Motley."

We never left the apartment. She cooked once, but the rest of the time we ordered in. We pretty much lived on pizza and Chinese food. The liquor store delivered bourbon, and she got the guy at the corner deli to send over a case of Tab.

Two days into it, Motley called. She answered in the living room and I picked up the extension in the bedroom. The conversation went something like this:

Motley: Hello, Elaine.

Elaine: Oh, hello.

Motley: You know who this is.

Elaine: Yes.

Motley: I wanted to talk to you. I wanted to make sure you were all right.

Elaine: Uh-huh.

Motley: Well? Are you?

Elaine: Am I what?

Motley: Are you all right?

Elaine: I guess so.

Motley: Good.

Elaine: Are you—

Motley: Am I what?

Elaine: Are you coming over?

Motley: Why?

Elaine: I just wondered.

Motley: Do you want me to come over?

Elaine: Well, I'm all alone. It's sort of lonesome here.

Motley: You could go out.

Elaine: I haven't felt like it.

Motley: No, you've been staying home all the time, haven't you? Are you afraid to go out?

Elaine: I guess so.

Motley: What are you afraid of?

Elaine: I don't know.

Motley: Speak up. I can't hear you.

Elaine: I said I don't know what I'm afraid of.

Motley: Are you afraid of me?

Elaine: Yes.

Motley: That's good. I'm glad to hear that. I'm not coming over now.

Elaine: Oh.

Motley: But I'll be over in a day or two. And I'll give you what you need, Elaine. I always give you what you need, don't I?

Elaine: I wish you would come over.

Motley: Soon, Elaine.

When he'd hung up I went back to the living room. She was on the leather sofa and she looked exhausted. She said, "I felt like a bird charmed by a snake. I was acting, of course. Trying to make him think he'd broken my spirit and he really did own me, body and soul. Do you think he bought it?"

"I don't know."

"Neither do I. It sounded as though he did, but maybe he was acting, too, playing my game with me. He knows I haven't left the apartment. Maybe he's watching it."

"It's possible."

"Maybe he's perched up somewhere with a pair of binoculars, maybe he can see in my fucking windows. You know something? I was pretending, but I wound up half convincing myself. It's like the rapture of the depths, it would be so goddamned easy to let go of my will and just drown. You know what I mean?"

"I think so."

"How do you suppose he got in? The other day, when I was fucking Whatsisname at the Sherry. He got past the doorman and then he got in the door. How did he do that?"

"It's not that hard to get past a doorman."

51

"I know, but they're pretty good here. And what about the door? You said there weren't any signs of forced entry."

"Maybe he had a key."

"How would he get a key? I for sure didn't give him one, and I'm not missing any."

"Did Connie have a key to your place?"

"What for, to water the plants? No, nobody had a key. You don't even have a key. You don't, do you? I never gave you one, did I?"

"No."

"I certainly never gave one to Connie. How did he get in? I've got a good lock on that door."

"Did you lock it with the key when you left?"

"I think so. I always do."

"Because if you didn't engage the deadbolt he could have loided his way in with a credit card. Or maybe he picked up your key long enough to make an impression in wax or soap. Or maybe he picks locks."

"Or maybe he just used his fingertips," she offered, "and pushed the door open."

My fourth night there, the phone rang at a quarter to four. I'd gone to sleep some two hours earlier, my gut full of Early Times and my whole system ragged with cabin fever. I heard the phone ring and willed myself awake, but my will wasn't strong enough to push through the fog. I thought I was awake but my body stayed in Elaine's bed and my mind in some sort of dream, and then Elaine was shaking me and urging me awake, and I threw back the covers and got my legs over the side of the bed.

"That was him on the phone," she said. "He's coming over." I asked what time it was and she told me. "I said give me an hour, a girl wants to look her best. He said half an hour, that should be plenty of time for me. He's on his way, Matt. What do we do now?"

I had her call the doorman and let him know she was expecting a guest. Send Mr. Motley right up, she told him, but be sure to ring and tell her he was on his way. She hung up and went into the bathroom, stood under the shower for two minutes, toweled off and started to get dressed. I don't remember what she chose, but she tried on a couple of different outfits, complaining about her own indecision all the while.

"This is crazy," she said. "You'd think I was getting ready for a date."

"Maybe you are."

"Yeah, a fucking date with destiny. Are you all right?"

"I'm a little slow off the mark," I admitted. "Maybe you could get some coffee going."

"Sure."

I got dressed, putting on the clothes I'd taken off two hours ago, the clothes I'd been wearing for the better part of a week. I generally wore a suit on the job in those days—I still do, more often than not—and I put it on. I had trouble getting my tie tied right and made two attempts before the inanity of it struck me and I pulled the tie out from under my collar and tossed it on a chair.

I had the .38 the city issued me in a shoulder holster. I drew it once or twice, then took off the jacket and the holster and wedged the gun under my belt, the butt nestled in the small of my back.

The bourbon bottle was on the table next to the bed. It was a fifth, and there was maybe half a pint left in it. I uncapped it and took a short pull straight from the bottle. Just a quick one, to get the old heart started.

I called to Elaine but she didn't answer. I put my suit jacket back on and practiced drawing the gun. The movement felt awkward, which can happen with any movement when you rehearse it to death. I moved the gun to the left side of my abdomen and practiced a crosshanded draw, but I liked that even less, and I thought about trying the shoulder holster again.

Maybe I wouldn't have to draw it. Maybe I could just keep the thing in my hand. We hadn't choreographed this show yet, hadn't decided where I was going to be when she let him in. I thought the simplest thing might be if I waited behind the door when she opened it, then stepped out with a drawn gun once he was inside. But maybe it made more sense to give him a little time alone with her first, while I waited in the kitchen or the bedroom for the right moment. There looked to be a psychological advantage in that, but there was more room in the script for something to go wrong. Her anxiety might tip him off, say, or he might just decide to do something weird. Crazy people, after all, are apt to do crazy things. It's their trademark.

I called her name again but evidently she had the water running and didn't hear me. I put the gun under my belt again, then drew it out and walked down the short hallway to the living room carrying it in my hand. I wanted coffee, if it was ready, and I wanted to work out how we were going to play the scene.

I walked into the living room and turned toward the kitchen and stopped in my tracks, because he was standing there with his back to the window and Elaine at his side and a little in front of him. He had one hand on her arm, just above the elbow, and with the other he was gripping her wrist.

He said, "Put the gun down. Now, right this minute, or I'll break her arm."

The gun wasn't pointed at him, and I wasn't holding it right, I didn't have my finger anywhere near the trigger. I was holding it in my hand the way you'd hold a plate of hors d'oeuvres.

I put the gun down.

* * *

She had described him well, the long angular body, spare of flesh but tight as a coiled spring, the narrow face, the eccentric haircut. Someone had used a clippers on everything outside the perimeter of the soup bowl, and his hair perched on his head like a skullcap. His nose was long, and fleshy at the tip, and his lips were quite full. His forehead sloped back, and beneath it his eyes were set deep under a prominent ridge of brow. The eyes were a sort of muddy brown, and I couldn't read anything in them.

His features and his hairstyle combined to give him a faintly medieval look, like an evil friar, but his clothes didn't fit the part. He wore an olive corduroy sport jacket with leather piping at the cuffs and lapels and tooled leather patches on the elbows. His pants were khaki, with a knife-edge crease, and he was wearing lizard boots with one-inch heels and silver caps on their pointed toes. His shirt was western style, with snaps instead of buttons, and he had one of those string ties with a turquoise slide.

"You must be Scudder," he said. "The pimping cop. Elaine wanted to let you know I was here, but I thought it would be nicer to surprise you. I told her I was sure you were a man who enjoyed surprises. I told Elaine not to make a sound, and so she didn't make a sound, not even when I hurt her. She does what I tell her. Do you know why?"

"Why?"

"Because she's beginning to realize I know what's best for her. I know what she needs."

His pallor was such that he didn't look to have any blood in his body. Beside him, Elaine was a matching shade; the blood had drained out of her face, and her strength and resolve looked to have gone with it. She looked like a zombie in a horror movie.

55

"I know what she needs," he said again, "and what she doesn't need is a dull-witted cop to pimp for her."

"I'm not her pimp."

"Oh? What are you then? Her lawfully wedded husband? Her demon lover? Her twin brother, separated from her at birth? Her long-lost bastard son? Tell me what you are."

It's funny what you notice. I kept looking at his hands. They still gripped her arm at the wrist and above the elbow. She'd told me how much strength he had in his hands, and I didn't doubt her word, but they didn't look that strong. They were large hands and his fingers were long, and knobby at the knuckle joints. The fingernails were short, clipped clear to the quick, and they had well-defined moons at their bases.

"I'm her friend," I said.

"*I'm* her friend," he said. "I'm her friends and her family." He paused for a moment, as if to relish the sound of that statement. He looked as though he liked it well enough. "She doesn't need anyone else. She certainly doesn't need you." He smiled just enough to show his prominent front teeth. They were large and slightly bucked. Horse teeth. Briskly he said, "Your services are no longer required. Your period of employment is terminated. You're out on your ass, you piece of shit. She doesn't want you around. Don't just stand there, with your face hanging out like bloomers on a tenement washline. Go. Scat!"

"Well, I don't know," I said. "I'm here at Elaine's invitation, not yours. Now if she wants me to leave—"

"Tell him, Elaine."

"Matt—"

"Tell him."

"Matt, maybe you'd better go."

I looked at her, trying to cue her with my eyes. "Do you really want me to leave?"

"I think you'd better."

I hesitated for a beat, then shrugged. "Whatever you say,"

56

I said, and moved toward the table where I'd set the gun down.

"Hold it! What do you think you're doing?"

"What does it look like I'm doing? I'm getting my gun."

"I can't allow that."

"Then I don't see how the hell I can leave," I said, reasonably. "That's my service revolver, and I'd be in shit up to my ears if I left it here."

"I'll break her arm."

"I don't care if you break her neck. I'm not going anywhere unless the gun goes with me." I thought for a moment. I said, "Look, I'll pick it up by the barrel. I'm not looking to shoot anybody with it. I just want to walk out of here with it."

While he worked it out I took another two steps and reached out to take the gun by the barrel. I kept the gun within his field of vision, so that he could see it was no danger to him. I couldn't have shot him anyway; he had Elaine positioned between us, and his fingers looked to be digging into her flesh. If she was in pain, I don't think she was aware of it. All that showed in her face was a mix of fear and despair.

Gun in hand, I angled forward and to my right. I was getting closer to him, but moving to put the coffee table between us. It was a flattened cube, of plywood I suppose, clad in white Formica. As I walked, I said, "I got to hand it to you, you made me look stupid. How did you get past the doorman?"

He just smiled.

"And through the door," I said. "That's a good lock there, and she swore you didn't have a key. Or did you? Or did she open it for you?"

"Put the gun away," he said. "And go."

"Oh, this? It bother you?"

"Just put it away."

"If it bothers you," I said, "here." And I tossed it at him.

He was holding her arm too hard, that was his mistake. It slowed his reaction time. He had to let go before he could do anything else, and instead his hands tightened reflexively and she cried out. He let go then, snatching at the gun, but by then I had a foot out to kick the coffee table at him, and I did, hard. It caromed into his shins even as I was launching myself over it and into him. The two of us sailed into a wall—we didn't miss the window by much—and the impact took the breath out of him. He wound up on his back and I wound up on top of him, and when I'd scrambled free he was still on the floor. I hit him on the chin, hard, and his eyes glazed. I grabbed him by the lapels and slammed him back against the wall and hit him three times in the middle. He was all muscle and all hard, but I put a lot into my punches and they got through. He sagged, and I swung a forearm and put my whole shoulder into it, and my elbow got him in the chin and put his lights out.

He lay on the floor like a rag doll, his head and shoulders propped against the white wall, one leg drawn up, one fully extended. I stood there, breathing hard, staring down at him. One of his hands lay on the floor, the fingers splayed. I remembered the look of the fingers gripping Elaine's arm, and I had the urge to move my foot a few inches so that it covered that hand, then lean my weight onto that foot and see if that didn't take some of the strength out of those steel fingers.

Instead I retrieved my piece and wedged it under my belt, then turned to Elaine. Some of the color had returned to her face. She didn't look wonderful, but she looked a lot better than she had when he was holding her arm.

She said, "When you said you didn't care if he broke my neck—"

"Oh, come on. You had to know I was setting him up."

"Yes, and I knew you must have something planned. But I was afraid it wouldn't work. And I was afraid he might break my neck, just out of curiosity, just to see whether you cared or not."

"He's not going to break anybody's neck," I said. "But I've got to figure out what to do with him."

"Aren't you going to arrest him?"

"Sure. But I'm afraid he'll walk."

"Are you kidding? After all this?"

"It's a tough case to prosecute," I told her. "You're a hooker, and juries tend not to get concerned about violence toward prostitutes. Not unless the girl dies."

"He said he killed a girl."

"Maybe he was just talking. Even if it's true, and I think it might be, we don't even know who she was or when he killed her, let alone have a case against him for it. We've got resisting arrest and assault on a police officer, but a half-decent defense attorney would make our relationship questionable."

"How?"

"He'd make it look as though I was your pimp. That would pretty much guarantee an acquittal. Even with the best slant on our relationship, it's a problem. You've got a married cop who's got this friendship with a call girl. You can imagine how that'll play in the courtroom. And in the papers."

"You said he's been arrested before."

"Right, and for the same kind of thing. But the jury won't know that."

"Why? Because charges were dropped?"

"They wouldn't know even if he'd been convicted and done time for it. Prior criminal history isn't admissible in criminal proceedings."

"Why the hell not?"

"I don't know," I said. "I've never understood it. It's supposed to be prejudicial, but isn't it part of the whole picture? Why shouldn't the jury know about it?" I shrugged. "Connie could testify," I said. "He hurt her and he threatened you. But would she stand up?"

"I don't know."

"I don't think she would."

"Probably not."

"I want to see something," I said, and I bent over Motley. He was still out cold. Maybe he had a glass jaw. There was a fighter like that, Bob Satterfield. He could take a punch with the best of them, but if you got his jaw just right he'd flop on his face for a ten count, so out of it he'd sleep through a Chinese fire drill.

I fumbled in his jacket pocket, straightened up, turned to show Elaine what I was holding. "This is a help," I said. "A baby automatic, looks like .25 caliber. It's sure to be unregistered, and there's no way in the world he'd have a carry permit. That's criminal possession of a deadly weapon in the second degree, that's a Class-C felony."

"Is that good?"

"It doesn't hurt. The thing is, I want to make sure his bail is too high for him to make, and I want him charged with something serious enough so that his lawyer can't plea-bargain the case down to nothing. I want him to do real time. He's a bad son of a bitch, he fucking well ought to go away." I looked at her. "Would you stand up?"

"What do you mean?"

"Would you testify?"

"Of course."

"There's more to it. Would you lie under oath?"

"What do you want me to say?"

I studied her for a moment. "I think you'll stand up," I said. "I'm going to take a chance."

"What do you mean?"

I wiped the gun clean of prints with my pocket handkerchief. I got an arm between Motley's shoulders and the wall and raised him up into a half-crouch. He was heavier than he looked, as thin as he was, and I could feel the hardness of his tissue. The muscles didn't relax fully even when he was out cold.

I fitted the gun into his right hand, got his index finger inside the trigger guard and curled it around the trigger. I found the safety, flicked it off. I wrapped my hand around his, levered his body a few degrees more erect, and saw where the gun was pointed. I was aiming right at one of the paintings, the one that later turned out to be worth fifty grand. I swung a little ways to the left and squeezed his finger against the trigger and put a hole in the wall. I placed the second shot a little higher, and angled the third almost into the ceiling. Then I let go of him and he fell back onto the floor and the wall, and the gun dropped from his hand to the floor beside him.

I said, "He was holding a gun on me. I kicked the coffee table at him. It knocked him off balance but he did get off three shots while he was falling, and then I crashed into him and took him down and out."

She was nodding, her face a study in concentration. If the gunshots had startled her, she seemed to have recovered quickly. Of course the shots hadn't been that loud, and the little bullets hadn't done much damage, just making neat little holes in the plaster.

"He fired a gun," I said. "He tried to kill a cop. That's not something he'll walk away from."

"I'll swear to it."

"I know you will," I said. "I know you'll stand up." I went over to her and held her for a minute or two. Then I went into the bedroom and got the bourbon bottle. I had a short one before I picked up the phone and called it in, and I had the rest of it while we waited for the cops to get there.

61

FOUR

She never did have to testify, not in court. She gave a sworn statement, perjuring herself cheerfully on paper, and she was letter perfect on that, telling an essentially unvarnished version of the truth up to the point where his gun came into play, and then laying it out for them the way we'd worked it out. My story was the same, and the physical evidence supported it. His fingerprints were on the gun, right where you'd expect to find them, and the paraffin test revealed nitrate deposits on his right hand, evidence that he'd fired a gun. It was indeed unregistered, and he had no license to possess a firearm, or to carry one on his person.

He swore he'd never seen the gun before, let alone fired it. His story was that he'd come to the Fifty-first Street premises after having made prior arrangements over the telephone to engage her services as a prostitute. He said he'd never seen her before the night in question, that he'd never had the opportunity to have sex with her because I had burst in and attempted to work a version of the badger game upon him, extorting him out of additional funds, and that when that failed I had launched an unprovoked attack upon him. Nobody bought any of this. If this was the first time he'd turned up in her life, why had she sworn out a complaint against him almost a week earlier? And his record might not be admissible evidence and the jurors might not be entitled to know about it, but the district attorney was damn well entitled and so was the judge who set bail at a quarter of a million dollars. His attorney protested this, arguing that his client had never been convicted of anything, but the judge looked at all those arrests for violence against women, along with a supporting statement that Connie Cooperman had been persuaded to give, and turned down a request for lower bail.

Motley stayed in a cell awaiting trial. The state brought a whole laundry list of charges against him, with attempted murder of a police officer up at the top. His lawyer took a good look at his client and the evidence against him and came around ready to cut a deal. The DA's Office was willing to play; the case was low-profile, the public didn't have a big emotional investment in it, and Elaine and I might come off looking pretty dirty after a round of intensive cross-examination, so why not plea-bargain the thing and save the state time and money? They reduced the main charge to an attempted violation of Section 120.11 of the penal code, aggravated assault upon a police officer. They dropped all the collateral charges, and in return James Leo Motley stood up in front of God and everybody and agreed that he was guilty as charged. The judge weighed his priors against the lack of convictions and came up with the Solomonic sentence of one-to-ten years in the state penitentiary, with credit for time served.

After sentence had been passed Motley asked the court if he could say something. The judge said he could, but not without reminding him he'd had the opportunity to make a statement prior to sentencing. Maybe it was shrewdness that had led him to hold his tongue until afterward; if he'd made the same statement earlier the judge would almost certainly have given him a sentence closer to the maximum.

What he said was, "That cop framed me, and I know it and he knows it, the pimping bastard. When I get out I got big plans for him and the two bitches." Then he turned to his left, tilting his head to point his long jaw at me. "That's you and all your women, Scudder. We got something to finish, you and me."

Lots of crooks threaten you. They're all going to get even, same as they're all innocent, they were all framed. You'd think nobody guilty ever went to prison.

He sounded as though he meant it, but that's how they all sound. And none of it ever comes to anything.

That had been something like a dozen years ago. It was another two or three years before I left the police force, for reasons that had nothing to do with Elaine Mardell or James Leo Motley. The precipitant, though perhaps not the cause, for my leaving was something that happened one night in Washington Heights. I was having a few quiet drinks at a tavern there when two men held up the place and shot the bartender dead on their way out. I ran out into the street after them and shot them both, killing one of them, but one shot went wide and fatally injured a six-year-old girl. I don't know that she had any business being there at that hour, but I suppose you could have said the same thing about me.

I didn't get any flak over the incident, as a matter of fact I got a departmental recognition, but from then on I had no heart for the job or my life. I quit the department, and around the same time I gave up trying to be a husband and father and moved into the city. I found a hotel room, and around the corner I found a saloon.

The next seven years are somewhat blurred in memory, although God knows they had their moments. The booze worked for a long time. Somewhere along the line it stopped working, but I drank it anyway because I seemed to have no choice. Then I started hitting detox wards and hospitals and losing three or four days at a time in blackouts, and I had a seizure and, well, things happened.

What it used to be like, what happened, and what it's like now . . .

"He's out there," she said.

"It seems impossible. He'd have been out years ago. It bothered me at the time that the judge gave him as short a sentence as he did."

"You didn't say anything."

"I didn't want to worry you. But he got one-to-ten, so he could have been on the street in less than a year. I never figured that would happen, he didn't strike me as the type to charm a parole board or get released after serving a minimum sentence, but even so you'd figure him to be out in three or four years, say five at the most. That's longer than most people can manage to nurse a grudge. But if he served five years that would mean he's been breathing free air for seven years now. Why would he wait this long to go after Connie?"

"I don't know."

"What do you want to do, Elaine?"

"I don't know that, either. I think what I want to do is throw some things in a suitcase and get a cab to JFK. I think that's what I want to do."

I could understand the impulse, but I told her it struck me as a little premature. "Let me make a few calls in the morning," I said. "It's possible he did something and wound up back in the joint. It'd be silly to fly to Brazil if he's locked up in Green Haven."

"Actually I was thinking more along the lines of Barbados."

"Or if he's dead," I said. "I thought at the time that he

was a good candidate to come out of there in a body bag. He's the type to make enemies, and it doesn't take a lot for someone to stick a knife in you."

"Then who sent me the clipping?"

"Let's not worry about that until we see if we can rule him out."

"All right. Matt? You'll stay here tonight?"

"Sure."

"I know I'm being silly but I'll feel better. You don't mind?"

"I don't mind."

She made up the couch for me with a couple of sheets and a blanket and a pillow. She'd offered me half the bed but I said I'd be more comfortable on the couch, that I felt restless and didn't want to worry about disturbing her with my tossing and turning. "You wouldn't disturb me," she said. "I'm going to take a Seconal, I take one about four times a year, and when I do nothing disturbs me that registers less than seven on the Richter scale. You want one? It's just the thing if you're wired. You'll be out cold before you even have time to relax."

I passed on the pill and took the couch instead. She went to bed and I stripped to my shorts and got under the covers. I couldn't keep my eyes closed. I kept opening them and looking at the lights of Queens across the river. A couple of times I thought with regret of the Seconal not taken, but it was never really an option. As a sober alcoholic, I couldn't take sleeping pills or tranquilizers or mood-elevators or any painkiller much stronger than aspirin. They interrupt sobriety and seem to undercut a person's commitment to recovery, and people who use them usually wind up drinking again.

I suppose I slept some, although it felt a lot like a white night. After a while the sun came up and slanted through the living-room window and I went into the kitchen and made a fresh pot of coffee. I toasted an English muffin and ate it and drank two cups of coffee.

I checked the bedroom. She was still sleeping, curled on her side with her face pressed into the pillow. I tiptoed past the bed and went into the bathroom and showered. It didn't wake her. I dried off and went back to the living room and got dressed, and by then it was time to make some telephone calls.

I had to make quite a few of them, and sometimes it took some doing to reach the person I had to speak with. I stayed at it until I found out what I needed to know, and then I looked in on Elaine again. She hadn't changed position, and I had a moment of wholly irrational panic, convinced that she was dead. He'd let himself in days ago, I decided, and he'd tampered with the Seconal, salting the capsule with cyanide. Or he'd let himself in just hours ago, slipping through walls like a ghost, slipping past me while I tossed on the leather couch, stabbing her in the heart and stealing away.

Of course it was nonsense, as I learned soon enough by dropping to a knee alongside the bed and listening to her steady shallow breathing. But it gave me a turn, and it showed me the state of my own mind. I went back to the living room, thumbed through the Yellow Pages, and made another couple of phone calls.

The locksmith got there around ten. I'd explained to him just what I wanted, and he brought along several models for me to look at. He went to work in the kitchen first, and he was halfway through in the living room when I heard her stirring. I went into the bedroom.

She said, "What's that noise? At first I thought you were using the vacuum cleaner."

"It's a drill. I'm having some locks installed. It's going to come to close to four hundred dollars. Do you want to write a check?"

"I'd rather give him cash." She went to the dresser and

took an envelope from the top drawer. Counting bills, she said, "Four hundred dollars? What are we getting, a vault?"

"Police locks."

"Police locks?" She arched an eyebrow. "To keep the police out? Or to keep the police in?"

"Whatever you decide."

"Here's five hundred," she said. "Get a receipt, okay?"

"Yes, ma'am."

"I don't know what my accountant does with them, but he's a bear for receipts."

She showered while I went out and kept the locksmith company. When he was done I paid him and got a receipt and put it and her change on the coffee table. She came out wearing baggy fatigues from Banana Republic and a short-sleeved red shirt with epaulets and metal buttons. I showed her how the locks worked. There were two of them on the living-room door and one in the kitchen.

"I think this is how he got in twelve years ago," I said, pointing to the service door in the kitchen. "I think he came in through the building's service entrance and up the back stairs. That's how he got past the doorman with no trouble. You've got a deadbolt lock on that door, but maybe it wasn't engaged at the time. Or maybe he had a key for it."

"I never use that door."

"So you wouldn't have known if it was locked or not."

"No, not really. It leads to the service elevator and the incinerator. Once in a blue moon I go out that way to the incinerator, but I don't like having to squeeze past the re-frigerator schlepping a bag of garbage, so I usually go out the front door and walk around."

"The first time he was here," I said, "he could have slipped into the kitchen and unlocked the door. Then it would have been open both times he let himself into the apartment. Sometime after that it would have been un-locked when you went to use it, but would you even have noticed it?"

"I don't think so. I would have just thought I forgot to lock it the last time I'd used it."

"Well, you don't have to use it at all for the time being." I demonstrated the lock, the steel bar that ran across the face of the door and lodged in a hasp on the doorframe. "This key locks and unlocks it," I said, "but I suggest you just leave it locked all the time. There's no way to unlock it from the outside. I had him install it without mounting a cylinder on the other side of the door. You never come in this way anyway, do you?"

"No, of course not."

"So it's permanently sealed now, for all practical purposes, but you can let yourself out with the key if you ever have to get out in a hurry. But if you do, you can't lock it after you. You can lock the deadbolt with the key, but not the police lock."

"I don't even know if I have a key for that door," she said. "Don't worry about it. I'll keep it closed all the time, and I'll keep the deadbolt and the police lock both locked."

"Good." We returned to the living room. "Now here," I said, "I had him mount two police locks. One of them's the same arrangement as you've got in the kitchen, a police lock that you can lock or unlock only from inside the apartment, with no cylinder on the outside. That way there's no lock out there for anybody to pick. When you're inside the apartment with both locks engaged there's no way anybody can get in without a battering ram. When you go out, you can lock the second police lock with a key. This is the key for it, with the bumps on it. The cylinder's supposed to be pick-proof, and the key itself can't be duplicated with ordinary equipment, so it would be a good idea not to lose it or your apartment will be secure against everyone, including you."

"There's a thought."

"You've got a lot of security here," I said. "He put an escutcheon plate over the cylinder so it can't be pried out, and the cylinder itself is some space-age alloy that you can't drill into. While he was at it I had him install a similar guard over the existing Segal deadbolt. All of this probably amounts to overkill, especially if you're planning to catch the next plane to Barbados, but I figured you could afford it. And you ought to have decent locks, Motley or no Motley."

"Speaking of him—"

"He's not dead and he's not in prison."

"When did he get out?"

"In July. The fifteenth of the month."

"Which July?" She looked at me and her eyes widened. "This July? He drew one-to-ten and served twelve years?"

"He wasn't what you'd call a model prisoner."

"Can they keep you there beyond the maximum sentence? Isn't that a violation of due process?"

"Not if you're a very bad boy. That sort of thing happens now and then. You can go to prison for ninety days and still be inside forty years later."

"God," she said. "I guess prison didn't rehabilitate him."

"It doesn't look that way."

"He got out in July. So that's plenty of time to find out where Connie went to and, and—"

"I guess it's time enough."

"And time to clip the story out of the paper and send it to me. And time to wait around while the fear builds. He gets off on fear, you know."

"It could still be a coincidence."

"How?"

"The way we said last night. A friend of hers knew you were her friend and wanted you to know what had happened."

"And didn't send a note? Or put on a return address?"

"Sometimes people don't want to get involved."

"And the New York postmark?"

I'd doped that out, too, lying on the couch and looking at Long Island City's skyline. "Maybe she didn't have your address. Maybe she put the clipping in an envelope and mailed the whole thing to someone she knew in New York, asking him or her to look up your address and send it on."

"That's pretty farfetched, isn't it?"

It had seemed plausible while I was stretched out watching dawn break. Now it did look like a stretch.

And it seemed even less likely an hour later, when I got back to my hotel. There weren't any messages in my box, but while I was checking I collected the letters I'd left behind the previous night. There was some junk mail, and a credit-card bill, and there was an envelope with no return address and my name and address block-printed in ballpoint.

It was the same story clipped from the same paper. No note with it, nothing scribbled in the margins. Something made me read it all the way through, word for word. The way you'll watch a sad old movie, hoping this time it'll have a happy ending.

FIVE

United had a nonstop out of La Guardia at 1:45 that was due into Cleveland at 2:59. I put a clean shirt and a change of socks and underwear in a briefcase along with a book I was trying to read and took a cab to the airport. I was early, but after I'd had a bite in the cafeteria and read the *Times* through and called Elaine I didn't have long to wait.

We were on time getting off and five minutes early at Cleveland-Hopkins International. Hertz had the car I'd reserved, a Ford Tempo, and the clerk gave me an area map with my route to Massillon marked out for me with a yellow highlighter. I followed her directions and made the drive in a little over an hour.

On the way, it occurred to me that it was just as well driving was one of those things you didn't forget how to do, because I'd done precious little of it in recent years. Unless there was a time I was forgetting, it had been over a year since I'd been behind a steering wheel. Last October Jan Keane and I had rented a car and driven to the Amish country around Lancaster, Pennsylvania, for a long weekend of turning leaves and folksy inns and Pennsylvania Dutch cooking. It started off well but we'd been having our problems and I suppose the weekend was an attempt to cure them, and that's a lot of weight for five days in the country to carry. Too much weight, as it turned out, because we were sullen and sour with each other by the time we got back to the city. We both knew it was over, and not just the weekend. In that sense you could say the trip accomplished what it was supposed to, though not what we wanted it to.

Police Headquarters in Massillon is housed in a modern building downtown on Tremont Avenue. I left the Tempo in a lot down the street and asked the desk officer for a Lieutenant Havlicek, who turned out to be a big man with close-cropped light brown hair and some extra weight in the gut and jowls. He wore a brown suit and a tie with brown and gold stripes, and he had a wedding ring on the appropriate finger and a Masonic ring on the other hand.

He had his own office, with pictures of his wife and children on his desk and framed testimonials from civic groups on one wall. He asked how I took my coffee, and he fetched it himself.

He said, "I was juggling three things when you called this morning, so let me see if I got it straight. You're with the NYPD?"

"I used to be."

"And you're working private now?"

"With Reliable," I said, and showed him a card. "But this matter doesn't involve them, and I don't have a client. I'm here because I think the Sturdevant killing might tie in with an old case of mine."

"How old?"

"Twelve years old."

"From when you were a police officer."

"That's right. I arrested a man with a history of violence toward women. He took a couple shots at me with a .25, so that was the major charge against him, and he wound up pleading to a reduced count of attempted aggravated assault. The judge gave him less time than I thought he deserved, but he got into trouble in prison and didn't get out until four months ago."

"I gather you figure it's a shame he got out at all."

"The warden at Dannemora says he killed two inmates for sure and was the odds-on suspect in three or four other homicides."

"Then why is he walking around?" He answered his own question. "Although there's a difference between knowing a man did something and being able to prove it, and I guess that goes double inside a state penitentiary." He shook his head, drank some coffee. "But how does he hook up with Phil Sturdevant and his wife? They weren't the kind of people lived in the same world as him."

"Mrs. Sturdevant lived in New York at the time. That was before her marriage, and she'd been on the receiving end of some of Motley's violence."

"That's his name? Motley?"

"James Leo Motley. Mrs. Sturdevant—her name was Miss Cooperman at the time—dictated a statement accusing Motley of assault and extortion, and after sentencing he swore he'd get even with her."

"That's pretty thin. That was what, twelve years ago?"

"About that."

"And all she did was give the police a statement?"

"Another woman did the same thing, and he made the same threat. Yesterday she got this in the mail." I handed him the clipping. Actually it was the copy I'd received, but I couldn't see that it made any difference.

"Oh, sure," he said. "This ran in the *Evening-Register*."

"It came all by itself in an envelope with no return address. And it was postmarked New York."

"Postmarked New York. Not back-stamped by the New

York post office, but marked to indicate it had been mailed there."

"That's right."

He took his time digesting this. "Well, I see why you thought it was worth getting on a plane," he said, "but I still don't see how your Mr. Motley could have been responsible for what happened in Walnut Hills the other night. Unless he was sending out hypnotic radio broadcasts and Phil Sturdevant was picking them up on the fillings in his teeth."

"It's that open-and-shut?"

"It sure as hell looks to be. You want to have a look at the murder scene?"

"Could I do that?"

"I don't see why not. We've got a key to the house somewhere. Let me get it and I'll take you over there and walk you through it."

The Sturdevant house was at the end of a cul-de-sac in a development consisting of expensive houses on lots of a half-acre or more. It was a one-story structure with a pitched roof and a fieldstone-and-redwood exterior. The property was nicely landscaped with evergreens, and there was a stand of birch trees near the property line.

Havlicek parked in the driveway and opened the front door with his key. We walked through an entrance hall into a large living room with a beamed cathedral ceiling. A fireplace ran the length of the far wall. It looked to be built of the same stone used for the house's exterior.

A gray broadloom carpet had been laid wall-to-wall in the living room, and there were some oriental area rugs laid here and there on top of it. One of these stretched in front of the fireplace. A chalk outline of a human being had been traced on the rug, with part of the legs extending onto the broadloom.

"That's where we found him," Havlicek said. "Way we

reconstruct it, he hung up the phone and came over to the fireplace. You see the gun rack. He kept a deer rifle and a .22 there, along with the twelve-gauge he used to kill himself. Of course we took both rifles along for safekeeping, in addition to the twelve-gauge. He would have been standing right there, and he'd have put the shotgun barrel in his mouth and triggered the weapon, and you can see the mess it made, blood and bone fragments and all. That's been cleaned up some, just for purposes of sanitation, but there's photographs on file if you need to see them."

"And that's where he fell. He landed face up?"

"That's right. The gun was lying alongside him, about where you'd expect to find it. Place has a charnel-house stink to it, doesn't it? Come on, I'll show you where we found the others."

The children had been murdered in their beds. They'd each had a room of their own, and in each room I got to look at blood-soaked bedding and another chalk outline, one smaller than the next. The same kitchen knife had been used on all three children and their mother, and it had been found in the bathroom off the master bedroom. In the bedroom itself they'd found the corpse of Connie Sturdevant. Bloody bedclothing indicated she'd been killed in bed, but the chalk outline was on the floor at the foot of the bed.

"We figure he killed her on the bed," Havlicek said, "and then threw her down on the floor. She was wearing a night-gown, so she'd evidently gone to sleep, or at least to bed."

"How was Sturdevant dressed?"

"Pajamas."

"Slippers on his feet?"

"Barefoot, I think. We can look at the photos. Why?"

"Just trying to get the picture. What phone did he use to call you people?"

"I don't know. There's extensions all over the house, and whatever one he used he hung it up afterward."

"Did you find bloody fingerprints on any of the phones?"

"No."

"He have blood on his hands?"

"Sturdevant? He had blood all over him, for God's sake. He blew the better part of his head all over his living room. You tend to lose a fair amount of blood that way."

"I know. Was all of it his?"

"What are you getting at? Oh, wait a minute, I can see where you're heading. You're saying he'd have had their blood on him."

"They seem to have done a lot of bleeding. You'd think he'd have got some of it on him."

"There was blood in the bathroom sink, where he must have washed his hands. As to whether he got blood on himself that he couldn't wash off, on his pajamas, say, well, I don't know. I don't even know if you could tell their blood apart. They could all have the same type, for all I know."

"There are other tests these days."

He nodded. "DNA matchups and that sort of thing. I know about that, of course, but an all-out forensic workup didn't appear indicated. I guess I see your point. If the only blood on him was his own, how did he manage to kill them without getting his hands dirty? Except he did get 'em dirty, we found where he tried washing up."

"Then there would have to be foreign bloodstains on his person."

"Foreign meaning not his. Why? Oh, because we know he had blood on him to wash off, and you never get all of it. So if there's none of their blood on his hands or his clothing, and if we do find traces of their blood in the bathroom sink, then somebody else killed them." He frowned and thought about it. "If there had been a single false note at the crime scene," he said. "If we had had the slightest reason to suspect this was anything other than what it looked to be, why, we might have taken a longer look at the physical evidence. But for God's sake, man, he called us up and told us what he'd done. We sent a car out and found him dead. When you've got a confession and the killer dead by his own hand, it tends to put a damper on further inquiry."

"I understand that," I said.

"And I haven't seen anything here today to change my mind. You saw the padlock on the front door. We put that on after, on account of we had to force the door when we got here. He had it locked with the chain on, the way you'll do when you're settled in for the night."

"The killer could have gone out another door."

"The back door was locked the same way, bolted from inside."

"He could have used a window and closed it after him. It wouldn't have been that hard to do. Sturdevant would already have been dead when the killer made the phone call. Do you automatically record calls to headquarters?"

"No. We log 'em, but we don't tape 'em. Is that how they do it in New York?"

"There's a tape made of all calls to 911."

"Then it's a shame he didn't do this in New York," he said, "so there'd be a record, same as your medical examiner could tell us what everybody had for breakfast. But I'm afraid we're a little backward here."

"I didn't say that."

He thought a moment. "No," he said. "I guess you didn't."

"They don't record calls into the individual precincts in New York, or at least they didn't when I was on the job. And they only started taping the 911 calls when it turned out that the operators were incompetent and kept screwing up. I'm not trying to play City Mouse, Country Mouse with you, Lieutenant. I don't think we'd have looked any harder at this case than you people did. As a matter of fact, the biggest difference between the way you've handled it and the way they'd have done it in New York is that you've been very decent and cooperative with me. If a cop or ex-cop from out

79

of town came to New York with the same story, he'd get a lot of doors shut in his face."

He didn't say anything just then. Back in the living room he said, "I can see where it might not be a bad idea to tape incoming calls. Shouldn't be all that costly to set up, either. What would it do for us in this instance? You're thinking voiceprint, but for that you'd need a recording of Sturdevant's voice for comparison purposes."

"Did he have an answering machine? He might have taped a message."

"I don't think so. Those machines aren't all that popular around here. Of course there might be some record of his voice somewhere. Home video, that sort of thing. I don't know if something like that would work for voiceprint comparison, though I don't see why not."

"If you had the call taped," I said, "you could find out one thing easily enough. You could find out if it was Motley."

"Well, you could at that," he said. "I never even thought of that, but when you've got an actual suspect it makes a difference, doesn't it? If you had a call taped and the voiceprint matched your Mr. Motley, you'd pretty much have him hanged, wouldn't you?"

"Not until we get a new governor."

"Oh, that's right. Your man keeps vetoing the death-penalty bills, doesn't he? But in a manner of speaking, you'd have your killer cold." He shook his head. "Speaking of voiceprints, you can probably guess we didn't do any dusting for fingerprints."

"Why should you? It looked open-and-shut."

"We do a lot of things routinely when there's not much point to them. Shame we didn't do that."

"I've a feeling Motley didn't leave any fingerprints."

"Still, it would be nice to know. I could get a crew in here now, but there've been so many people through here by this time I don't think we'd have much luck. Besides, it'd mean reopening the case, and I have to say you haven't given me cause to do that." He hooked his thumbs in his belt and looked at me. "You honestly think he did it?"

"Yes."

"Can you point to any kind of corroborating evidence? A clipping in the mail and a New York postmark, that may be enough to get you thinking, but it doesn't do a lot to change how the case looks from here."

I thought about that one while we left the house. Havlicek drew the door shut and snapped the padlock. It was cooler now, and the birch trees cast long shadows across the lawn. I asked when the killings had taken place. Wednesday night, he said.

"So it's been a week."

"Will be in a matter of hours. The call came in around midnight. I could give you the time to the minute, if it matters, because as I said we keep a log."

"I just wondered about the date," I said. "There was no indication on the clipping. I suppose the story would have run in Thursday night's paper."

"That's right, and there were follow-up stories the next day or two, but they won't tell you anything. Nothing else came to light, so there wasn't much for them to write about. Just that people were surprised, no indication he was under that kind of stress. The usual things you get from friends and neighbors."

"What kind of a workup did your medical examiner do?"

"The chief of pathology over at the hospital does our medical exams. I don't think he did much beyond looking at the bodies and confirming that the wounds were consistent with the way we read the case. Why?"

"You still have the bodies on hand?"

"I don't believe they've been released yet. I don't know that we're clear on who we're supposed to release them to, far as that goes. You got something specific in mind?"

"I was wondering if he'd happened to check for semen."

81

"Jesus God. You think he raped her?"

"It's possible."

"No signs of a struggle."

"Well, he's very strong, and she might not have tried to fight him off. You were asking about corroborative evidence. If there were semen traces, and if the lab work established the semen didn't come from Sturdevant—"

"That'd be corroboration, wouldn't it? You might even wind up matching the semen to your suspect. I'll tell you, I'm not even going to apologize for not ordering a check for pecker tracks. That's about the last thing that would have occurred to me."

"If you've still got the bodies—"

"We can get him to run tests now. I was already thinking that. I don't guess she happened to douche in the past few days, do you?"

"I wouldn't think so."

"Well, let's find out," he said. "Let's see if we can catch the doc before he goes home for dinner. God, his line of work's got to be hell on a man's appetite. Police work's bad enough. Though I seem to manage, don't I?" He clapped a hand to his gut and flashed a rueful grin. "Let's go," he said. "Maybe we'll get lucky."

The pathologist had left for the day. "He'll be in eight o'clock tomorrow morning," Havlicek said. "You did say you were staying over, didn't you, Matt?"

We were Matt and Tom now. I said I was booked on a late-afternoon flight the following day.

"The Great Western's the best place to stay," he said. "It's east of town on Lincoln Way. If you like Italian food you can't go wrong at Padula's, that's right at First Street, or there's a restaurant at the motel that's not bad. Or here's a better idea, let me call my wife and see if she can't set an extra place at the table."

"That's decent of you," I said, "but I think I'm going to beg off. I had about two hours' sleep last night and I'm afraid I might fall asleep at the table. Suppose you let me take you to lunch tomorrow?"

"We'll have to argue about who takes who, but it's a date. You want to meet me first thing in the morning and we'll go see the doc? Is eight o'clock too early for you?"

"Eight o'clock is fine," I said.

I got my car from the lot where I'd left it and found my way to the motel he'd recommended. I got a room on the second floor and took a shower, then watched the news on CNN. They had cable reception and pulled in thirty channels. After the newscast I worked the dial and found a prizefight on some cable channel I'd never heard of. A pair of Hispanic welterweights were spending most of their time in clinches. I watched until I realized that I wasn't paying any attention to what I was seeing. I went to the restaurant and had a veal chop and a baked potato and coffee and went back to the room.

I called Elaine. Her machine answered, and when I identified myself she picked up and turned the machine off. She was doing fine, she said, sitting behind her barricades and waiting. So far there'd been no untoward phone calls and nothing unlikely in the day's mail. I told her what I'd done, and that I'd be seeing the pathologist in the morning, that I'd ask him to look for semen traces.

"Make sure he checks in back," she said.

We talked a little more. She sounded all right. I told her I'd call when I got back to the city, and then I rang off and worked my way around the TV dial without finding anything that grabbed me.

I got my book from my briefcase. It was *The Meditations of Marcus Aurelius*. Jim Faber, my AA sponsor, had recommended it to me, quoting a couple of lines that had sounded interesting, and one day I'd stopped at the Strand and picked up a used copy of the Modern Library edition for a couple of dollars. I'd been finding it slow going. I liked some of the things he said, but a lot of the time I would have trouble tracking his argument, and when I did hit a sentence that resonated for me I would have to put the book aside and think about it for a half hour or so.

This time I read a page or two, and then I hit this passage: *Whatever happens at all happens as it should; thou wilt find this true, if thou shouldst watch narrowly.*

I closed the book and put it on the table next to me. I tried to imagine the events at the Sturdevant home a week ago. I wasn't sure what order he did them in, but for the sake of argument I decided he'd taken Sturdevant out first because he'd have presented the greatest danger.

Still, the report of the shotgun would have awakened everybody else. So maybe he'd have gone to the kids' rooms first, working his way down the hallway, moving from one room to the next, stabbing the two boys and the girl in turn.

Then Connie? No, he'd have saved her for last. He'd washed up in the bathroom off the master bedroom. Let's say he immobilized her, got her husband into the living room at gun- or knife-point, killed him with the shotgun, then went back and did Connie. And raped her while he was at it? Well, I'd find out tomorrow, if you could still detect the presence of semen a week after the fact.

Then a phone call, and then a quick trip through the house to get rid of fingerprints. And, finally, a quick and silent exit through a window, and he was on his way. Five people dead, three of them small children. A whole family gone because twelve years ago a woman had sworn out a statement against a man who'd forced himself on her.

I thought about Connie. Prostitution isn't necessarily a bad life, not at the level she and Elaine had practiced it, with East Side apartments and an executive clientele. But she had taken her shot at a much better life, and she'd been living it in the house in Walnut Hills.

Then it ended. And Jesus, the *way* that it ended . . .

Whatever happens at all happens as it should. Maybe it would be nice to reach the point where I found that true, but I wasn't there yet. Perhaps I just wasn't watching narrowly enough.

I got my wake-up call in the morning and checked out after breakfast. At eight sharp I gave my name to the desk officer. He had been told to expect me, and sent me back to Havlicek's office.

He was wearing a gray suit this morning, and another striped tie, this one red and navy. He came out from behind his desk to shake hands and asked me if I'd had coffee. I said I had.

"Then we might as well go see Doc Wohlmuth," he said.

I suppose there are older buildings in Massillon, but in my short time there everything I saw looked to have been built within the past ten years. The hospital was new, its walls bright with fresh pastel shades, its floors antiseptically clean. The pathology department was in the basement. We rode down in a silent elevator and walked the length of a hallway. Havlicek knew the route and I tagged along.

I don't know why, but I expected Doc Wohlmuth to be a cantankerous old bastard a few years past retirement age. He turned out to be around thirty-five, with a mop of streaky blond hair and a receding chin and an open boyish face off a Norman Rockwell cover. He shook hands when Havlicek introduced me, then stood there gamely through a round of the badinage cops and pathologists visit upon one another. When Havlicek asked him if he'd found traces of semen or any other evidence of recent sexual activity upon the corpse of Cornelia Sturdevant, he didn't mind showing that the question came as a surprise.

"Well, hell," he said. "I didn't know I was supposed to look for it."

"There's a possibility the case is more complicated than it looked at first," I said. "Do you have the body on hand?"

"Sure do."

"Could you check?"

"I don't see why not. She's not going anywhere."

He was halfway to the door when I remembered my conversation with Elaine. "Check for anal as well as vaginal entry," I suggested. He stopped in mid-stride, but he didn't turn around so I don't know what showed on his face.

"Will do," he said.

Tom Havlicek and I sat around waiting for him. Wohlmuth had some family snapshots in a lucite cube on his desk. That inspired Tom to tell me that Harvey Wohlmuth had himself a real sweetheart of a wife. I admired her photograph, and he asked me if I was a family man.

"I used to be," I said. "The marriage didn't last."

"Oh, I'm sorry."

"It was a long time ago. She's remarried, and my boys are pretty much grown. One's in school and the other's in the service."

"You have much contact with them?"

"Not as much as I'd like."

That was a stopper, and the silence hung for a moment before he picked up the ball and talked about his own children, a girl and a boy, both of them in high school. We moved from family to police work, and then we were just a pair of old cops telling stories. We were still at it when Wohlmuth returned, an owlish expression on his face, to tell us that he'd found semen traces in Mrs. Sturdevant's anus.

"Well, you called that," Havlicek said.

Wohlmuth said he hadn't expected to find anything. "There was no evidence of struggle," he said. "Nothing. No skin particles under her nails, no bruises on her hands or forearms."

Havlicek wanted to know if he could type the sperm and prove that it was or wasn't Sturdevant's.

"It might be possible," Wohlmuth said. "I'm not sure, with all the time that's gone by. We can't do it here, I can tell you that much. What I want to do is send slides and specimens and tissue samples to Booth Memorial in Cleveland. They can do a workup beyond what we're capable of here."

"I'll be interested in the results."

"So will I," Wohlmuth said. I asked if there'd been anything else remarkable about the body. He said she appeared to be in good health, which has always struck me as a curious thing to say about a dead person. I asked if he'd spotted any contusions, especially around the rib cage or the thighs.

Havlicek said, "I don't get it, Matt. What would bruises there indicate?"

"Motley had a lot of strength in his hands," I said. "He liked to use his fingers on a spot on the rib cage."

Wohlmuth said he hadn't noticed anything out of the ordinary in that respect, but that bruises weren't always that pronounced if the victim died shortly after the injury was inflicted. The injured area didn't discolor a day later in the same way.

"But you could have a look for yourself," he offered. "You want to come see?"

I didn't really, but I dutifully followed him down a hall and through a door into a room as cold as a meat locker, and with a not entirely dissimilar odor to it. He led me to a table where a body lay beneath a sheet of translucent plastic and drew the sheet aside.

It was Connie, all right. I don't know that I'd have recognized her alive, let alone dead, but knowing who she was I was able to see the girl I'd met a few times a dozen years ago. I felt a sickness deep in my gut, not nausea so much as a deep acidic sorrow.

I wanted to look for contusions, but it was hard for me to violate her nakedness with my eyes, and impossible to lay hands on her. Wohlmuth had no such compunctions, and a good thing, given the line of work he was in. Without ceremony he shunted a breast aside and palpated the sides of the rib cage, and his fingers found something. "Right here," he said. "See?"

I couldn't see anything. He took my hand and guided my fingers to a spot. She was cold to the touch, of course, and there was a flaccidity to her flesh. I could see what he'd found; there was a spot where the flesh was softer, less resilient. There wasn't much in the way of discoloration, however.

"And you said the inside of the thigh? Let's have a look. Hmmm. Here's something. I don't know if it would be a particularly sensitive pressure point for pain. Not an area I've got much expertise in. But there's been some trauma here. You want to see?"

I shook my head. I was unwilling to look between her parted thighs, let alone touch her. I didn't want to see any more, didn't want to be in that room any longer. Havlicek evidently felt the same way, and Wohlmuth sensed it and led us back to his office.

There he said, "I, uh, checked the children for semen."

"Christ!" Havlicek said.

"I didn't find any," Wohlmuth added quickly. "I thought I ought to check, though."

"Couldn't hurt."

"You saw the stab wounds, right?"

"They'd have been hard to miss."

"Right." He hesitated. "Well, they were all inflicted from the front. Three stab wounds between the ribs and into the heart, and any one of them would have done it."

"So?"

"What did he do, sodomize her and then roll her over and kill her?"

"Maybe."

"How did you find her? Lying on her back?"

Havlicek frowned, summoning the memory. "On her back," he said. "She'd slid down off the foot of the bed.

Stabbed through the nightgown, and it covered her to her knees. Maybe that semen was from much earlier."

"No way to tell."

"Or later," I suggested. They looked at me. "Try it this way. She's on her back in bed and he stabs her. Then he rolls her over onto her stomach, lifts her nightgown, and pulls her halfway off the bed so he can get at her better. He sodomizes and turns her over and pulls her nightgown down, and in the process she slides the rest of the way off the bed. Then he goes into the bathroom to wash up and rinses the knife while he's at it. That would account for the evident lack of struggle, wouldn't it? They don't offer a whole lot of resistance when they're already dead."

"No," Wohlmuth agreed. "They don't insist on a whole lot of foreplay, either. I don't have any knowledge of the man you're talking about. Is that kind of behavior consistent with what you know about him? Because I don't think it's in conflict with the physical evidence."

I thought of what he'd said to Elaine, about dead girls being as good as live ones if you got them early on. "It's consistent," I said.

"So you're talking about a monster."

"Well, Jesus God," Tom Havlicek said. "It wasn't Saint Francis of Assisi killed those kids."

SIX

"James Leo Motley," Havlicek said. "Tell me about him."

"You know about his priors and what he went away for. What else do you want to know?"

"How old is he?"

"Forty or forty-one. He was twenty-eight when I arrested him."

"You got a photo of him?"

I shook my head. "I could probably dig up a photo but it would be twelve years old." I described Motley as I remembered him, his height and build, his facial features, his haircut. "But I don't know if he still looks like that. His face wouldn't have changed much, not with the kind of strong features he had. But he could have gained or lost weight in prison, and he might not still have the haircut. As far as that goes, he could have lost the hair. It's been a long time."

"Some prisons will photograph a prisoner at the time of his release."

"I don't know if that's policy at Dannemora or not. I'll have to find out."

"That's where they had him? At Dannemora?"

"That's where he finished up. He started at Attica, but after a couple of years they transferred him."

"Attica's where they had the riot, isn't it? But that would have been before his time. The years seem to go by faster and faster, don't they?"

We were having lunch at the Italian place he'd recommended the night before. The food was good enough but the decor had a determinedly ethnic feel to it, and it came off like a stage set from one of the *Godfather* movies. Tom had turned down the waitress's suggestion of wine or a cocktail. "I'm not much of a drinker," he said to me, "but you go right ahead."

I'd said it was a little early for me. Now he apologized for having stranded me after we'd left Wohlmuth. "Hope you found things to keep you busy," he said. I told him I'd had a chance to read the newspapers and walk around town a little. "What I should have told you," he said, "is we've got the Pro Football Hall of Fame right off Seventy-seven in Canton. If you're any kind of a football fan, it's something you wouldn't want to miss."

That got us onto football, and that carried us through to the coffee and cheesecake. Massillon, he said, was like Kansas during the Civil War, with brother against brother when it came to the Browns and the Bengals. And they both had good teams this year, and if Kosar stayed healthy both teams ought to make the playoffs, and that was about as much excitement as the town could be expected to handle. They'd never face each other in the Super Bowl, not with both of them being in the same conference, but it was conceivable that they'd be matched up for the conference championship, and wouldn't that be something?

"We were talking about a subway series this year," I said. "The Mets and the Yankees, but the Mets lost out in the playoffs and the Yankees were out of it completely."

"I wish I had the time to follow baseball," he said. "But I

just don't. Football, I have about half my Sundays off, and I'm almost always free to watch the Monday night games."

Then, over coffee, we got back on track. "Why I asked about a photo," he said, "is at this point you haven't given me enough to justify reopening the case. We'll have to see what we get from the lab work they'll be doing at Booth in Cleveland. If they can say for sure that semen's from some-body else, maybe that'll tilt the balance. Meanwhile, what we got is a piece of mail mailed and delivered in New York City, and that doesn't mean a lot to my chief here in Massillon."

"I can understand that."

"Let's assume you've got the right reading on this and your man did it. The murders took place a week ago last night. I'd say he'd have had to've been in town a few days beforehand, and possibly as much as a week. I suppose it's theoretically possible that he committed the murders the day he arrived, but I'd say it was more likely he took some time to look the situation over."

"I would certainly think so. He's a planner, and he had twelve years to let it all ripen. He'd figure to take his time."

"And he left town with a clipping from Thursday night's paper, so he was still here when the paper hit the street that afternoon. There's a downtown newsstand that gets it around four, but most places don't have it for sale until five or six. So he was here that long, and maybe overnight. When was the postmark?"

"Saturday."

"So he clipped a newspaper Thursday night in Massillon and mailed it Saturday in New York. And it was delivered Monday?"

"Tuesday."

"Well, that's not so bad. Sometimes they take a week, don't they? You know what the post office and the Florsheim Shoe Company got in common?" I didn't. "Half a million loafers they'd love to unload but nobody wants 'em. Why I asked about the postmark, if he mailed it Friday we could be pretty sure he flew from here to New York. Not a hundred percent, because you can drive it in ten hours if you push it. You happen to know if he has a car?"

I shook my head. "I don't even know where he lives, or what he's been doing since they cut him loose."

"I was thinking we could check with the airlines, look for his name on the passenger manifests. You think he'd use his right name?"

"No. I think he'd pay cash and use an alias."

"Or pay with a stolen credit card, and that wouldn't have his right name on it, either. He probably put up at a hotel or motel here, and again I don't suppose we'll find James Leo Motley signed on any registration cards, but if we had a photo to circulate somebody might recognize his picture."

"I'll see what I can do."

"If he flew, he'd have needed a car to get around. He could have come by bus from Cleveland but he'd still need a car in Massillon. You have to show a license and a credit card to rent one."

"He could have stolen one."

"Could have. Lot of things to check, and I don't know what any of 'em might prove. I don't know how much effort I can get the department to put into checking, either. If the right word comes back from Booth Memorial, then we might do something. Otherwise I have to say our effort will most likely be minimal."

"I can understand that."

"When you've only got so many man-hours available to you," he said, "and when you're looking at a case you were able to close half an hour after it opened, well, you can see how you wouldn't be in a hurry to open it up again."

Afterward he gave me precise directions to the Hall of Fame in Canton. I listened, but without paying much attention. I was willing to believe it was fascinating, but I wasn't in the mood to stare through plate glass at Bronko Nagurski's old jersey and Sid Luckman's leather helmet. Besides, I had to turn in the Tempo in Cleveland or Hertz would charge me for a second day.

I gave it back to them with time to spare. My flight turned out to be overbooked, and before boarding they asked for volunteers to relinquish their seats and take a later flight, with the reward of a free trip anywhere in the continental United States. I couldn't think of anyplace I wanted to go. Evidently enough other people could, because they got their volunteers in short order.

I fastened my seat belt, opened my book, read a paragraph of Marcus Aurelius, and promptly fell asleep with the book in my lap. I didn't stir until we were making our descent into La Guardia.

My seat companion, wearing granny glasses and a Western Reserve sweatshirt, pointed to my book and asked me if it was something like TM. Sort of, I said.

"I guess it really works," she said enviously. "You were truly spaced."

I took a bus and a subway into Manhattan; the rush hour was in full swing, and that figured to be faster than a cab, and twenty dollars cheaper. I went straight to my hotel and checked my mail and messages, none of them important. I went upstairs and took a shower and called Elaine and brought her up to date. We didn't talk long, and then I went downstairs and had a bite and went over to St. Paul's for a meeting.

The speaker was a regular member of the group, sober a good number of years, and instead of telling an elaborate drinking story he talked this time about what he'd been going through lately. He'd had conflicts at work, and one of his kids was in bad trouble with drugs and alcohol. He wound up talking a lot about acceptance, and that became

the meeting's unofficial topic. I thought about Marcus Aurelius's wise words on the subject, about everything happening the way it was supposed to happen, and during the
discussion period I considered talking about that, and relating it to what had happened in a picture-book suburb of
Massillon, Ohio. But the meeting ended before I got around
to raising my hand.

In the morning I called Reliable and told them I wouldn't
be able to come in that day. I'd told them the same thing the
day before, and the person I spoke to asked me to hold, and
then the fellow I reported to came on the line.

"I had some work for you yesterday and today," he said.
"Can I expect you tomorrow?"

"I'm not sure. Probably not."

"Probably not. What's the story, you working a case of
your own?"

"No, it's something personal."

"Something personal. How about Monday?" I hesitated,
and before I could reply he said, "You know, there's a lot
of guys out there can do this kind of work and are glad to
get it."

"I know that."

"It's not a regular job, you're not on the payroll, but all
the same I need people I can count on to come in when I got
work for them."

"I appreciate that," I said. "I don't think you're going to
be able to count on me for the next little while."

"The next little while. How long is that?"

"I don't know. It depends how things work out."

There was a long pause, then a sudden bark of laughter.
He said, "You're drinking again, aren't you? Jesus, why
didn't you just say so in the first place? Give me a call when
you've got it out of your system and I'll see if I've got anything for you."

Rage boiled up within me, immediate and volcanic. I
choked on it until I heard him break the connection, then
slammed the receiver down. I stalked away from the phone,

my blood singing with the implacable fury of the falsely accused. I thought of a dozen things to tell him. First, though, I'd go over there and throw all his tables and chairs out the window. Then I'd tell him how he could change my per diem into nickels, and just where he could put it. And then—

What I did was call Jim Faber at work. He heard me out, and then he laughed at me. "You know," he said reasonably, "if you weren't an alcoholic in the first place, you wouldn't give a shit."

"He's got no right to think I'm drunk."

"How is it your business what he thinks?"

"Are you saying I haven't got a right to be angry?"

"I'm saying you can't afford it. How close are you to picking up a drink?"

"I'm not going to pick up a drink."

"No, but you're closer than you were before you talked with the son of a bitch. That's what you really felt like doing, isn't it? Before you called me instead."

I thought about it. "Maybe," I said.

"But you picked up the phone, and now you're starting to cool off."

We talked for a few minutes, and by the time I hung up my anger had lost its edge. Who was I really angry at? The guy at Reliable, who'd as much as said he was willing to hire me again after my bender had run its course? Not likely.

Motley, I decided. Motley, for starting all this in the first place.

Or myself, maybe. For being powerless to do anything about it.

The hell with it. I picked up the phone and made some calls, and then I went over to Midtown North to talk to Joe Durkin.

I never met Joe Durkin while I was on the job, although our years of service overlapped. I'd known him now for three or four years, and he'd become as good a friend as I had in the

NYPD. We'd done each other a little good over the years. Once or twice he'd steered a client in my direction, and a few times I'd turned up something useful and passed it on to him.

When I first met him he was counting the months toward his twenty years, figuring to put in his papers the day he hit that magic number. He couldn't wait, he always said, to get off the job and out of the goddamned city. He was still saying the same thing, but the number had changed to twenty-five, now that he'd passed the twenty-year mark.

The years have packed meat around his middle and thinned the dark hair that he combs flat across his head, and his face shows the florid cheeks and broken blood vessels of the heavy hitter. He had quit cigarettes for a while, but now he was smoking again. His ashtray overflowed onto the desktop, and he had a fresh cigarette burning. He put it out before I was halfway through with my story, and he had another one going before I was finished.

When I was done he tilted his chair back and blew a trio of smoke rings. There wasn't a lot of air moving in the detective squad room that morning. The rings drifted to the ceiling without losing their shape.

"Hell of a story," he said.

"Isn't it?"

"This guy in Ohio sounds like a pretty decent fellow. What's his name, Havlicek? Wasn't there a guy with the same name played for the Celtics?"

"That's right."

"Also named Tom, if I'm not mistaken."

"No, I think it was John."

"You sure? Maybe you're right. Your guy any relation?"

"I didn't ask him."

"No? Well, you had other things on your mind. What is it you want to do, Matt?"

"I want to put that son of a bitch back where he belongs."

"Yeah, well, he did what he could to stay there. A guy like that's a good bet to die inside the walls. You think they can make any kind of a case against him in Massillon?"

"I don't know. You know, he got a big break when they read it as murder-suicide and closed it out on the spot."

"It sounds as though we'd have done the same thing."

"Maybe, or maybe not. We'd have had his call on file, for one thing. Taped, with a chance of voiceprint ID. We'd have run more elaborate forensic workups on all five victims as a matter of course."

"You still wouldn't necessarily find sperm up her ass, not unless you were looking for it."

I shrugged. "It doesn't matter," I said. "For Christ's sake, we'd have been able to say if the husband had any blood on him besides his own."

"Yeah, we'd have probably done that. Except we tend to fuck up a lot too, Matt. You've been away from it long enough to forget that side of it."

"Maybe."

He leaned forward, stubbed out his cigarette. "Every time I quit these things," he said, "I'm a heavier smoker when I go back to them. I think quitting's dangerous to my health. If that semen turns out not to be the husband's, you figure they'll open the case?"

"I don't know."

"Because they're light years away from having a case against him. You can't prove he was in Ohio. Where is he now, you got any idea?"

I shook my head. "I called the DMV. He doesn't own a car and he doesn't have a license."

"They just told you all that?"

"They may have assumed I had official status."

He gave me a look. "Of course you weren't impersonating a police officer."

"I didn't identify myself as such."

"You want to look up the statute, it says you can't act in

such a manner as will lead people to believe you're a peace officer."

"That's with intent to defraud, isn't it?"

"To defraud or to induce people to do for you that which they wouldn't do otherwise. Doesn't matter, I'm just being a hard-on. No car, no license. Of course he could be the unlicensed driver of an unregistered vehicle. Where's he living?"

"I don't know."

"He's not on parole so he doesn't have to tell anybody. What's his last known address?"

"A hotel on upper Broadway, but that was more than twelve years ago."

"I don't suppose they held his room."

"I called there," I said. "Just on the off-chance."

"And he's not registered."

"Not under his own name."

"Yeah, that's another thing," he said. "False ID. He could have a full set. Twelve years in the joint, he's got to know a lot of dirty people. He's been out since when, the middle of July? He could have everything from an American Express card to a Swiss passport by now."

"I thought of that."

"You're pretty sure he's in town."

"Has to be."

"And you think he's gonna make a try for the other girl. What's her name again?"

"Elaine Mardell."

"And then he'll nail you for the hat trick." He gave it some thought. "If we had an official request from Massillon," he said, "we could maybe put a couple of uniforms on it, try to turn him up. But that's if they open the case and issue a warrant for the fucker."

"I think Havlicek would like to do that," I said. "If he could run it past his chief."

"He'd like to while the two of you are eating rigatoni and talking football. Now you're five hundred miles away and he's got a million other things that need doing. It gets easier for him to say the hell with it. Nobody likes to open a closed file."

"I know."

He got a cigarette from his pack, tapped it against his thumbnail, put it back in the pack. He said, "What about a photo? They got one at Dannemora?"

"From his intake interview eight years ago."

"You mean twelve, don't you?"

"Eight. He was at Attica first."

"Right, you said so."

"So the only photograph they have is eight years old. I asked if they could send me a copy. The guy I spoke to seemed doubtful. He wasn't sure whether that was policy or not."

"I guess he didn't somehow assume you were a police officer."

"No."

"I could call," he said, "but I don't know how much good it would do. Those people generally cooperate, but it's hard to light a fire under them. They tend to take their time. Of course you don't need the photo until your friend in Ohio gets clearance to reopen the case, and that doesn't happen until they get the new forensic report."

"And maybe not then."

"And maybe not then. But by that time you'll probably have the photo from Dannemora. Unless, of course, they decide not to send it to you."

"I don't want to wait that long."

"Why not?"

"Because I want to be able to go out and look for him."

"So you want a photo to show."

"Or a sketch," I said.

He looked at me. "That's a funny idea," he said. "You mean one of our artists."

"I figured you might know somebody who wouldn't mind a little extra work."

"Moonlighting, you mean. Draw a picture, pick up a couple of extra bucks."

"Right."

"I might at that. So you'll sit down with him and get him to draw a picture of somebody you haven't laid eyes on in a dozen years."

"It's a face you don't forget."

"Uh-huh."

"And there was a picture that ran in the papers at the time of the arrest."

"You didn't keep a copy, did you?"

"No, but I could look at the microfilm over at the library. Refresh my memory."

"And then sit down with the artist."

"Right."

"Of course you don't know if the guy looks the same, all these years, but at least you'd have a picture of what he used to look like."

"The artist could age him a little. They can do that."

"Amazing what they can do. Maybe you'd all three get together, you and the artist and Whatsername."

"Elaine."

"Right, Elaine."

"I hadn't thought of that," I said, "but it's a good idea."

"Yeah, well, I'm a bottomless well of good ideas. It's my trademark. Offhand I can think of three guys who could do this for you, but there's one I'll call first, see if I can track him down. You wouldn't get upset if this ran you a hundred bucks?"

"Not at all. More if necessary."

"A hundred ought to be plenty." He picked up the phone. "The guy I'm thinking of is pretty good," he said. "More important, I think he might like the challenge."

SEVEN

Ray Galindez looked more like a cop than an artist. He was medium height and stocky, with bushy eyebrows mounted over brown cocker spaniel eyes. At first I put him in his late thirties, but that was an effect of the weight he carried and a certain solemnity to his manner, and after a few minutes I lowered that estimate by ten or twelve years.

As arranged, he met us at Elaine's that evening at seven-thirty. I'd arrived earlier, in time for her to make a pot of coffee and me to drink a cup of it. Galindez didn't want any coffee. When Elaine offered him a beer he said, "Maybe later, ma'am. If I could just have a glass of water now that'd be great."

He called us sir and ma'am, and doodled on a scratch pad while I explained the nature of the problem. Then he asked for a brief description of Motley and I gave him one.

"This ought to work," he said. "What you're describing is a very distinctive individual. That makes it much easier for me. What's the worst thing is when you got an eyewitness and he says, 'Oh, this was just an average person, real ordinary-looking, he just looked like everybody else.' That means one of two things. Either your suspect had a face with nothing there to grab onto, or your witness wasn't really seeing what he was looking at. That happens a lot when you've got different races. Your white witness looks at a black suspect and all he sees is a black person. You see the color and you don't see the face."

Before he did any drawing, Galindez led us in an eyes-closed visualization exercise. "The better you see him," he said, "the more we get on the page." Then he had me describe Motley in detail, and as I did so he worked up a sketch with a soft pencil and an Art-Gum eraser. I'd managed to get to the Forty-second Street library early that afternoon, and I'd located two newsphotos of Motley, one taken at the time of his arrest, the other during his trial. I don't know that my memory needed refreshing, but I think they had helped clarify the visual image I'd had of him, the way you'd skim off the grime of the ages to restore an old painting.

It was remarkable, watching the face take shape on the sketch pad. He had both of us pointing out whatever looked off about the sketch, and he'd go to work with the eraser and make a slight change, and gradually the image came into focus with our memory. Then, when we couldn't find anything else to object to, he brought the sketch up to date.

"What we've got here," he said, "is already a man who looks older than twenty-eight years of age. Partly that's because all three of us know for a fact that he's forty or forty-one now, so our minds have been making little unconscious adjustments to our memory. Still, there's more we can do. One thing that happens as you age, your features get more prominent. You take a young person and draw a caricature of him, ten or twenty years later it doesn't look so exaggerated. I had an instructor once, she said we grow up to be caricatures of ourselves. What we'll do here, we'll make the nose a little bit larger, we'll sink the eyes a little beneath the brow." He did all this with a hint of shadow here, a change of line there. It was quite a demonstration.

"And gravity starts working on you," he went on. "Pulls you down here and there." A flick of the eraser, a stroke of the soft pencil. "And the hairline. Now here we're in the dark on account of we lack information. Did he keep his hair? Is he bald as an egg? We just don't know. But let's say he did like most people do, most men, that is, and he's got the beginnings of male-pattern baldness with the receding hairline. That doesn't mean he's going to look bald, or even well on his way. All it means is his hairline's changed and he's got himself a higher forehead, might look something like this."

He added a suggestion of lines around the eyes, creases at the corners of the mouth. He increased the definition of the cheekbones, held the pad at arm's length, made a minute adjustment with eraser and pencil.

"Well?" he said. "What do you think? Suitable for framing?"

His work done, Galindez accepted a Heineken. Elaine and I split a Perrier. He talked a little about himself, reluctantly at first, but Elaine was masterful at drawing him out. I suppose it was a professional talent of hers. He told us how drawing had always been something he could do, how he'd taken it so utterly for granted that it had never occurred to him to make a career of it. He'd always wanted to be a cop, had a favorite uncle in the department, and took the test for admission as soon as he finished up a two-year hitch at Kingsborough Community College.

He went on sketching for his own amusement, doing portraits and caricatures of his fellow officers, and one day in the absence of a regular police artist he was pressed into service to produce a sketch of a rapist. Now that was the bulk of what he did, and he loved it, but he felt himself being drawn away from police work. People had been suggesting that he might have the potential for an artistic career far greater than anything he could expect to realize in law enforcement, and he wasn't sure how he felt about that.

He said no to Elaine's offer of a second beer, thanked me for the two fifties I handed him, and told us he hoped we'd let him know how things turned out. "When you take him down," he said, "I hope I get a chance to see him, or at least a photo of him. Just to see how close I came. Sometimes you'll see the actual guy and he's nothing like what you drew, and other times anybody'd swear you must have been working from a model."

When he left Elaine closed the door after him and engaged all the locks. "I feel silly doing this," she said, "but I've been doing it anyway."

"There are people all over town with half a dozen locks on every door, and alarm systems and everything else. And they don't have somebody who's threatened to kill them."

"I suppose it's comforting to know that," she said. "He's a nice kid, Ray. I wonder if he'll stay a cop."

"Hard to say."

"Was there ever anything else you wanted to be? Besides a cop?"

"I never even wanted to be a cop. It was something I drifted into, and before I was out of the Academy I realized it was what I'd been born for. But I never knew that early on. When I was a kid I wanted to be Joe DiMaggio when I grew up, but that's what every kid wanted, and I never had the moves to go with the desire."

"You could have married Marilyn Monroe."

"And sold coffee makers on television. There but for the grace of God."

She carried our empty glasses into the kitchen and I trailed along behind her. She rinsed them under the tap, placed them in the strainer. "I think I'm getting stir-crazy," she said. "What are you doing tonight? Do you have any-place you have to be?"

I looked at my watch. I usually go to St. Paul's on Fridays for the eight-thirty step meeting, but it was too late now, they'd already started. And I had caught a noon meeting downtown already that day. I told her I didn't have anything planned.

"Well, how about a movie? How does that sound?"

It sounded fine. We walked over to Sixtieth and Third to a first-run house. It was the weekend so there was a line, but there was a pretty decent film at the end of it, a slick caper movie with Kevin Costner and Michelle Pfeiffer. "She's not really pretty," Elaine said afterward, "but there's something about her, isn't there? If I were a man, I'd want to fuck her."

"Repeatedly," I said.

"Oh, she does it for you, huh?"

"She's all right."

"'Repeatedly,'" she said, and chuckled. Around us, Third Avenue was thronged with young people who looked as though the country were every bit as prosperous as the Re-publicans kept telling us it was. "I'm hungry," Elaine an-nounced. "You want to get a bite? My treat."

"Sure, but why is it your treat?"

"You paid for the movie. Can you think of a place? Friday night in this neighborhood, wherever we go we're going to be up to our tits in yuppies."

"There's a place in my neighborhood. Great hamburgers and cottage fries. Oh, wait a minute. You don't eat ham-burgers, do you? The fish is good there, but I forget if you said you eat fish."

"Not anymore. How's their salad?"

"They serve a good salad, but is that enough for you?"

She said it would be plenty, especially if she stole a few of my cottage fries. There were no empty cabs and the streets were full of people trying to hail one. We started to walk, then caught a bus on Fifty-seventh Street and got off at Ninth Avenue. The place I had in mind, Paris Green, was five blocks downtown. The bartender, a lanky fellow with a brown beard that hung down like an oriole's nest, gave a wave as we cleared the threshold. His name was Gary, and he'd helped me out a few months ago when I'd been hired to find a girl who'd done some of her drinking there. The manager, whose name was Bryce, had been a little less helpful then, but he was helpful enough now, greeting us with a smile and showing us to a good table. A waitress with a short skirt and long legs came over to take our drink order, went away, and came back with Perrier for me and a Virgin Mary for Elaine. I must have been watching the girl's departure, because Elaine tapped my glass with hers and advised me to stick to Michelle Pfeiffer.

"I was just thinking," I said.

"I'm sure you were."

When the girl returned Elaine ordered the large garden salad. I had what I generally have there, a Jarlsberg cheeseburger and well-done fries. When the food came I had what felt like *déjà vu* until I realized I was getting echoes of Tuesday night, when I'd had a late bite at Armstrong's with Toni. The two restaurants weren't that much alike, and neither were the women. Maybe it was the cheeseburgers.

Halfway through mine I thought to ask her if it bothered her that I was eating a cheeseburger. She looked at me as though I were crazy and asked why it should bother her.

"I don't know," I said. "You don't eat meat, and I just wondered."

"You must be kidding. Not eating meat is just a choice I make, that's all. My doctor didn't order me to quit, and it wasn't an addiction I had to struggle with."

"And you don't have to go to the meetings?"

"What meetings?"

"Carnivores Anonymous."

"What a thought," she said, and laughed. Then her eyes

narrowed and she looked appraisingly at me. "Is that what you did? AA?"

"Uh-huh."

"I thought that was probably how you did it. Matt, would it have bothered you if I'd ordered a drink?"

"You did."

"Right, a Virgin Mary. Would it have—"

"You know what the British call it? Instead of a Virgin Mary?"

"A Bloody Shame."

"Right. No, it wouldn't have bothered me if you'd ordered a real drink. You can order one now if you want."

"I don't."

"Is that why you ordered a Virgin Mary? Because you thought it might bother me otherwise?"

"It didn't even occur to me, as a matter of fact. I hardly ever drink alcohol these days. I hardly ever did. The only reason I asked was because *you* asked about the cheeseburger, and while we've been discussing meat and drink I've been sneaking your cottage fries."

"While my attention was diverted elsewhere. We could probably arrange to get you some of your own."

She shook her head. "Stolen sweets are best," she said. "Didn't your mother ever tell you that?"

She wouldn't let me take the check, and then rejected my suggestion that we split it. "I invited you," she said. "Besides, I owe you money."

"How do you figure that?"

"Ray Galindez. I owe you a hundred bucks."

"The hell you do."

"The hell I don't. Some maniac's trying to kill me and you're protecting me. I ought to be paying your regular rate, you know that?"

"I don't have a regular rate."

109

"Well, I ought to be paying you what a client pays. I certainly ought to be covering the expenses. Speaking of which, you flew to Cleveland and back, you stayed over at a hotel—"

"I can afford it."

"I'm sure you can, but so what?"

"And I'm not just acting on your behalf," I went on. "I'm his target at least as much as you are."

"You think so? He's probably a lot less likely to fuck you in the ass."

"You never know what he learned in prison. I'm serious, Elaine. I'm operating in my own interest here."

"You're also acting in mine. And it's depriving you of income, you already said how you're not working at the detective agency in order to make time for this. If you're contributing your time, the least I can do is cover all the expenses."

"Why don't we split them?"

"Because that's not fair. You're the one running around, you're the one putting your regular work on the shelf for the duration. Besides, I can afford it better than you can. Don't pout, for Christ's sake, it's no reflection on your manhood, it's just a simple statement of fact. I've got a lot of money."

"Well, you earned it."

"Me and Smith Barney, making our money the old-fashioned way. I earned it and I kept it and I invested it, and I'm not rich, honey, but I'll never be poor. I own a lot of property. I own my apartment, I bought right away when the building went co-op, and I own houses and multiple dwellings in Queens. Jackson Heights, mostly, and some in Woodside. I get checks every month from the management company, and every now and then my accountant tells me I've got too big a balance in my money-market account and I have to go out and buy another piece of property."

"A woman of independent means."

"You bet your ass."

✳   ✳   ✳

She paid the check. On the way out we stopped at the bar and I introduced her to Gary. He wanted to know if I was working on a case. "He let me play Watson once," he told Elaine. "Now I live in hope of another opportunity."

"One of these days."

He draped his long body over the bar, dropped his voice low. "He brings suspects here for grilling," he confided. "We grill them over mesquite."

She rolled her eyes and he apologized. We got out of there, and she said, "God, it's glorious out, isn't it? I wonder how long this weather can last."

"As long as it wants, as far as I'm concerned."

"It's hard to believe it's something like six weeks until Christmas. I don't feel like going home. Is there someplace else we can go? That we can walk to?"

I thought for a moment. "There's a bar I like."

"You go to bars?"

"Not usually. The place I'm thinking of is kind of lowlife. The owner—I was going to say he was a friend of mine, but that may not be the right word."

"Now you've got me intrigued," she said.

We walked over to Grogan's. We took a table, and I went over to the bar to get our drinks. They don't have waiters there. You fetch what you want yourself.

The fellow behind the stick was called Burke. If he had a first name, I'd never heard it. Without moving his lips he said, "If you're looking for the big fella, he was just here. I couldn't say if he'll be back or not."

I brought two glasses of club soda back to the table. While we nursed them I told her a couple of stories about Mick Ballou. The most colorful one involved a man named Paddy Farrelly, who'd done something to arouse Ballou's ire. Then one night Ballou went in and out of every Irish saloon on the West Side. He was carrying a bowling bag, so they

111

said, and he kept opening it to show off Paddy Farrelly's disembodied head.

"I heard that story," Elaine said. "Wasn't there something about it in the papers?"

"I think one of the columnists used it. Mick refuses to confirm or deny. In any event, Farrelly's never been seen since."

"Do you think he did it?"

"I think he killed Farrelly. I don't think there's any real question of that. I think he went around showing off a bowling bag. I don't know for sure that he ever opened it, though, or that there was anything in it."

She thought it over. "Interesting friends you have," she said.

Before our club soda ran out, she got a chance to meet him. He came in with two much smaller men in tow, two men dressed alike in jeans and leather flier's jackets. He gave me a slight nod as he led the two the length of the room and through a door at the rear. Some five minutes later the three reappeared. The two smaller men walked on out of the bar and headed south on Tenth Avenue, and Ballou stopped at the bar, then came over to our table with a glass of twelve-year-old Jameson in his hand.

"Matthew," he said. "Good man." I pointed to a chair but he shook his head. "I can't," he said. "I have business. The man who's his own boss always winds up working for a slavedriver."

I said, "Elaine, this is Mick Ballou. Elaine Mardell."

"A pleasure," Ballou said. "Matthew, I've been saying I wished you would come by, and here you are and I have to be off. Come back again, will you?"

"I will."

"We'll tell tales all night and go to mass in the morning. Miss Mardell, I'll hope to see you again as well."

He turned away. Almost as an afterthought he raised his

glass and drained it. On his way out he left the glass on an empty table.

After the door closed behind him Elaine said, "I wasn't prepared for the size of him. He's huge, isn't he? He looks like one of those statues on Easter Island."

"I know."

"Rough-hewn from granite. What did he mean about going to mass in the morning? Is that code for something?"

I shook my head. "His father was a meatcutter in the Washington Street market. Every once in a while Mick likes to put on his father's old apron and go to the eight o'clock mass at St. Bernard's."

"And you go with him?"

"I did once."

"You bring a girl to the most remarkable places," she said, "and introduce her to the most remarkable people."

Outside again, she said, "You live near here, don't you, Matt? You can just put me in a cab. I'll be all right."

"I'll see you home."

"You don't have to."

"I don't mind."

"Are you sure?"

"Positive," I said. "Besides, I'm going to need that sketch Galindez made. I want to get it photocopied first thing in the morning and start showing it to people."

"Oh, right."

There were plenty of cabs now, and I flagged one and we rode across town in silence. Her doorman opened the cab door for us, then hurried ahead to hold the door to the lobby.

As we rode up in the elevator she said, "You could have had the cab wait."

"There are cabs all over the place."

"That's true."

"It's easier to get another one than pay his waiting time. Besides, I might walk home."

"At this hour?"

"Sure."

"It's a long walk."

"I like long walks."

She unfastened both locks, the Segal deadbolt and the Fox police lock, and when we were inside she fastened them all again, the two she'd just unlocked and the other, the police lock that could only be engaged from inside. It was a lot to go through given that I was going to be leaving in a minute, but I was pleased to see her do it. I wanted her to get in the habit of setting all the locks the minute she walked into the place. And not just most of the time. All of the time.

"Don't forget the cab," she said.

"What about the cab?"

"All the cabs," she said. "You want to keep track, so I can reimburse you."

"Oh, for Christ's sake," I said.

"What's the matter?"

"I can't bother with that kind of chickenshit," I said. "I don't go through that when I have a client."

"What do you do?"

"I set some kind of arbitrary flat rate and it includes my expenses. I can't make myself keep receipts and write down every time I get on the subway. It drives me crazy."

"What about when you do a day's work for Reliable?"

"I keep track as well as I can, and it makes me a little bit nuts, but I put up with it because I have to. I may be done working for them anyway, after the conversation I had with one of the bosses this morning."

"What happened?"

"It's not important. He was a little miffed that I was taking some time off, and I'm not sure he'll want me back when it's over. Then again, I'm not sure I'll want to go back."

114

"Well, you'll work it out," she said. She walked over to the coffee table, picked up a little bronze statue of a cat, and turned it over in her hands. "I don't mean keep receipts," she said. "I don't mean itemize everything to the penny. I just want you to get paid back for whatever out-of-pocket expenses you have. I don't care how you arrive at a figure, just so you don't cheat yourself."

"I understand."

She walked over to the window, still passing the little cat from hand to hand. I moved alongside her and we looked at Queens together. "Someday," I said, "all of this will be yours."

"Funny man. I want to thank you for tonight."

"No thanks are due."

"I think they are. You saved me from a severe case of cabin fever. I had to get out of here, but it was more than that. I had a good time."

"So did I."

"Well, I'm grateful. Taking me to places in your neighborhood, Paris Green and Grogan's. You didn't have to let me into your world like that."

"I had at least as good a time as you did," I said. "And it doesn't exactly hurt my image to be seen with a beautiful woman on my arm."

"I'm not beautiful."

"The hell you're not. What do you want, reassurance? You must know what you look like."

"I know I'm not a bow-wow," she said. "But I'm certainly not beautiful."

"Oh, come on. How'd you get all those houses across the river?"

"You don't have to look like Elizabeth Taylor to make it in the life, for God's sake. You ought to know that. You just have to be a person a man'll want to spend time with. I'll tell you a secret. It's mental work."

"Whatever you say."

She turned away, put the cat back on the coffee table. With her back to me she said, "Do you really think I'm beautiful?"

"I've always thought so."

"That's so sweet."

"I'm not trying to be sweet. I just—"

"I know."

Neither of us said anything for a moment, and the room turned deeply silent. There had been a moment like that in the film we saw, when the music stopped and the sound track went soundless. It heightened the suspense, as I recall.

I said, "I'd better take that sketch."

"You'd better. I want to put it in something, though, so it won't smudge. Let me go pee first, okay?"

While she was gone, I stood in the middle of the room looking at James Leo Motley as Ray Galindez had drawn him and trying to read the expression in his eyes. That didn't make much sense, given that I was looking at an artist's drawing instead of a photo, and that Motley's eyes had been opaque and unreadable even in person.

I wondered what he was doing out there. Maybe he was holed up in an abandoned building sucking on a crack pipe. Maybe he was living with a woman, hurting her with the tips of his fingers, taking her money, telling her she liked it. Maybe he was out of town, shooting craps in Atlantic City, lying on a beach in Miami.

I went on gazing at the sketch, trying to let my old animal instincts tell me where he was and what he was doing, and Elaine returned to the room and moved to stand beside me. I felt the gentle pressure of her shoulder against my side and breathed in her scent.

She said, "I thought a cardboard tube. That way you wouldn't have to fold it, you could just roll it, and it won't get smudged."

"How do you happen to have a cardboard tube on hand? I thought you didn't keep stuff."

"I don't, but if I pull the rest of the paper towels off the roll I'll have a tube."

"Clever."

"I thought so."

"If you think it's worth it."

"How much is a roll of paper towels? A buck nineteen, something like that?"

"I don't know."

"Well, it's something like that. Of course it's worth it." She extended a forefinger, touched the sketch. "When this is over," she said, "I want this."

"What for?"

"I want it matted and framed. Remember what he said, 'Suitable for framing'? He was joking, but that's because he doesn't take his work seriously yet. This is art."

"You're serious."

"You bet I am. I should have gotten him to sign it. Maybe I'll get in touch with him later, ask him if he'd be willing. What do you think?"

"I think he'd be flattered. Listen, I was going to have a few Xerox copies made, but now you're giving me ideas. What I'll do is I'll run an edition of fifty and number them."

"Very funny," she said. She moved her hand and laid it gently on top of mine. "Funny man."

"That's me."

"Uh-huh."

There was more of that utter silence, and I cleared my throat to break it. "You put perfume on," I said.

"Yes, I did."

"Just now?"

"Uh-huh."

"It smells nice."

"I'm glad you like it."

I turned to put the sketch on the table, then straightened up again. My arm moved around her waist and my hand set-

117

tled on her hip. She sighed almost imperceptibly and leaned against me, her head on my shoulder.

"I feel beautiful," she said.

"You should."

"I didn't just put on perfume," she said. "I got undressed."

"You're dressed now."

"Yes, I am. But before I was wearing a bra and panties, and now I'm not. So it's just me under these clothes."

"Just you."

"Just me and a little perfume." She swung around to face me. "And I brushed my teeth," she said, tilting her head, looking up at me with her lips slightly parted. Her eyes held mine for a moment, and then she closed them.

I took her in my arms.

It was quite wonderful, urgent yet unhurried, passionate yet comfortable, familiar yet surprising. We had the ease of old lovers and the eagerness of new ones. We had always been good together, and the years had been kind. We were better than ever.

Afterward she said, "I was thinking about this all night. I thought, gee, I like this guy, I always liked him, and wouldn't it be nice to find out if the gears still mesh after all these years. So in a manner of speaking I had this planned, but it was all in the mind. Do you know what I mean?"

"I think so."

"My mind was excited at the prospect. Then you told me I was beautiful and all of a sudden I'm standing there with wet panties."

"Honestly?"

"Yeah, instant arousal. Like magic."

"The way to a woman's heart—"

"Is through her panties. Can't you see new worlds opening up for you? All you have to do is tell us we're beautiful."

She put her hand on my arm. "I think the reason it worked is you made me believe it. Not that I am, but that you think I am."

"You are."

"That's your story," she said, "and you stick to it. You know that story about Pinocchio? The girl sits on his face and says, 'Lie to me, lie to me.'"

"When did I ever lie to you?"

"Ah, baby," she said, "I figured it'd be fun to do this, and I knew it was going to happen one of these days, but who would have guessed we'd be so hot for each other?"

"I know."

"When was the last time we were together like this? The last time you were over here was three years ago, but we didn't go to bed then."

"No, it was a few years before then."

"So it could have been seven years ago?"

"Maybe even eight."

"Well, that explains it. The cells in your body change completely every seven years. Isn't that what they say?"

"That's what they say."

"So your cells and my cells had never met before. I never understood that, the cells changing every seven years. What the hell does it mean? If you get a scar you've still got it several years later."

"Or a tattoo. The cells change but the ink stays between them."

"How does it know how to do that?"

"I don't know."

"That's what I can't figure out. How does it know? You don't have any tattoos, do you?"

"No."

"And you call yourself an alcoholic. Isn't that when people get them, when they're tanked?"

"Well, it never struck me as the reasoned act of a sober man."

"No, I wouldn't think so. I read somewhere that a high percentage of murderers are heavily tattooed. Have you ever heard that?"

"It sounds familiar."

"I wonder why that would be. Something to do with self-image?"

"Maybe."

"Did Motley have any?"

"Self-image?"

"Tattoos, you dimwit."

"Sorry. Did he have any tattoos? I don't remember. You ought to know, you saw more of his body than I did."

"Thanks for reminding me. I don't remember any tattoos. He had scars on his back. Did I tell you about that?"

"Not that I remember."

"Bands of scar tissue across his back. He was probably physically abused in childhood."

"It happens."

"Uh-huh. Are you sleepy?"

"Sort of."

"And I'm not letting you doze off. That's the thing about fucking, it wakes women up and puts men to sleep. You're an old bear and I won't let you hibernate."

"Ummmmm."

"I'm glad you don't have any tattoos. I'll let you alone now. Good night, baby."

I slept, and sometime during the night I awoke. I was dreaming, and then the dream had slipped away beyond recall and I was awake. Her body was drawn close to mine and I could feel her heat, and I was breathing her smell. I ran a hand along her flank, feeling the wonderful smoothness of her skin, and the suddenness of my own physical response surprised me.

I filled my hands with her and stroked her, and after a

moment she made a sound not unlike a cat's purr and rolled onto her back, shifting to accommodate me. I eased onto her and into her and our bodies found their rhythm and labored together, endlessly rocking.

Afterward she laughed softly in the darkness. I asked her what was so funny.

"'Repeatedly,'" she said.

In the morning I slipped out of bed and showered and dressed, then woke her to let me out and lock up after me. She wanted to make sure I had the sketch. I held up the cardboard core from a roll of paper towels, Galindez's effort coiled within.

"Don't forget I want it back," she said.

I told her I'd take good care of it.

"And of yourself," she said. "Promise?"

I promised.

EIGHT

I walked back to my hotel. On the way I found a copy shop that hadn't closed for the weekend and got them to run a hundred copies of the sketch. I dropped most of them in my room, along with the original, which I'd rolled and reinserted in its cardboard sleeve. I kept a dozen or so copies and took along a batch of business cards, the ones Jim Faber had printed up for me, not the ones from Reliable. These had my name and phone number, nothing else.

I took the Broadway local uptown and got off at Eighty-sixth. My first stop was the Bretton Hall, Motley's last known address at the time of his arrest. I already knew he wasn't registered there under his own name, but I tried his picture on the man behind the desk. He studied it solemnly and shook his head. I left the picture with him, along with one of my cards. "Be something in it for you," I said. "If you can help me out."

I worked my way up the east side of Broadway to 110th Street, hitting the residential hotels on Broadway itself and on the side streets. Then I crossed to the other side and did the same thing, working my way back down to Eighty-sixth and continuing on down to around Seventy-second Street. I stopped for a plate of black beans and yellow rice at a Cuban-Chinese lunch counter, then worked the east side of Broadway back up to where I'd started. I passed out more business cards than pictures, but I still managed to get rid of all but one of the copies of the sketch and wished I'd brought more. They'd only cost me a nickel apiece, and at that rate I could have afforded to paper the city with them.

A couple of people told me Motley looked familiar. At one welfare hotel, the Benjamin Davis on Ninety-fourth, the clerk knew him immediately. "He was here," he said. "Man stayed here this summer."

"What dates?"

"I don't know as I could say. He was here more than a couple weeks, but I couldn't tell you when he came or when he moved out."

"Could you check your records?"

"I might could, if I recollected his name."

"His real name's James Leo Motley."

"You don't always get real names here. I don't suppose I have to tell you that." He flipped to the front of the register, but the volume only went back to early September. He went into a back room and came back with the preceding volume in hand. "Motley," he said to himself, and started paging through the entries. "I don't see it here. I got to say I don't think that was the name he used. I disremember his name, but I would know it if I heard it, you know what I'm saying? And when I hear Motley it don't ring no bells."

He went through the book all the same, running his finger down the pages slowly, moving his lips slightly as he scanned the names of lodgers. The whole process drew some attention, and a couple of others, tenants or hangers-on, drifted over to see what was occupying us.

"You know this man," the clerk said to one of them. "Stayed here over the summer. What was the name he called hisself?"

The man he'd asked took the sketch and held it so the light fell on it. "This ain't a photograph," he said. "This is like a picture somebody drawn of him."

"That's right."

"Yeah, I know him," he said. "Looks just like him. What name was you calling him?"

"Motley. James Leo Motley."

He shook his head. "Wasn't no Motley. Wasn't no James anything." He turned to his friend. "Rydell, what was this dude's name? You remember him."

"Oh, yeah," Rydell said.

"So what was his name?"

"Looks just like him," Rydell said. "On'y his hair was different."

"How?"

"Short," Rydell told me. "Short on top, on the sides, short all over."

"Real short," his friend agreed. "Like maybe he used to be someplace where they give you a real short haircut."

"Where they just use that old clippers," Rydell said, "and all's they do is buzz you up one side of your head and down the other. I swear I'd know his name. If I was to hear it I'd know it."

"So would I," the other man said.

"Coleman," Rydell said.

"Wasn't Coleman."

"No, but it was like Coleman. Colton? Copeland!"

"Think you're right."

"Ronald Copeland," Rydell said triumphantly. "Reason I said Coleman, you know that actor, used to be, name of Ronald Colman? Dude here was Ronald Copeland."

And, amazingly, his name was in the book, with a check-in date of July 27, twelve days after he cleared the gate at Dannemora. For previous address he'd put Mason City, Iowa. I couldn't imagine why, but I dutifully noted it in my notebook.

They had an odd system of record-keeping at the Benjamin Davis, and there was no indication in the book of his date of departure. The clerk had to consult a card file to find that out. It turned out he'd been there exactly four weeks, checking out on the twenty-fourth of August. He had not left a forwarding address, and the desk clerk couldn't recall that there'd been anything that needed forwarding, or that he'd received any mail during his stay, or had any callers.

None of them could recall a conversation with him. "Man kept to hisself," Rydell said. "Time you'd see him, he'd be going to his room or out to the street. What I'm saying, he was never just standing around talking to you."

His friend said, "Something about him, you didn't start up no conversation with him."

"Way he looked at you."

"Hell, yes."

"He could look at you," Rydell said, "and it was like you'd get a chill. Not a hard look, neither, or a dirty look. Just cold."

"Ice-cold."

"Like he'd kill you for any reason at all. You want my opinion, man's a stone killer. I didn't never know nobody looked at you like that and wasn't."

"I knew a woman once had that kind of look," his friend said.

"Shit, I don't want to meet no woman like that."

"You didn't want to meet this one," his friend said. "Not on the shortest day of your life."

We talked some more, and I gave them each a card and told them it would be worth something to know where he was now, or if he turned up again in the neighborhood. Rydell offered the opinion that the conversation we'd just had ought to be worth something already, and I wasn't inclined to argue the point. I gave ten dollars to each of them, him and his

friend and the desk clerk. Rydell allowed as to how it might
have been worth more than that, but he didn't seem surprised when that was all he got.

"You see those dudes on the TV," he said, "and they be
passing out twenty dollars here, twenty dollars there, 'fore
nobody even tells 'em anything. Why is it you never see no
dudes like that around here?"

"They spend all their money," his friend said, "before
they get this far uptown. This gentleman here, this gentleman's a man knows how to pace hisself."

I paced myself all up and down Broadway, and that was the
only time I had occasion to hand out any money. It was also
as close as I came to getting a lead, and I suppose it was
progress of a sort. I could place him with certainty in New
York for four weeks ending August 24. I had an alias for
him, and had the inferential evidence that he was dirty. If he
was clean, what did he need with an alias?

More important, I'd established that Galindez's drawing
was recognizably close to Motley's present appearance. His
hair had been shorter, but by now his prison haircut would
have grown out. Then too, he might have sideburns or facial
hair, but he very likely didn't; he hadn't had them before he
went away, and he hadn't started growing them by the time
he checked out of the Davis, six weeks after they let him out
of prison.

By the time I made the circle back to the Bretton Hall my
legs were feeling the mileage. And that was the least of it.
That kind of legwork takes its toll. You have the same conversation with dozens of people, and most of the time it's like
talking to plants. The only bright spot that day had come at
the Benjamin Davis, with a long dry spell before it and a
longer drier one after. That was typical. When you make
rounds like that—knocking on doors, cops call it, but on this
occasion I'd had no doors to knock on—when you do this,

you know that you're wasting at a minimum ninety-five percent of your time and effort. There doesn't seem to be any
way around this, because you can't do the useful five percent
without the other. It's like shooting birds with a scattergun.
Most of the pellets miss, but you don't mind as long as the
bird falls. And you couldn't expect to bring him down with a
.22. He's too small, and there's too much sky around him.

Still, it takes it out of you. I took the bus and went back
to my hotel room and turned on the television. There was a
late college game underway, two Pac-10 teams, and one of
them had a quarterback who was being hyped for the
Heisman Trophy. I sat down and started watching, and I
could understand what the fuss was about. He was a white
boy, too, and big enough for pro ball. Something gave me
the feeling that his income over the next ten years was going
to be higher than mine.

I must have dozed off watching, because I was having
some kind of dream when the phone rang. I opened my eyes,
turned the sound down on the TV, and answered the phone.

It was Elaine. She said, "Hi, sweetie. I called earlier but
they said you were out."

"I didn't get a message."

"I didn't leave one. I just wanted to thank you and I
didn't want to do that by message. You're a sweet man, but I
suppose everybody tells you that."

"Not quite everybody," I said. "I talked to dozens of people today and not one of them told me that. Most of them
didn't tell me a thing."

"What were you doing?"

"Looking for our friend. I found a hotel where he spent a
month after he got out of prison."

"Where?"

"A flop in the West Nineties. The Benjamin Davis, but I
don't think you'd know it."

"Would I want to?"

"Probably not. Our sketch is good, I managed to establish that much, and it may be the most important thing I learned today."

"Did you get the original back?"

"You still want it, huh?"

"Of course I do. What are you doing tonight? Do you want to bring it over?'

"I've got some more legwork to do."

"And I bet you give great leg, don't you?"

"And I want to get to a meeting," I said. "I'll call later, if it's not too late. And maybe I'll come by, if you feel like late company."

"Good," she said. "And Matt? That was sweet."

"For me too."

"Did you used to be such a romantic? Well, I just wanted you to know I appreciate it."

I put the phone down and turned the sound up. The game was well into the fourth quarter, so I'd evidently been asleep for a while. It was no contest at this stage, but I watched the rest of it anyway, then went out to get something to eat.

I took a batch of copies of Motley's likeness and an inch-thick stack of business cards, and after I ate I went on downtown. I worked the SRO hotels and rooming houses in Chelsea, then walked on down to the Village. I timed things so I could catch a meeting in a storefront on Perry Street. There were about seventy people jammed into a room that would have held half that number comfortably, and the seats were all spoken for by the time I got there. There was standing room only, and precious little of that. The meeting was lively, though, and I got a seat when the place thinned out at the break.

The meeting broke at ten and I made the rounds of some of the leather bars, Boots and Saddles on Christopher, the Chuckwagon on Greenwich, and a couple of lowdown riverfront joints on West Street. The gay bars catering to the S & M crowd had always had a murky ambience, but now in the Age of AIDS I found their atmosphere particularly unsettling. Part of this, I suppose, came from the perception that a large proportion of the men I saw, looking so gracefully casual in denim and cowhide, smoking their Marlboros and nursing their Coors, were walking time bombs, infected with the virus and odds-on to come down with the disease within months or years. Armed with this knowledge, or perhaps disarmed by it, it was all too easy for me to see the skull beneath the skin.

I was there on a hunch, and a thin one at that. The day Motley surprised us at Elaine's apartment, the first time I'd seen him, he'd been togged out like some sort of urban cowboy, all the way down to his metal-tipped boots. This was a long way from making him a leather queen, I had to admit, but I didn't have any trouble picturing him in those bars, leaning sinuously against something, those long strong fingers curled around a beer bottle, those flat cold eyes staring, measuring, challenging. As far as I knew, women were Motley's victims, but I couldn't be sure how discriminating he was in that particular regard. If he didn't care whether his partners were alive or dead, how important could their gender be to him?

So I showed his likeness around and asked the questions that went with it. Two bartenders thought Motley looked familiar, although neither could ID him for certain. At one of the West Street dives, they had a dress code on weekends; you had to be wearing denim or leather, and a bouncer wearing both stopped me in my suit and pointed to the sign explaining the policy.

I suppose it's fair play. Look at all the people in jeans and bomber jackets who don't get to have a drink at the Plaza. "It's not a social call," I told him. I showed him Motley's picture and asked if he knew him.

"What's he done?'

"He hurt some people."

"We get our share of rough trade."

"This is rougher than you'd want."

"Let me see that," he said, raising his sunglasses, bringing the sketch up to his eyes for a closer look. "Oh, yes," he said.

"You know him?"

"I've seen him. You wouldn't call him a frequent flier, but I've got a bitching memory for faces. Among other body parts."

"How many times has he been here?"

"I don't know. Four times? Five times? First time I saw him must have been around Labor Day. Maybe a little earlier than that. And he's been here, oh, four times since. Now he could come in early in the day and I wouldn't know it, because I don't start until nine o'clock."

"How was he dressed?"

"Our friend here? I don't remember. Nothing specific sticks in my mind. Jeans and boots, for a guess. I never had to challenge him, so whatever he was wearing must have been appropriate."

I asked some more questions and gave him my card and told him to keep the sketch. I said I'd like to go inside and show the sketch to the bartender, if I could do so without too severely breaching decorum.

"We have to make certain exceptions," he said. "After all, you're a police officer, aren't you?"

"Private," I said. I don't know what made me say it.

"Oh, a private dick! That's even better, isn't it?"

"Is it?"

"I'd have to say it's about as butch as it gets." He sighed theatrically. "Honey," he said, "I'd let *you* past the rope even if you were wearing taffeta."

It was well past midnight by the time I ran out of leather bars. There were other places I could have tried, after-hours cellars clubs that were just getting started at that hour, but most of the ones I knew about were gone now, shut down in reaction to the gay plague, barn doors securely padlocked now that the horse was gone. One or two had survived, though, and I'd learned of some new ones that night, and for all I knew James Leo Motley was in one of them at that very moment, waiting for an invitation into the darkened back room.

But it was late and I was tired and I didn't have the stomach to go looking for him. I walked for a dozen blocks, trying to clear my nostrils of the reek of stale beer and backed-up drains and sweat-soaked leather and amyl nitrate, an amalgam of smells with a base note of lust. Walking helped, and I'd have walked all the way home if I hadn't already been feeling the miles I'd clocked earlier in the day. I walked until a cab came along, then rode the rest of the way.

In my room I thought of Elaine, but it was much too late to call her. I spent a long time under the shower and went to bed.

NINE

Church bells woke me. I must have been sleeping right on the surface of consciousness or I wouldn't have heard them. But I did, and I stirred myself and sat on the edge of my bed. Something was bothering me and I didn't know what it was.

I called Elaine. Her line was busy. I tried her again after I'd finished shaving and got another busy signal. I decided I'd try her again after breakfast.

There are three places I'm apt to have breakfast, but only one of them is open on Sundays. I went there and all the tables were taken. I didn't feel like waiting. I walked a couple of blocks to a place that had opened within the past several months. This was my first meal there, and I ordered a full breakfast and ate about half of it. The food didn't satisfy my appetite but it did a good job of killing it, and by the time I got out of there I'd forgotten about calling Elaine.

Instead I continued on down Eighth Avenue and started making the rounds of the Times Square hotels. There used to be more of them. A lot of the buildings have come down to make way for bigger ones, and most of the landlords would tear theirs down if they could. For a few years now there's been a moratorium on the conversion or demolition of SRO hotels, the city's attempt to keep the homelessness problem from getting worse than it is.

The closer you get to Forty-second Street, the nastier it gets in the lobbies. Something in the air announces that everyone within the walls has a couple of wants out on him. Even the semi-respectable places, third-class hotels charging fifty or sixty dollars a night, have a sour and desperate aura. As you move down in class, more and more signs turn up above the desk and taped to the glass partitions. No guests after eight o'clock. No cooking in the rooms. No firearms allowed on premises. Maximum stay twenty-eight days—this to prevent anyone's attaining the status of a permanent resident, and thus acquiring a statutory immunity to steep rent increases.

I put in a couple of hours and handed out a fair number of cards and pictures. The desk clerks were either wary or uninterested, and some of them managed to be both at once. By the time I'd worked my way past the Port Authority bus terminal, everybody looked like a crack addict to me. If Motley was staying in one of these dumps, what was the point in trying to ferret him out? I could just wait a while and the city would kill him for me.

I found a phone, dialed Elaine's number. She had the machine on but picked up after I'd announced myself. "I had a late night last night," I said. "That's why I didn't call."

"It's just as well. I made it an early night and slept like a log."

"You probably needed it."

"I probably did." A pause. "Your flowers are beautiful today."

I kept my voice neutral. "Are they?"

"Absolutely. I think they're like home-made soup, I think they're actually better on the second day."

Across the street two teenagers leaned against the steel shutter of an army-surplus store, alternately scanning the street and sending casual glances toward me. I said, "I'd like to come over."

"I'd like that. Can you give me an hour or so?"

"I suppose so."

She laughed. "But you don't sound happy about it. Let's see, it's a quarter to twelve. Why don't you come over at one o'clock or a few minutes after. Is that all right?"

"Sure."

I hung up the phone. The two boys across the street were still keeping an eye on me. I had the sudden urge to go over there and ask them what the hell they were staring at. That would have been asking for trouble, but I felt like it all the same.

Instead I turned and walked away. When I'd gone half a block I turned and looked over my shoulder at them. They were still lounging against the same steel shutter, and they didn't appear to have moved.

Maybe they hadn't been looking at me at all.

I gave her the hour and fifteen minutes she'd asked for. I spent half of it as productively as the two idlers on Eighth Avenue, lurking in a doorway of my own across the street from Elaine's apartment building. People came and went, all of them strangers to me. I don't know what I was looking for. Motley, I suppose, but he didn't show.

I made myself wait until precisely one o'clock before I went over there and presented myself to her doorman. He called upstairs, handed me the phone. She asked me who had drawn the sketch, and I went blank for an instant, then told her it was Galindez. I gave the phone back to the doorman and let her tell him it was okay to let me come up. When I knocked on her door she checked the judas first, then unfastened all the locks.

"Sorry," she said. "I suppose it's silly to go through all that—"

"That's all right." I walked over to the coffee table, where a floral arrangement was a riot of color among all that black and white. I didn't know the names of all the flowers, but I recognized a couple of exotics, bird-of-paradise and antherium, and I figured I had to be looking at seventy-five dollars' worth of floral affection.

She came over and kissed me. She was wearing a yellow silk blouse over black harem pants, and her feet were bare. She said, "See what I mean? They're prettier than yesterday."

"If you say so."

"Some of the buds are starting to open, I think that's what it is." Then I guess she picked up on the tone of what I'd said and she looked at me and asked if something was the matter.

"They're not my flowers," I said.

"Did you pick out something different?"

"I didn't send any flowers, Elaine."

It didn't take her long. I looked at her face and watched the wheels turn in her mind. She said, "Jesus Christ. You're not kidding around, are you, Matt?"

"Of course not."

"There was no note, but it never even occurred to me that they weren't from you. For God's sake, I thanked you for them. Yesterday. I called you, remember?"

"You didn't mention flowers."

"I didn't?"

"Not specifically. You thanked me for being romantic."

"What did you think I meant?"

"I don't know. I was a little groggy at the time, I'd dozed off in front of the TV set. I guess I just thought you were referring to the night we'd had together."

"Well, I was," she said. "Sort of. The night and the flowers. In my mind they more or less went together."

"There was no note?"

"Of course not. I figured you didn't bother with a

note because you knew I'd know who sent them. And I did, but—"

"But I hadn't."

"Evidently not." She had paled at the news, but her color was back now. She said, "I'm having a little trouble adjusting to this. I've spent the past twenty-four hours enjoying the flowers and thinking warm thoughts about you for having sent them, and now they're not your flowers at all. I suppose they're from him, aren't they?"

"Unless someone else sent them to you."

She shook her head. "My gentlemen friends don't send flowers, I'm afraid. God. I feel like throwing them out."

"They're the same flowers they were ten minutes ago."

"I know, but—"

"What time did they get here?"

"When did I call you, around five o'clock?"

"Something like that."

"They came an hour or two before then."

"Who delivered them?"

"I don't know."

"Well, was it a kid from the florist or what? And did you happen to get the name of the florist? Was there anything on the wrapper?"

She was shaking her head. "Nobody delivered them."

"What do you mean? They couldn't have just turned up on your doorstep."

"That's exactly what they did."

"And you opened the door and there they were?"

"Just about. I had a visitor, and when I let him in he handed them to me. For a split second I thought they were from him, which didn't make any sense, and then he explained they'd been sitting on my welcome mat when he arrived. At which point I immediately assumed they were from you."

"You figured I just dropped them on your doorstep and left?"

"I thought you probably had them delivered. And then I was in the shower and didn't hear the bell, so the delivery boy left them. Or he left them with the doorman, and the doorman left them there when I didn't respond to the bell." She laid a hand on my arm. "To tell the truth," she said, "I didn't give the matter that much thought. I was just, well, moved, you know? Impressed."

"And touched that I had sent you flowers."

"Yes, that's right."

"It certainly makes me wish they were mine."

"Oh, Matt, I don't—"

"It does. And they're beautiful flowers, you can't get around it. I should have kept my mouth shut and taken credit for them."

"Think so, huh?"

"Why not? They're a hell of a good romantic gesture. I can see where a guy could get laid on the strength of something like that."

Her face softened, and her arm moved to circle my waist. "Ah, baby," she said. "What makes you think you need flowers?"

Afterward we lay quietly together for a long while, not asleep but not entirely awake. At one point I thought of something and laughed softly to myself. Not softly enough, because she asked me what was so funny.

I said, "Some vegetarian."

"Some what? Oh." She rolled onto her side and opened her big eyes at me. "A person who abstains entirely from animal matter," she said, "runs the risk over a long period of time of developing a vitamin B-12 deficiency."

"Is that serious?"

"It can lead to pernicious anemia."

"That doesn't sound good."

"It shouldn't. It's fatal."

"Really?"

"So they tell me."

"Well, you wouldn't want to chance that," I said. "And you can get that on a strict vegetarian diet?"

"According to what I've read."

"Can't you get B-12 from dairy products?"

"I think you can, yes."

"And don't you eat dairy? There's milk in the fridge, and yogurt, as I recall."

She nodded. "I eat dairy," she said, "and you're supposed to be able to get B-12 from dairy products, but I figure you can't be too careful, you know what I mean?"

"I think you're right."

"Because why leave something like that to chance? Pernicious anemia just doesn't sound like something a person would want to have."

"And an ounce of prevention—"

"I don't think it was an ounce," she said. "I think it was more like a spoonful."

I must have drifted off because the next thing I knew I was alone in the bed and the shower was running in the bathroom. She emerged from it a few minutes later wrapped in a towel. I took a shower myself, dried off, and got dressed, and when I went into the living room there was coffee poured for me and a plate on the table with cut-up raw vegetables and bite-size chunks of cheese. We sat at the dinette table and nibbled at the food. Across the room, the floral arrangement was as dazzling as ever in the soft light of late afternoon.

I said, "The guy who handed you the flowers."

"What about him?"

"Who was he?"

139

"Just a guy."

"Because if Motley deliberately used him to get the flowers to you, he might be a lead back to him."

"He didn't."

"How can you be sure?"

She shook her head. "Believe me," she said, "there's no connection. He's a fellow I've known for a couple of years."

"And he just happened to drop in?"

"No, he had an appointment."

"An appointment? What kind of an appointment?"

"Oh, for God's sake," she said. "What kind of an appointment do you think he had with me? He wanted to come over and spend an hour discussing Wittgenstein."

"He was a john."

"Of course he was a john." She looked at me sharply. "Does that bother you?"

"Why should it bother me?"

"I don't know. Does it?"

"No."

"Because it's what I do," she said. "I turn tricks. This is not new information. It's what I did when you met me and it's what I still do."

"I know."

"So why do I get the impression that it bothers you?"

"I don't know," I said. "I just thought—"

"What?"

"Well, that you were keeping the doors barred for the time being."

"I am."

"I see."

"I *am*, Matt. I'm not taking any hotel dates, I turned down a couple of people already. And I'm not letting anybody in the door that I don't know. But the fellow who came over yesterday afternoon, he's been a regular date of mine for a few years. He'll show up one or two Saturdays a month, he's no trouble, and why shouldn't I let him in?"

140

"No reason."

"So what's the problem?"

"No problem. A girl's got to make a living, right?"

"Matt—"

"Got to accumulate some more ready cash, got to buy some more apartment houses. Right?"

"You've got no right to be like that."

"Like what?"

"You've got no right."

"I'm sorry," I said. I picked up a piece of cheese. It was a dairy product, and a likely source of vitamin B-12. I put it back down on the plate.

I said, "When I called this morning."

"And?"

"You told me not to come over right away."

"I told you to give me an hour."

"An hour and fifteen minutes, I think it was."

"I'll take your word for it. So?"

"Did you have someone over here?"

"If I'd had someone here I wouldn't have answered the phone. I'd have put the mute on and let the machine pick it up in silence, the way I did when you and I went into the bedroom."

"Why did you tell me to wait for an hour and a quarter?"

"You won't let it alone, will you? I had a fellow coming at noon."

"So you did have somebody coming."

"That's what I just told you. He called me just a few minutes before you did, as a matter of fact. He made a date to come over at noon."

"At noon on a Sunday?"

"He always comes on Sunday, usually late morning or early afternoon. He lives in the neighborhood, he tells his wife he's going out to buy the paper. He comes over here, and I suppose he picks up the *Times* on his way home. I

141

suppose that's part of the kick for him, putting one over on her that way."

"So you told me—"

"To give me until one o'clock. I knew he'd be on time, and I knew he'd be out of here within a half hour. He always is. And I wanted a half hour after that so that I could take a shower and freshen up and be—"

"And be what?"

"And be nice for you," she said. "What the fuck is this, will you tell me that? Why are you attacking me?"

"I'm not."

"The hell you're not. And why am I defending myself, that's the real question. Why the hell should I have to defend myself?"

"I don't know." I picked up my coffee cup, but it was empty. I put it down again and picked up a piece of cheese and put that down, too. I said, "So you already had your B-12 today."

For a moment she didn't say anything, and I had time to regret the line. Then she said, "No, as a matter of fact I didn't, because that's not what we did. Why? Would you like to know what we did?"

"No."

"I'll tell you anyway. We did what we always do. I sat on his face and he ate me while he jerked himself off. That's what he likes, that's what we always do when he comes over here."

"Stop it."

"Why the hell should I? What else would you like to know? Did I come? No, but I faked it, that's what gets him over the edge. Anything else you'd like for me to tell you? You want to know how big his cock was? *And don't you dare hit me, Matt Scudder!*"

"I wasn't going to hit you."

"You wanted to."

"I never even raised my hand, for God's sake."

"You wanted to."

"No."

"Yes. And I wanted you to. Not to hit me, but to want to." Her eyes were huge, brimming with tears at their corners. Softly, wonderingly, she said, "What's the matter with us? Why are we doing this to each other?"

"I don't know."

"I do," she said. "We're mad, that's why. You're mad at me because I'm still a whore. And I'm pissed off at you because you didn't send me flowers."

She said, "I think I know what happened. We've been under a strain, both of us. I think it's made us more vulnerable than we realized. And we wound up casting each other in roles we couldn't play. I thought you were Sir Galahad and I don't know who you got me mixed up with."

"I don't know either. Maybe the Lady of Shalott."

She looked at me.

"How does the poem go? 'Elaine the fair, Elaine the lovable, Elaine, the lily maid of Astolat.'"

"Stop it."

The sky had gone dark outside her window. Above the lights of Queens I saw the winking red lights of an airplane making its approach to land at La Guardia.

After a moment she said, "We read that in high school. Tennyson. I used to pretend it was about me."

"You told me once."

"Did I?" Her gaze turned inward as she took a long look at an old memory. Then, crisply, she said, "Well, I'm no lily maid, baby, and your armor's lost its shine. And it was Sir Lancelot the Lady of Shalott was hung up on, not Sir Galahad, and we're not either of them. All we are is two people who always liked each other and always did each other some good. That's not the worst thing in the world, is it?"

143

"I never thought so."

"And now we've got a crazy man who wants to kill us, so it's the wrong time for either of us to get hinky. Agreed?"

"Agreed."

"So let's get the money part handled. Can we do that?"

We could and did. I figured out my expenses to date and she reminded me of some I'd forgotten, then rounded the figure upward and cut off my arguments with a sharp glance. She went into the bedroom and came back with a handful of fifties and hundreds. I watched as she counted out two thousand dollars and shoved the stack across the table at me.

I didn't reach for it. "That's not the number you mentioned," I said.

"I know. Matt, you really shouldn't have to keep track of what you lay out, and you shouldn't have to come back to ask me for more money. Take this, and when it starts running thin tell me and I'll give you more. Please don't argue. Money's what I've got, and I damn well earned it, and if you can't use it at a time like this, what's the point of having it?"

I picked up the money.

"Good," she said. "That's settled. I don't know about the emotional part. I was always better at the business side. I think we'll just have to play it by ear and take it a day at a time. What do you think?"

I got to my feet. "I think I'll have one more cup of coffee," I said, "and then I'll get out of here."

"You don't have to."

"Yes I do. I want to go play detective and spend some of the money you gave me. I think you're right, I think we'll play it by ear. I'm sorry about before."

"So am I."

When I came back with the coffee she said, "Jesus, I've got six messages on my machine."

"When did the calls come? When we were in bed?"

"Must have. Is it all right if I play them back?"

"Why shouldn't it be?"

144

She shrugged and pressed the appropriate button. There was a whirring sound, some background noise, then a click. "A hang-up," she said. "That's what I get most of the time. A lot of people don't like to leave a message."

There was another hang-up. Then a man said, very crisply and confidently, "Elaine, this is Jerry Pines, I'll give you a call in a day or so." Then another hang-up, and then a caller who cleared his throat forcefully, took a long moment trying to think of something to say, and rang off without a word.

Then the sixth caller. A fairly long pause, with the tape running and only background noise audible. Then a whisper:

"Hello, Elaine. Did you like the flowers?"

Another pause, as long as the first. Throughout it the background noise, actually quite low in volume, sounded like the roar of a subway train.

And then, in the same forceful whisper, he said, "I was thinking of you earlier. But it's not your turn yet. You have to wait your turn, you know. I'm saving you for last." A pause, but a brief one. "I mean second-last. He'll be the last."

That was all he had to say, but the tape ran another twenty or thirty seconds before he broke the connection. Then the answering machine clicked and whirred and readied itself to handle incoming calls again, and we sat there in a silence that hung in the air like smoke.

TEN

I was back in my hotel room before dawn, but I didn't beat the sun by much. It was well past four by the time I got there, and I'd spent the whole night running all over the city, going places I hadn't been in years. Some of them were long gone, and some of the people I was looking for were gone, too, dead or in jail or in some other world. But there were new places and new people, and I found my way to enough of them to keep busy.

I found Danny Boy Bell in Poogan's. He is a short albino Negro, precise in his gestures and polite in his manners. He has always worn conservatively cut three-piece suits and he has always kept vampire's hours, never leaving his house between sunrise and sunset. His habits hadn't changed, and he still drank Russian vodka straight up and ice-cold. The bars that were home to him, Poogan's Pub and the Top Knot, always kept a bottle on ice for him. The Top Knot's gone now.

"There's a French restaurant there now," he told me. "High-priced and not very good. I'm here a lot these days. Or I'll be at Mother Goose on Amsterdam. They got a nice little trio, plays there six nights a week. The drummer uses the brushes and he never takes a solo. And they keep the lights right."

Right meant dimmed way down. Danny Boy wears dark glasses all the time, and he'd probably wear them at the bottom of a coal mine. "The world's too loud and too bright," I'd heard him say more than once. "They should put in a dimmer switch. They should turn the volume down."

He didn't recognize the sketch, but Motley's name struck a chord with him. I started to fill him in and he remembered the case. "So he's coming back at you," he said. "Why don't you just grab a plane, go someplace warm while he cools off? Guy like that, give him a few weeks and he'll step on his cock and wind up back in slam. You won't have to worry about him for another ten years."

"I think he's gotten pretty shrewd."

"Went up for one-to-ten and served twelve, how much of a genius can he be?" He finished his drink and moved his hand a few inches, which was all he had to do to get the waitress's attention. After she'd filled his glass and assured herself that I was still all right, he said, "I'll pass the word and keep my ears open, Matt. All I can do."

"I appreciate it."

"Hard to know where he might hang out, or who he might rub up against. Still, there's places you could check."

He gave me some leads and I went out and chased them around the city. I went to a chicken-and-ribs joint on Lenox Avenue and a bar down the street from it where a lot of the uptown players did their drinking. I caught a cab downtown to a place called Patchwork on Third Avenue in the Twenties, where Early American quilts hung on the exposed brick walls. I told the bartender I was there to see a man named Tommy Vincent. "He's not in just now," I was told, "but he usually comes in around this time, if you'd care to wait for him."

I ordered a Coke and waited at the bar. The back-bar

mirror let me keep an eye on the door without turning around. I watched some people come in and some others leave, and by the time I had nothing in my glass but ice cubes, a fat man two stools down from me came over and put an arm around me as if we were old friends. "I'm Tommy V.," he said. "Something I can do for you?"

I walked on Park Avenue in the Twenties, Third just below Fourteenth Street, Broadway in the high Eighties, Lexington between Forty-seventh and Fiftieth. That's where the street girls were hard at it, decorously turned out in hot pants and peekaboo halters and orange wigs. I talked to dozens of them, and I let them think I was a cop; they wouldn't have believed a denial anyway. I showed Motley's picture around and said he was a man who liked to hurt working girls, and a likely killer. I said he might be a john, or at least play the part of one, but that he fancied himself a pimp and might try to corral an outlaw girl.

A sallow blonde on Third, her dark roots giving her a two-tone hairdo, thought she recognized him. "Saw him a time ago," she said. "Looks but don't buy. One time he's got these questions. What will I do, what won't I do, what do I like, what don't I like." She made a fist, held it at her crotch, moved it in a pumping motion. "Jerking me around. Got no time for that, you know? Time I see him after that, I just walk on by."

A girl on Broadway, with an overblown body and a Deep South accent, said she'd seen him around, but not lately. Last she'd seen of him he'd gone off with a girl named Bunny. And where was Bunny? She'd gone off somewhere, disappeared, hadn't been around in weeks. "On some other stroll," she said. "Or maybe something happened." Like what? She shrugged. "Anything," she said. "You see somebody," she said, "and then you don't. And you don't miss them right away, and then you say, 'Hey, what happened to that person?' And nobody knows." Had she seen Bunny again since she'd gone off with Motley? She thought it over and couldn't say one way or the other. And maybe it hadn't been Motley that Bunny had gone with. The more she thought about it, the vaguer she seemed to get.

Somewhere along the way I managed to get to the midnight meeting at Alanon House, a sort of clubhouse occupying a suite of offices on the third floor of a decaying building on West Forty-sixth Street. They get a young crowd at that meeting, many of them newly and shakily sober, and a majority having a history of heavy drug use along with alcoholism. The crowd that night was a lot like the people outside, the biggest single difference being the direction they were headed. The ones at the meeting were staying clean and sober, or trying to. The ones out there on the street were slipping off the edge of the world.

I got there a few minutes late. The speaker had gotten as far as her twelfth birthday, by which time she'd been drinking for two years and had just started smoking marijuana. The story went on to include all the popular chemical mood-changers, not excepting IV heroin and cocaine, along with shoplifting, street prostitution, and the black-market sale of her infant son. It took a while to tell but it hadn't taken all that long to live; she was only nineteen now.

The meeting lasted an hour and I stayed until the end. My attention faded after the speaker finished up, and I didn't contribute anything to the discussion, which was ostensibly on the topic of anger. I tuned in now and then when some speaker's anger was voluble enough to break in on my reverie, but for the most part I just let my mind drift and took emotional sanctuary in the meeting. It was a nasty world outside and I'd been seeking out the nastiest part of it for the past few hours, but in here I was just another alcoholic trying to stay sober, same as everyone else, and that made it a very safe place to be.

Then we all stood and said the prayer, and then I went back out into the goddamned streets.

*　　*　　*

I slept for around five hours Monday morning and woke up hung over, which didn't seem fair. I'd slopped down quarts of bad coffee and watered Coke and breathed in acres of secondhand smoke, so I don't suppose it was out of the ordinary that I wasn't ready to greet the day like Little Mary Sunshine, but I liked to think I'd given up mornings like this along with the booze. Instead my head ached and my mouth and throat were dry and every minute took three or four minutes to pass.

I swallowed some aspirin, showered and shaved, and went downstairs and around the corner for orange juice and coffee. When the aspirin and coffee kicked in I walked a few blocks and bought a paper. I carried it back to the Flame and ordered solid food. By the time it came all the physical symptoms of the hangover were gone. I still felt a profound weariness of the spirit, but I would just have to learn to live with that.

The paper didn't do a lot to elevate my outlook. The front-page story was a massacre in Jamaica Heights, an entire family of Venezuelans shot and stabbed, four adults and six children dead and the house torched, with the fire spreading to a pair of neighboring dwellings. Various evidence seemed to indicate that the deaths were drug-related, which meant, I suppose, that the general public could feel free to shrug it off and the cops wouldn't have to bust their humps trying to solve it.

The news was no more encouraging in the sports pages, with both of the New York teams losing, the Jets by a lot, the Giants dropping a squeaker to the Eagles. The only good thing about the sports news was that it was trivial; nobody died, and when all was said and done, who really gave a damn who won or lost?

Not I, but then I didn't seem to give a damn about very

much. I flipped back to the news pages and read about another drug-related homicide, this one in the Marine Park section of Brooklyn, where someone had used a sawed-off
shotgun on a twenty-four-year-old black male with a long
record of drug busts. That didn't elate me either, but I have
to admit it disheartened me a little less than the loss to Phila-
delphia, which hadn't torn me up all that much in the first
place.

There was a honey of a story on page 7.

A twenty-two-year-old man named Michael Fitzroy had
attended mass at St. Malachy's with his girlfriend. She was
an actress with a couple of commercials to her credit, and
she had an apartment in Manhattan Plaza, the subsidized
housing for actors at Forty-second and Ninth. They were on
their way to her place, walking hand in hand down Forty-
ninth Street, at about the same time that a woman named
Antoinette Cleary decided she'd had enough of life as we
know it.

She acted on this decision by opening her window and
throwing herself out of it. Her apartment, as luck would have
it, was twenty-two stories up, and she picked up speed on the
way down according to that formula they teach you in high
school physics class, the one nobody remembers. In any
event, she was going fast enough at the moment of impact to
kill herself, and to do the same for Michael Fitzroy, who got
to her predestined spot on the pavement just a second before
she did. His girlfriend, one Andrea Dautsch, was uninjured,
but the story said she became hysterical. It seemed to me she
had every right.

I flipped through the rest of the paper. The mayor of
Baltimore had recently proposed the legalization of drugs,
and I read what Bill Reel had to say on the subject. I read the
comics without cracking a smile. Then something made me
turn back to page 7, and I read once more about the last
moments of Michael Fitzroy.

I don't know why the story moved me as much as it did.

The fact that it happened so close to home may have had something to do with it. The Cleary woman had lived at 301 West Forty-ninth, a building I'd walked past hundreds of times. I'd passed it yesterday morning on my way to scout out the Times Square hotels. If I'd slept a little longer I might have been there when it happened.

I thought of Marcus Aurelius, and how everything happened the way it was supposed to. I tried to figure out how this had been true for Michael Fitzroy, as he trudged the road of happy destiny to his girlfriend's apartment. The *News* reported that the woman who fell on him was thirty-eight years old. It also provided the information that she had taken off all her clothes prior to jumping.

They say God's will is unfathomable, and it certainly looked that way to me. Some celestial force had evidently decided that twenty-two was as old as Michael Fitzroy was supposed to get, and that the highest good of all concerned would be best served by having him struck down in his prime by a rapidly descending naked lady.

Life, I'd heard someone say, is a comedy for those who think and a tragedy for those who feel. It seemed to me that it was both at once, even for those of us who don't do much of either.

Early that afternoon I called Tom Havlicek in Massillon and caught him at his desk. "Say, I was meaning to call you," he said. "How's Fun City?"

It had been a while since I'd heard it called that. "About the same," I said.

"How about those Bengals?"

I hadn't even noticed whether they'd won or lost. "Really something," I said.

"You bet. How's it going at your end?"

"He's in New York. I keep cutting his trail, but it's a big

153

city. He threatened a woman yesterday, an old friend of Connie Sturdevant's."

"Nice."

"Yeah, he's a sweetheart. I was wondering if you heard
anything from Cleveland."

"You mean from the lab work." He cleared his throat.
"We got a blood type on the semen."

"That's great."

"I don't know how great it is, Matt. It's A-positive, and
that's the same type as the husband. If it's your guy who left
the tracks, well, that wouldn't be too much of a coincidence.
That's the most common blood type. In fact all three kids
were A-positive, which means we couldn't tell whose blood
Sturdevant had on him when he died, if some of it was theirs
or if it was all his from the shotgun wound."

"Can't they do a DNA profile on the semen?"

"They maybe could have," he said, "*if* they got the job
right away instead of waiting over a week for it. Way it
stands, all you can prove is that your suspect didn't leave
sperm in the woman. If he's something other than A-
positive, he's off the hook."

"For sodomy. Not necessarily for homicide."

"Well, I guess. Anyway, that's all the lab evidence does. It
might get him off the hook, depending on his blood type,
but it sure don't get him on it."

"I see," I said. "Well, that's disappointing, but I'll find out
what Motley's blood type is. His prison records ought to
have it. Oh, by the way, I sent you something Express Mail
this morning, you ought to get it tomorrow. It's an artist's
sketch of Motley along with an alias he used in New York a
few months ago. Something for you to use when you run a
check on hotels and airports."

There was a silence. Then he said, "Well, Matt, I don't
know that we'll be doing that."

"Oh?"

"The way it shapes up from here, we don't have any

grounds to reopen the case. Even if the semen wasn't the husband's, what does that prove? Maybe she's having an affair, maybe she's got a boyfriend waits tables at a Greek restaurant, maybe her husband found out about it and that's what set him off. Point is, we haven't got a reason in the world to invest manpower in a case that still looks open-and-shut."

We batted it around some. If he could just get a warrant issued, I said, the New York cops could pull Motley off the street before he killed somebody else. He'd love to oblige, he told me, but his chief would never go for it, and even if he did a judge might not agree that they had grounds for a warrant.

"You say he threatened somebody," he said. "Can't you get her to sign a complaint?"

"It's possible. He didn't speak to her directly. He left a message on her answering machine."

"So much the better. You got evidence. Unless she went and erased it."

"No, I kept the tape. But I don't know what it's evidence of. It's a threat, but the language is veiled. And you'd be hard put to prove it's his voice. He whispered."

"So it would sound spookier? Or to keep her from recognizing his voice?"

"Not that. He wanted her to know who it was. I think he was being careful about voiceprints. Damn it, he was careless and stupid twelve years ago. Prison turned him crafty."

"It'll do that," he said. "It may not rehabilitate them, but it sure will make better criminals out of them."

Around three it started raining. I bought a five-dollar umbrella on the street and it blew inside out before I got back to the hotel. I left it in a trash basket and took shelter under a canopy until the storm leveled off some, then walked the remaining few blocks home. I got out of my wet clothes and made a few phone calls, then stretched out and took a nap.

It was eight o'clock when I opened my eyes, and just past eight-thirty when I entered the basement meeting room at St. Paul's. The speaker had just been introduced. I got a cup of coffee and found a seat and listened to a good old-fashioned low-bottom drinking story. Jobs lost, relationships ruined, dozens of trips to detox, panhandling in a bottle gang, innumerable exposures to AA. Then one day something clicked, and now the son of a bitch was standing there in a suit and tie with his face shaved and his hair combed, looking nothing like the story he was telling.

The discussion was round-robin at that particular meeting, and they started in the back of the room, so it got to be my turn early on. I was going to pass, but he'd talked a lot about hangovers, and how if all sobriety meant was a permanent respite from hangovers, it was worth it.

I said, "My name is Matt and I'm an alcoholic, and my hangovers used to be bad, too. I figured I was done with them in sobriety, so I felt a little resentful when I woke up with one this morning. It didn't seem fair, and I started off the day with a pretty good resentment. Then I reminded myself that I used to feel that way every morning of my life, and that I took it for granted, I didn't even object to it very strongly. My God, a normal person who woke up feeling like that would have gone to a hospital, and I would just pull up my socks and go work."

A few other people spoke, and then it was the turn of a woman named Carole. "I never woke up with a hangover since I've been sober," she said, "but I identify with what Matt said in another sense. Because I like to believe that everything works out for us once we stop drinking, that bad things don't happen to us anymore. And that's not true. The miracle of sobriety isn't just that our lives get better, but that we stay sober even when they get bad. But it still tears me up when bad things happen. When Cody got AIDS I couldn't believe how unfair it was. Sober people aren't supposed to get AIDS! But the thing is they do, and when they do they die, just like everybody else. And sober people don't commit suicide. My God, all the times I tried to kill myself when I was drinking, and I don't do that anymore, and I thought nobody did, not sober. And then today I learned how Tony committed suicide, and I thought, that's not supposed to happen. But anything can happen, and I still can't pick up a drink."

I went up to Carole on the break and asked if Tony had been a member of our group. "Came here all the time," she said. "Sober three years. Tony Cleary."

"I can't place him."

"Her. I'm sure you knew her, Matt. Tall, dark hair, around my age. Worked in the garment center, I forget doing what but she used to talk about how she was having an affair with her boss. I'm positive you knew her."

"My God," I said.

"She never struck me as suicidal. But I guess you never know, do you?"

"We went out and spoke together in Queens less than a week ago," I said. "The two of us and Richie Gelman, we went all the way out to Richmond Hill together." I scanned the room looking for Richie, as if he could help confirm what I was saying. I didn't see him. "She seemed in great shape," I said. "She sounded fine."

"I saw her Friday night and she seemed fine then. I don't remember what she said but she didn't seem depressed or anything."

"We had a bite afterward. She seemed solid and content, happy with her life. What was it, pills?"

She shook her head. "She went out a window. It was in the paper and there was something on the six o'clock news

157

tonight. It was freaky, because she landed on some kid fresh out of church services and he was killed, too. Crazy, isn't it?"

Call your cousin, the message read.

This time I didn't have to go through the answering machine. She picked up on the first ring. "He called," she said.

"And?"

"He said, 'Elaine, I know you're there. Pick up the telephone and turn off your machine.' And I did."

"Why?"

"I don't know why. He told me to do it and I did it. He said he had a message for you."

"What was the message?"

"Matt, why did I turn off the machine? He told me to do it and I did it. What if he tells me to unlock the door and let him in? Am I going to do it?"

"No, you're not."

"How do you know that?"

"Because that would be unsafe and you'd know not to do it. It didn't put you in any danger to turn off the machine. There's a difference."

"I wonder."

So did I, but I would keep my doubts to myself. I said, "What was the message?"

"Oh, right. It didn't make any sense, at least I don't think it did. To me. I wrote it down right after he hung up so I wouldn't forget it. Where did I put it?"

I suppose I knew what it was. I must have.

"Here it is," she said. "'Tell him I'm going to take all his women away. Tell him yesterday was number two. No extra charge for the kid on the street. He was a dividend.' Does any of that make any sense to you?"

"No," I said. "But I know what it means."

ELEVEN

I called Anita. She had remarried, and it was her husband who answered the phone. I apologized for calling so late and asked to speak to Mrs. Carmichael. It felt strange calling her that, but the whole call felt strange.

I told her I was probably bothering her for nothing, but that there was a situation she ought to know about. I went through it quickly, explaining that a man I'd put away years ago was carrying on a psychopathic vendetta, trying to get back at me by killing all my women.

"Except I don't have any," I said, "so he's been forced to interpret the phrase loosely. He killed one woman who was a witness against him twelve years ago, and he killed another who was the most casual acquaintance of mine you could imagine. I didn't even know her last name."

"But he killed her. Why don't the police arrest him?"

"I'm hoping they will. But in the meantime—"

"You think I'm in danger?"

"I honestly don't know. He may not know you exist, and if he does there's no reason to assume he'd know your married name or your new address. But the guy's resourceful."

159

"What about the boys?"

One was in the service, the other in college on the other side of the country. "They don't have anything to worry about," I said. "It's women he's really interested in."

"In killing, you mean. God. What do you think I should do?"

I made some suggestions. That she think about taking a vacation, if it was convenient. Failing that, that she notify the local police and see what protection they could provide. She and her husband might even want to think about hiring private security guards. And they should certainly pay attention and see if they were being followed or watched, and should avoid opening doors to strangers, and—

"God *damn* it," she said. "We're divorced. I'm married to somebody else. Doesn't that make a difference?"

"I don't know," I said. "He may be like the Catholic church. He may not recognize divorce."

We talked some more, and then I had her put her husband on the line and went through the whole thing with him. He seemed sensible and decisive and I hung up feeling that he'd think it through and do something positive. I only wished I could say the same for myself.

I went over to the window and looked out at the city. When I moved in you could see the World Trade Center towers from my window, but since then various builders have come along, eating up different portions of the sky. I still have a fairly decent view, but it's not what it used to be.

It was raining again. I wondered if he was out there. Maybe he'd get wet, maybe he'd catch his death.

I picked up the phone and called Jan.

She is a sculptor, with a loft south of Canal on Lispenard Street. I had met her back when we were both drinking, and we did some good drinking at her place, she and I. Then she got sober and we stopped seeing each other, and then I got sober and we began again. And then it stopped working, and then it ended, and neither of us ever quite understood why.

When she answered I said, "Jan, it's Matt. I'm sorry to be calling so late."

"It is late," she said. "Is something the matter?"

"Definitely," I said. "I'm not sure whether or not it affects you. My fear is that it might."

"I don't understand."

I went through it in a little more detail than I had with Anita. Jan had seen the TV coverage of Toni's death, but of course she hadn't suspected that it was anything other than the suicide it appeared to be. Nor had she known that Toni was in the program.

"I wonder if I ever met her."

"You could have. You came to St. Paul's a few times. And she got around some, spoke at other meetings."

"And you went on a speaking date with her? You told me where but it slipped my mind."

"Richmond Hill."

"Where is that, somewhere in Queens?"

"Somewhere in Queens, yes."

"And that's why he killed her? Or were the two of you sort of an item?"

"Not at all. She wasn't my type and she was involved with someone at her job. We weren't even buddies particularly. I'd talk to her at meetings, but that speaking engagement was the only real time we ever spent together."

"And on the strength of that—"

"Right."

"You're sure it wasn't suicide? Of course you are. That's a stupid question. Do you think—"

"I'm not sure what I think," I said. "He got out of prison four months ago. He could have spent the whole four months tagging along behind me and he wouldn't have seen me spending time with you. But I don't know what he

161

knows, who he talked to, what kind of research he might have done. You want to know what I think you should do?"

"Yes."

"I think you should get on a plane first thing in the morning. Pay cash for your ticket and don't tell anyone where you're going."

"You're serious."

"Yes."

"I have good locks on the door. I could—"

"No," I said. "Your building's not secure, and this is a man who gets in and out of places and makes it look easy. You can decide to take your chances, but don't kid yourself that you can stay in the city and be safe."

She thought for a moment. "I've been meaning to visit my—"

"Don't tell me," I cut in.

"You think the line is tapped?"

"I think it's better if nobody knows where you're going, myself included."

"I see." She sighed. "Well, Matthew, you've got me taking it seriously. I might as well start packing right now. How will I know when it's safe to come back? Can I call you?"

"Anytime. But don't leave your number."

"I feel like a spy, and an inept one at that. Suppose I can't reach you? How will I know when to come in from the cold?"

"A couple of weeks should do it," I said. "One way or the other."

On the phone with her, talking with her, I had to fight the urge to grab a cab to Lispenard Street and set about the business of protecting her. We could spend a few hours drinking gallons of coffee and having one of the intense conversations that had characterized our relationship from the night we met.

162

I missed those conversations. I missed her, and sometimes I thought about trying to make it work again, but we had already made that attempt a couple of times and the reality of the situation seemed to be that we were through with each other. We didn't *feel* through with each other, but that was how it seemed to be.

Back when it all fell apart I'd called Jim Faber. "It's just hard for me to grasp," I told him. "The whole idea that it's over between us. I honestly thought it would work out."

"It did," he said. "This is *how* it worked out."

I almost called him now.

I could have. Our arrangement was that I wouldn't call him after midnight, and it was well past that. On the other hand, I could call him at any hour of the day or night if it was an emergency.

I thought about it and decided the present circumstances didn't qualify as an emergency. I wasn't in danger of taking a drink, which is the only sort of emergency I could think of that would justify waking the guy up. Curiously enough, I didn't even feel like drinking. I felt like hitting someone, or screaming, or kicking the wall down, but I didn't much feel like picking up a drink.

I went out and walked around. The rain had tuned itself down to a light drizzle. I walked over to Eighth Avenue and let myself be drawn eight blocks downtown. I knew her building, I'd walked her home. It was on the northwest corner, but I didn't know whether her apartment fronted on the street or the avenue so I couldn't tell just where she'd come down.

Sometimes a jumper lands with enough force to break up the concrete. I didn't see any broken pavement. Of course she'd had Fitzroy there to break her fall and absorb most of the force of it.

No stains on the pavement. There would have been

163

blood, probably a lot of it, but there had been plenty of rain to clean up whatever the janitorial crew might have missed. Of course it doesn't always wash away. Sometimes it soaks in.

Maybe there was blood there and I just wasn't seeing it. It was night, after all, and the pavement was wet. You wouldn't be likely to spot bloodstains under such conditions, especially if you weren't sure exactly where to look for them.

There are bloodstains all over the city, if you know where to look.

All over the world, I suppose.

I must have spent an hour walking. I thought of stopping at Grogan's but I knew that wasn't a good idea. I wasn't up for conversation, nor did I want to allow myself the self-indulgence of barroom solitude. I just kept on walking, and when the rain picked up I didn't even mind. I walked on through it and let it soak me.

All your women, Scudder. Jesus, a madman wanted to take from me women I didn't have. I had barely known Connie Cooperman and hadn't thought of her in years. And who were his other targets? Elaine, who played a shopworn Lady of Shalott to my corroded Lancelot. Anita, my wife years and years ago, and Jan, my girlfriend months and months ago. And Toni Cleary, who'd had the bad judgment to go out for a hamburger with me.

He must have followed us that night. Could he have trailed us all the way out to Richmond Hill? It seemed impossible. Maybe he'd just been in the neighborhood, lurking, and he picked us up on our way to Armstrong's, or walking toward her place.

I kept walking around, trying to sort it out.

I packed it in, finally, went back to my hotel room and hung my wet clothes up to dry. It had turned cold out there and I had paid as little heed to that as to the rain, and I was chilled to the bone. I stood under a hot shower and then crawled into bed.

Lying there, I had a thought, or skirted close to the edge of one. He was out there, menacing all of these women who used to be mine, and here I was, running around like a juggler trying to keep all the balls in the air. Trying to save them, trying to protect them, Elaine and Anita and Jan, and in the process trying to hold on to them. Trying, in a sense, to confirm their status as what he labeled them—my women, mine.

Trying in the process to deny the truth, to turn a blind eye on reality. To overlook the bitter fact that these women were not mine, and probably never had been mine. That I didn't have anybody, and likely never would.

That I was all alone.

TWELVE

In daylight you could see the bloodstains, although you would have had to be looking for them to know what they were. I went over there with Joe Durkin, and the doorman pointed out Toni's landing site. It was on the side street, perhaps twenty yards west of the building's entrance.

The doorman was an Hispanic kid, his shoulders too narrow for the jacket of his uniform, his mustache sparse and tentative. He'd had Sunday off but I showed him the sketch of Motley anyway. He looked at it and shook his head.

Durkin got a passkey and we went upstairs and let ourselves into her apartment. No one had troubled to close the window and it had rained in some the previous day. I leaned out over the sill and tried to see the spot where she came down. I couldn't see anything, and a rush of vertigo made me pull my head in and straighten up.

Durkin went over to the bed. It was made, and some clothing was folded neatly at its foot. A navy skirt, an off-white blouse, a dark gray cable-knit cardigan. A pair of lacy white panties. A bra, also white, with large cups.

He picked up the bra, examined it, put it back.

"Big girl," he said, and glanced my way to check my reaction. I don't suppose I showed much. He lit a cigarette, shook out the match, and looked around for an ashtray. There weren't any. He blew on the match to make sure it was cool and set it down carefully on the edge of the night table."

"Your guy said he killed her," he said. "That right?"

"That's what he told Elaine."

"Elaine's the witness against him? That's twelve years back when all this shit started?"

"That's right."

"You don't think he's like some of these Arab terrorists, do you? Plane comes down, they're on the phone claiming credit for it."

"I don't think so."

He drew on his cigarette and blew out smoke. "No, I guess not," he said. "Well, it could have been murder. I don't see how you can rule it out. Somebody goes out a high window, how are you going to say whose idea it was?" He walked over to the door. "She had this locked, had the deadbolt on. What's that prove either way? Doesn't make a locked-room case out of it. You can engage the deadbolt from inside by turning this thing here, or you can do it when you leave by locking it with the key. He puts her out the window, he picks up a key, he locks up after himself on his way out. Proves nothing."

"No."

"Of course there's no note. I never like a suicide without a note. There ought to be a law."

"What would you have for a penalty?"

"You gotta come back and live." He looked around reflexively for an ashtray, then flicked ashes on the parquet floor. "Used to be a crime to attempt suicide, though I never heard of anyone prosecuted for it. Idiot statute. Makes it a crime to attempt something that's not a crime if you succeed at it. Here's one for you, the kind of dimwit question turns up on the sergeants' exam. Say she falls out the window and hits the Fitzroy kid. He dies but he breaks her fall and she lives. What's she guilty of?"

"I don't know."

"I suppose it's either criminally negligent homicide or manslaughter two. And there's been incidents like that. Not from twenty-odd stories up, but when someone jumps from say four stories up. You never get a prosecution, though."

"No."

"Unsound mind'd be a pretty good defense, I would think. What I'll do, I'll call and get a lab crew in here. Be a gift from God to find some of his prints on the window frame, wouldn't it now?"

"Or anywhere in the apartment."

"Anywhere," he agreed. "But I don't think we'll get lucky that way, do you?"

"No."

"Be sweet if we did. Couple of uniforms from our house were first on the scene, so if there's a case it's our case, and I'd fucking love to hang it on your guy's neck. But everything says this is a guy who doesn't leave prints. He called her twice, right? First time he whispered."

"That's right."

"And that's what you got on tape, an unidentified male whispering and saying he sent flowers. And a vague threat, says it's not her turn yet but doesn't say her turn for what. Try making a case out of that."

He looked for someplace to get rid of his cigarette. His eyes went to the floor, then to the open window. He went instead to the kitchen sink and held the cigarette under the tap, then dropped the butt in the trash.

He said, "Then when he does threaten her and talks in a normal voice it's after he tells her to turn off the machine, and of course she does what he says and turns it off. So we got her word he threatened her, and her word that he confessed to killing Cleary and Fitzroy. And even that's thin, because he didn't say exactly what he did or mention anybody by name."

"Right."

"So unless we've got some physical evidence, I don't see that we've got a thing. I'll copy that sketch and we'll try it on the doorman, the guy who was on that morning, and the rest of the crew, too, just in case somebody spotted him lurking around the premises the past few days. I wouldn't expect much, though. And placing him in the area, or even in the building, is a long way from convicting him of her murder. First you've got to establish that there's been a murder, and I don't know how you can do that."

"What about the medical evidence?"

"What about it?"

"What was the cause of death?"

He looked at me.

"Wasn't there an autopsy?"

"It's required. You know that. But you also know what they look like after they fall that far. You want medical evidence? Cleary fell headfirst, and her head collided with Fitzroy's head. Don't even think about the odds of that, but it happened. You know what both their heads look like? Long as the ME doesn't find a bullet in her, he's going to put down that she died from injuries sustained in the fall. You're thinking he may have killed her first."

"It seems likely."

"Yeah, but go prove it. It's just as likely he knocked her out and tossed her out unconscious. What are you going to find, marks on her throat? Evidence of a blow to the head?"

"How about semen? He left some in the woman in Ohio."

"Yeah, and they couldn't even say whose it was. I'll tell you something, Matt, if they find semen in Cleary it could even be Fitzroy's, the way the two of them shared their last moments and all. And say it's Motley's, what does that prove? It's not against the law to go to bed with a woman.

170

It's not even against the law to fuck her in the ass." He reached for another cigarette, changed his mind. "I'll tell you," he said, "we're not gonna get this guy for Cleary. Not without very strong fingerprint evidence, and probably not even with that. Placing him on the scene, even in the room with her, doesn't make it a murder or him a murderer."

"What does?" He looked at me. "Just what do we have to do, wait for a corpse with his signature on it?"

"He'll fuck up, Matt."

"Maybe," I said. "I don't know that I can wait."

Durkin was good. He might not believe the case had a chance of amounting to anything but he went through the motions all the same, and without wasting time. He got some lab techs over there right away, and that afternoon he called me with a report.

The bad news was that they hadn't turned up a single print of Motley's anywhere in the Cleary apartment. The good news, if you wanted to call it that, was the lack of prints at strategic spots on the frame and sill of the window she went out of, which tended to indicate that someone had either taken care not to leave prints or had wiped them away after the body cleared the window. You couldn't call it evidence, people don't leave a print every time they touch a surface, but it helped confirm for us something we already knew. That Toni Cleary hadn't killed herself. That she'd had help.

All I could think of to do was what I'd already been doing. Talking to people. Knocking on doors. Showing his sketch around, and passing out copies of it, along with cards from my diminishing supply.

That made me think of Jim Faber, who'd printed them as a gift to me. Call your sponsor—that's what you heard all the time in meetings. Don't drink, go to meetings, read the Big Book, call your sponsor. I wasn't drinking and I'd been going to meetings. I couldn't think what the Big Book might have to say about playing hide-and-seek with a vengeful psychopath, nor did I figure Jim was an authority on the subject. I called him anyway.

"Maybe there's nothing you can do," he said.

"That's a helpful thought."

"I don't know if it's helpful or not. It's probably not very encouraging."

"Not very, no."

"But maybe it is. Maybe it's just a way of acknowledging that you're already taking all the appropriate actions. Finding a man who doesn't want to be found in a city the size of New York must be like finding the proverbial needle in the equally proverbial haystack."

"Something like that."

"Of course, if you could involve the police—"

"I've been trying. There's a limit to what they can do at this stage."

"So it sounds as though you're doing everything you can, and beating yourself up because you can't do more. And worrying because the whole thing's out of your control."

"Well, it is."

"Of course it is. We can't control how things turn out. You know that. All we can do is take the action and turn over the results."

"Just take your best shot and walk away from it."

"That's right."

I thought about it. "If my best shot's not good enough, other people get it in the neck."

"I get it. You can't let go of the controls because the stakes are too high."

"Well—"

"You remember the Third Step?" I did, of course, but he felt compelled to quote it anyway. "'Made a decision to turn

172

our will and our lives over to the care of God, as we understood Him.' You can turn over the small stuff, but when it's
nitty-gritty time you have to take control of it yourself."

"I get the point."

"You want to get a handle on the Third Step? Here's a
two-point program for you. A—just turn over the small
stuff. B—it's all small stuff."

"Thanks," I said.

"You all right, Matt? You're not going to drink, are you?"

"No. I'm not going to drink."

"Then you're all right."

"Yeah, I'm terrific," I said. "You know, someday I'm going
to call you and you're going to tell me what I want to hear."

"Entirely possible. But the day that happens is the day
you better get yourself another sponsor."

I checked the desk around six and there was a message to call
Joe Durkin. He'd left for the day but I had his home number.
"I just thought you'd want to know," he said. "I talked to the
assistant medical examiner and he said forget it. He said it
was hard to tell where one of them started and the other left
off. He said, 'Tell your friend to go up to the top of the
Empire State Building and throw down a grapefruit. Then
tell him to go on down to the sidewalk and try to figure out
what part of Florida it came from.'"

"Well, we tried," I said. "That's the important thing."

I hung up, thinking that Jim would have been proud of
me. My attitude was improving by leaps and bounds, and
any minute now I'd be a prime candidate for canonization.

Of course it didn't change anything. We still had nothing,
and were going nowhere.

I went to a meeting that night.

My feet, creatures of habit, started heading for St. Paul's

shortly after eight. I got to within a block of the big old church and something stopped me.

I wondered whom I'd be endangering by showing up there.

The thought sent a chill through me, as though someone had drawn a piece of chalk squeaking across the Great Blackboard in the Sky. My aunt Peg, God rest her, would have said that a goose just walked over my grave.

I felt like a leper, a Typhoid Mary, carrying a virus that could turn the innocent into homicide victims. For the first time since I'd walked in the door, it was unsafe for me to go to a meeting of my home group. Not unsafe for me, but unsafe for others.

I told myself it didn't make sense, but I couldn't shake the feeling. I turned and retreated to the corner of Fifty-eighth and Ninth and tried to think straight. It was Tuesday. Who else had a meeting on Tuesday night?

I caught a cab and got out at Cabrini Hospital, on East Twentieth. The meeting was in a conference room on the third floor. The speaker had a full head of wavy gray hair and an engaging smile. He was a former advertising account executive and he had been married six times. He had sired a total of fourteen children with his various wives, and he had not filed an income-tax return since 1973.

"Things got a little out of hand," he said.

Now he was a sporting-goods salesman in a discount retail store on Park Avenue South, and he lived alone. "All my life I was afraid of being alone," he said, "and now I've discovered that I like it."

Good for you, I thought.

There was no one I knew at the meeting, although there were a few familiar faces in the room. I didn't raise my hand during the discussion and I ducked out before the closing prayer, slipping away without saying a word to anybody.

It was cold out. I walked a few blocks, then caught a bus.

＊　　＊　　＊

Jacob was on duty, and he told me I'd had some phone calls. I glanced at my box. There was nothing in it.

"She didn't leave a message."

"It was a woman?"

"Believe so. Same one each time, asked for you, said she would call back. Seems like she calls every fifteen, twenty minutes."

I went upstairs and called Elaine, but it hadn't been her. We talked for a few minutes. Then I hung up and the phone rang.

The voice was a rich contralto. Without preamble she said, "I'm taking a big chance."

"How?"

"If he knew about this," she said, "I'd be dead. He's a killer."

"Who is?"

"You ought to know. Your name is Scudder, isn't it? Aren't you the man's been showing his picture all over the street?"

"I'm the man."

There was a stretch of silence. I could tell she hadn't hung up, but I wondered if she might have set the phone down and walked away. Then, her voice little more than a whisper, she said, "I can't talk now. Stay where you are. I'll call back in ten minutes."

It was more like fifteen. This time she said, "I'm scared, man. He'd kill me in a hot second."

"Then why call me?"

"'Cause he might kill me anyway."

"Just tell me where I can find him. It won't get back to you."

"Yeah?" She considered this. "You got to meet me," she said.

"All right."

"We got to talk, you know? Before I tell you anything."

"All right. Pick a time and a place."

"Shit. What time is it now? Close to eleven. Meet me at midnight. Can you do that?"

"Where?"

"You know the Lower East Side?"

"I can find my way around."

"Meet me at—shit, I'm crazy to do this." I waited her out. "Place called the Garden Grill. That's on Ridge Street just below Stanton. You know where that is?"

"I'll find it."

"It's on the right-hand side of the street if you're going downtown. And there's steps leading down from the street. If you're not looking for it you could miss it."

"I'll find it. You said midnight? How will I know you?"

"Look for me at the bar. Long legs and auburn hair, and I'll be drinking a Rob Roy straight up." A throaty chuckle. "You could buy me a refill."

Ridge Street runs south from Houston Street seven or eight blocks east of First Avenue. It's not a good neighborhood, but then it never was. Over a century ago the narrow streets began filling up with mean tenements, thrown up in a hurry to house the mob of immigrants arriving from Eastern Europe. The buildings left a lot to be desired when they were new, and the years have not been good to them.

Many of them are gone. Stretches of the Lower East Side have seen the tenements give way to low-income housing projects, which have arguably become worse places to live than the hovels they replaced. Ridge Street, though, remained an unbroken double row of five-story tenements, with an occasional gap in the form of a rubble-strewn lot where someone had torn down a building after someone else had burned it out.

My cab dropped me at the corner of Ridge and Houston

a few minutes before twelve. I stood there while the driver made a quick U-turn and looked for greener pastures. The streets were empty, and of course all of the shops on Houston were dark, and most of them shuttered, their corrugated-steel shutters black with undecipherable graffiti.

I walked south on Ridge. On the other side of the street a woman was berating a child in Spanish. A few houses further on, a trio of youths in leather jackets looked me over and evidently decided I was more trouble than I was worth.

I crossed Stanton Street. The Garden Grill, not all that hard to find if you were looking for it, was in the fourth building from the corner. A scrap of neon in an otherwise opaque window announced its name. I walked a dozen yards past it and checked to see if I was attracting any attention. I didn't seem to be.

I retraced my steps and descended a half-flight of stairs to a heavy door with steel mesh over its window. The glass itself was darkened, but through it I could see the interior of a barroom. I opened the door and walked into a real bucket of blood.

A bar ran the length of a long narrow room. There were twelve or fifteen people standing or occupying backed stools, and a few heads turned at my entrance but no one took an undue interest. A dozen tables ranged across from the bar, and perhaps half of them were occupied. The lighting was dim, and the air was thick with smoke, most of it tobacco but some of it marijuana. At one of the tables a man and woman were sharing a joint, passing it back and forth, holding it in an elaborate roach clip. They didn't look in fear of arrest, and no wonder; busting someone in here for possession of marijuana would be like handing out jaywalking summonses in the middle of a race riot.

One woman sat alone at the bar, drinking something out of a stemmed glass. Her shoulder-length hair was chestnut, and the red highlights were like bloodstains in the subdued lighting. She wore red hot pants over black mesh tights.

I went over and stood at the bar, leaving an empty stool between us. When the bartender came over I turned and caught her eye. I asked her what she was drinking.

"A Rob Roy," she said.

It was the voice I'd heard over the phone, low and throaty. I told the bartender to give her another, and ordered a Coke for myself. He brought the drinks and I took a sip of mine and made a face.

"The Coke's flat here," she said. "I should have said something."

"It doesn't matter."

"You must be Scudder."

"You didn't tell me your name."

She considered this and I took a moment to look at her. She was tall, with a broad forehead and a sharply defined widow's peak. She was wearing a short bolero jacket over a halter the same color as her hot pants. Her midriff was bare. She had a full-lipped mouth with bright red lipstick, and she had large hands with bright red polish on her nails.

She looked for all the world like a whore, and I didn't see how she could possibly be anything else. She also looked like a woman, unless you paid attention to the timbre of the voice, the size of the hands, the contour of the throat.

"You can call me Candy," she said.

"All right."

"If he finds out I called you—"

"He won't find out from me, Candy."

"Because he'd kill me. He wouldn't have to think long and hard to do it, either."

"Who else has he killed?"

She pursed her lips, blew out a soundless whistle. "I'm not saying," she said.

"All right."

"What I can do, I can take you around, show you where he's staying."

"Is he there now?"

"'Course not. He's somewhere uptown. Man, if he was anywheres this side of Fourteenth Street, I wouldn't be here talking to you." She raised a hand to her mouth, blew on her fingernails as if they were freshly painted and she wanted to speed their drying. "I ought to get something for this," she said.

"What do you want?"

"I don't know. What's anybody always want? Money, I guess. Afterward, when you get him. Something."

"There'll be something for you, Candy."

"Money's not why I'm doing this," she said. "But you do something like this, you ought to get something for it."

"You will."

She nodded shortly, got to her feet. Her glass was still half-full, and she knocked it back and swallowed, her Adam's apple bobbing as she did so. She was a male, or at least she'd been born one.

In some parts of town a majority of the street girls are men in drag. Most of them are getting hormones, and quite a few have had silicone breast implants; like Candy, they're equipped with more impressive chests than most of their genuinely female competitors. Some have had sex-change surgery, but most of the ones on the street aren't that far along yet, and they may have hit the pavement in order to save up for their operations. For some of them, the surgery will eventually include a procedure to shave the Adam's apple. I don't think there's anything available yet to reduce the size of hands and feet, but there's probably a doctor somewhere working on it.

"Give me five minutes," she said. "Then come along to the corner of Stanton and Attorney. I'll be walking slow. Catch up with me as I get to the corner and we'll go from there."

"Where will we be going?"

"It's not but a couple blocks."

I sipped my flat Coke and gave her the head start she'd

179

asked for. Then I picked up my change and left a buck on the bar. I went out the door, up the stairs to the street.

The cold air was bracing after the warm fug inside the Garden Grill. I took a good look around before I walked to the corner of Stanton and looked east toward Attorney. She had covered half the block already, walking in that hip-rolling stroll that's as good as a neon sign. I picked up my own pace and caught her a few yards before the corner.

She didn't look at me. "We turn here," she said, and hung a left at Attorney. It looked a lot like Ridge Street, the same crumbling tenements, the same air of unquiet desperation. Under a streetlamp, a Ford a few years old sat low on the ground, all four of its wheels removed. The streetlamp across the way was out, and so was another further down the block.

I said, "I haven't got much money with me. Under fifty dollars."

"I said you could pay me later."

"I know. But if this was a setup, there's not enough money to make it worthwhile."

She looked at me, a pained expression on her face. "You think that's what this is about? Man, I make more in a half hour than I could ever roll you for, and the men I make it from are all smiles when they give it to me."

"Whatever you say. Where are we going?"

"Next block. You'll see. Say, that picture of him? Somebody drew it, right?"

"That's right."

"Looks just like him. Got the eyes just right, too. Man, he looks at you, those eyes just go right on through you, you know what I mean?"

I didn't like it. Something felt wrong, something hadn't felt right since I walked down the dark stairwell and into the bar. I didn't know how much of it was my own cop instinct and how much was contagious anxiety that I'd picked up from Candy. Whatever it was, I didn't like it.

"This way," she said, reaching for my arm. I jerked my

arm free and she drew back and stared at me. "What's the matter, you can't stand to be touched?"

"Where are we going?"

"Right through there."

We were at the mouth of an empty lot where a tenement had once stood. Now cyclone fence barred the way, topped with concertina wire, but someone had cut a gate into the fence. Beyond it I could see some discarded furniture, a burned-out sofa and some cast-off mattresses.

"There's a back house to one of the buildings on the next block," she said, her voice little more than a whisper. "Except it's sealed off, you can't get in from the other street. The only way's through the lot here. You could live on this block and never know about it."

"And that's where he is?"

"That's where he stays. Look, man, just come with me to where you can see the entrance. You'd never find it if I don't point it out to you."

I stood still for a moment, listening. I don't know what I expected to hear. Candy stepped through the opening in the fence, not even looking back at me, and when she was a few yards ahead I started in after her. I knew better, but it didn't seem to matter. I felt like Elaine. He'd told her to pick up the phone and turn off the answering machine, and knowing better didn't help. She did what he told her.

I walked slowly, picking my way through the debris underfoot. The street had been dark to begin with, and it got darker with every step I took into the lot. I couldn't have been more than ten yards in when I heard footsteps.

Before I could turn a voice said, "That's just fine, Scudder. Hold it right there."

THIRTEEN

I started to pivot around to my right. Before I'd moved any distance, before I'd even begun to move, his hand fastened on my left arm just above the elbow. His grip tightened and his fingers had found something—a nerve, a pressure point—because pain knifed through me and my arm went dead from the elbow on down. His other hand moved to grasp my right arm, but higher up, close to the shoulder, with his thumb probing the armpit. He bore down and I felt another stab of pain, along with a wave of nausea rolling up from the pit of my stomach.

I didn't make a sound, or move a muscle. I heard more footsteps, and broken glass crunched underfoot as Candy returned to appear a few feet in front of me. A stray shaft of light glinted off one of her gold hoop earrings.

"Sorry," she said. There was no mockery in her tone, but no apology either.

"Pat him down," Motley said.

"He hasn't got a gun, silly. He's just glad to see me."

"Pat him down."

Her hands fluttered like little birds, patting at my chest

▲ Lawrence Block ▲

and sides, circling my waist to grope for a gun tucked beneath my belt. She dropped to her knees before me to trace the outside of my legs to the ankle, then ran her hands up along the inside of the legs to the groin. There her hands lingered for a long moment, cupping, patting. The touch was at once a violation and a caress.

"Definitely pre-op," she announced. "And no gun. Or would you like me to do a strip search, J.L.?"

"That's enough."

"Are you sure? He could have a weapon up his heinie, J.L. He could have a whole bazooka up there."

"You can go now."

"I'd be willing to look for it."

"I said you could go now."

She pouted, then dropped the attitude and settled her big hands on my shoulders. I could smell her perfume, heady and floral, overlaid upon a body scent of indeterminate gender. She raised up a little on her toes and leaned forward to kiss me flush on the mouth. Her lips were parted and her tongue flicked out. Then she let go of me and drew away. Her expression was clouded, unreadable in the dimness.

"I really am sorry," she said. And then she slipped past me and was gone.

"I could kill you right now," he said. His tone was flat, cold, unemphatic. "With my hands. I could paralyze you with pain. And then write you out a ticket to the boneyard."

He was still holding me as before, one hand above the left elbow, the other at the right shoulder. The pressure he was exerting was painful but bearable.

"But I promised to save you for last. First all your women. And then you."

"Why?"

"Ladies first. It's only polite."

184

"Why any of this?"

He laughed, but it didn't come out sounding like laughter. He might have been reading a string of syllables off a cue card, ha ha ha ha ha. "You took twelve years of my life," he said. "They locked me up. Do you know what it's like to be locked up?"

"It didn't have to be twelve years. You could have been back on the street in a year or two. You're the one who decided to make it hard time."

His grip tightened and my knees buckled. I might have fallen if he hadn't been holding on. "I shouldn't have served a day," he said. "'Aggravated assault upon a police officer.' I never assaulted you. You assaulted me, and then you framed me. They sent the wrong man to jail."

"You belonged there."

"Why? Because I was moving in on one of your women and you couldn't keep her? You weren't strong enough to hold her on your own. Therefore you didn't deserve her, but you couldn't accept that. Could you?"

I didn't say anything.

"Ah, but you made a mistake framing me. You thought prison would destroy me. It destroys a lot of men, but you have to understand how it operates. It weakens the weaklings and strengthens the strong."

"Is that how it works?"

"Almost always. Cops don't last in prison. They almost never get out alive. They're weak, they need guns and badges and blue uniforms to survive, and they don't have any of those props in prison, and they die within the walls. But the strong just get stronger. You know what Nietzsche said? 'That which does not destroy me makes me stronger.' Attica, Dannemora, every joint I was in just made me stronger."

"Then you should be grateful to me for putting you there."

He let go of my shoulder. I shifted my weight, looking to balance myself so that I could thrust behind me with my foot, raking his shin, stomping on his instep. Before I could begin to move he jabbed a finger into my kidney. He might as well have used a sword. I cried out in agony and fell forward, landing hard on my knees.

"I was always strong," he said. "I always had great strength in my hands. I never worked at it. It was always there." He grabbed me by my upper arms, hoisted me to my feet. I couldn't even think about kicking out at him. My legs lacked the strength to keep me upright, and if he'd let go of me I think I'd have fallen.

"But I worked out in prison," he went on. "They had weights in the exercise yard and some of us would work out all day long. Especially the niggers. You'd see them with the sweat pouring off them, stinking like hogs, pumping themselves up, turning themselves into muscle-bound freaks. I worked twice as hard as they did but all I added was strength, not bulk. Endless sets, high reps. I never got any bigger but I turned myself into wrought iron. I just got stronger and stronger."

"You needed a knife in Ohio. And a gun."

"I didn't need them. I used them. The husband was soft, like the Pillsbury Doughboy. I could have put my fingers clear through him. I walked him into his living room and killed him with his own gun." He was silent for a moment, and when he spoke again his voice was softer. "I used the knife on Connie just to make it look good. By then she was already dead in her soul. There wasn't much left of her to kill."

"And the children?"

"Just tidying up." One hand slid over my rib cage, and he didn't take long to find the spot he wanted. He pressed with a fingertip and the pain was like an electric shock, radiating down my arms and legs, taking the resistance right out of me. He waited a moment, then pressed just a little bit harder in the same spot. I felt myself swaying at the brink of unconsciousness, dizzy with vertigo as I stared down into the blackness.

I didn't know what the hell to do. My options were limited—I couldn't try anything physical. He was every bit as strong as he claimed to be, as far as I could tell, and I could barely keep myself upright, let alone mount an attack. Whatever I tried would have to be psychological in nature, and I felt similarly overmatched in that department. I didn't know what strategy was best, whether to talk or to remain silent, whether opposition or agreement was called for.

I tried silence for the time being, perhaps for lack of anything to say. He didn't speak either, letting his fingers do the talking, pressing various spots on my rib cage and around my shoulder blades and collarbone. His touch was painful, even as his instinct was unerring in guiding him to the best targets, but he wasn't putting the pressure on. His fingers toyed with me like a mandarin's with a worry stone.

He said, "I didn't need a knife with Antoinette. Or a gun."

"Why did you kill her?"

"She was one of your women."

"I barely knew her."

"I killed her with my hands," he said, speaking the words as if savoring the memory. "Stupid cow. She never knew who I was or why I was punishing her. 'I'll give you money,' she said. 'I'll do anything you want,' she said. She wasn't a bad fuck. But you already know that."

"I never slept with her."

"I didn't sleep with her," he said. "I just screwed her like you'd screw a sheep. Or a chicken. You wring their necks as you come, that's how you do it with chickens. I didn't wring her neck. I broke it. Snap, like a twig breaking."

I didn't say anything.

187

"And then out the window. It was just luck she hit the boy on the way down."

"Luck."

"I was trying for Andrea."

"Who?"

"His girlfriend. Of course I didn't expect to hit anybody, but I was trying for her."

"Why?"

"I'd rather kill a woman," he said.

I told him he was crazy. I said he was an animal, that he belonged in a cage. He hurt me again, then crossed a leg in front of mine and gave me a shove. I went sprawling on my hands and knees. I scuttled forward, scraping my hands on gravel and broken glass, stumbling over things I couldn't make out, then spinning around, setting myself, bracing for his approach. He rushed me and I threw a right at him, putting whatever I had into the punch.

He slipped the blow. The follow-through carried me past him and took me right off my feet. I managed one step, then lost it completely and fell full-length upon the ground.

I lay there, gasping for breath, waiting for whatever was coming next.

He let me wait. Then, softly, he said, "I could kill you right now."

"Why don't you."

"You wish I would, don't you? Good. In a week you'll beg me."

I tried to get up onto my hands and knees. He kicked me in the side, just below the rib cage. I scarcely felt it, the pain refused to register, but I stopped trying to get up.

He knelt at my side and put a hand at the back of my head, cupping the base of the skull. His thumb found the hollow behind the earlobe. He was talking to me but my mind was unable to track his sentences.

His thumb dug into the spot he'd found. The pain reached a new level, but I had gone somehow beyond pain.

It was as though I were standing to one side, observing the sensation as a phenomenon, experiencing more awe than agony.

Then he turned up the gain a notch. There was already nothing but blackness in front of my eyes, but now the blackness spread behind my eyes as well. There was just one drop of fiery red against a sea of inky black. Then the red shrank to a pinpoint and went out.

FOURTEEN

I couldn't have been out long. I came to abruptly, as if someone had thrown a switch. I used to come to like that after a
long night of drinking. There was a period of time when I
never fell asleep and never woke up. Instead I would pass out
and come to.

Everything hurt. I lay still at first, taking an inventory of
the pain, trying to assess the extent of the damage. It took me
a while, too, to make sure that I was alone. He could have
been hunkered down alongside me, waiting for me to move.

When I did get up I did so slowly and tentatively, partly
out of prudence, partly of necessity. My body didn't seem
capable of fast movement or sustained activity. When I got
up onto my knees, for example, I had to stay there until I
summoned up the strength to stand. Then, on my feet at last,
I had to wait until the dizziness passed or I would have fallen
back down again.

Eventually I found my way through the obstacle course of
litter to the fence and groped along it until I got to where the
opening had been cut. I emerged on Attorney Street. I remembered that was where I was, but I'd lost all sense of di-

rection and couldn't tell which way was uptown. I walked to the corner, which turned out to be Rivington, and then I must have turned east instead of west because I wound up back at Ridge Street. I turned left at Ridge and walked two blocks and finally got to Houston Street, and I didn't have to stand there too long before a cab came along.

I held up a hand and he drew up and slowed down. I started toward him, and I guess he got a good look at me then and didn't like what he saw, because he stepped on the gas and peeled off.

I would have cursed him if I'd had the strength.

Instead it was all I could do to remain on my feet. There was a mailbox nearby and I walked over and let it take some of my weight. I looked down at myself and was glad I hadn't wasted breath cursing the cabbie. I was a mess, with both trouser legs laid open at the knee, my jacket and shirtfront filthy, my hands dark with dried blood and embedded dirt and grit. No cabdriver in his right mind would have wanted me in his hack.

But one did, and I can't say he came across as particularly demented. I stayed there at Ridge and Houston for ten or fifteen minutes, not because I really expected anyone to stop for me but because I couldn't figure out where the nearest subway entrance might be, or trust myself to cope with it once I did. Three more cabs passed me up, and then one stopped. He may have thought I was a police officer. I was trying my best to give that impression, holding up my billfold as if to display a shield.

When he stopped for me I got the rear door open before he could change his mind. "I'm sober and I'm not bleeding," I assured him. "I won't mess up your cab."

"Fuck the cab," he said. "I don't own this heap of shit, and so what if I did? Wha'd they do, jump you and roll you? This is no place for you at this hour, man."

"Why didn't you tell me that a couple of hours ago?"

"Hey, you're not too bad off if you got your sense of

humor. I better get you to a hospital. Bellevue's closest, but maybe you'd rather go someplace else?"

"The Northwestern Hotel," I said. "That's on Fifty-seventh and—"

"I know where it's at, I got a regular pickup five days a week across the street at the Parc Vendome. But are you sure you wouldn't be better off going to a hospital?"

"No," I said. "I just want to go home."

Jacob was at the desk when I stopped to check for messages. If he noticed anything unusual about my appearance, nothing in his manner showed it. Either he was more diplomatic than I'd ever realized or he'd reached that point in the terpin-hydrate bottle where relatively few things got his attention.

No calls, thank God. I went to my room, closed the door, and put the chain on. I'd done that once before, a few years back, only to discover that a man who wanted to kill me was waiting for me in the bathroom. I'd only managed to lock myself in with him.

This time, though, all that was waiting for me in the bathroom was the tub, and I couldn't wait to get into it. But first I braced myself and looked in the mirror.

It wasn't as bad as I'd feared. I was carrying some bruises and superficial scrapes and scratches, and some of the grit I'd rolled in, but I hadn't lost any teeth or broken anything or sustained any bad cuts.

I looked like hell all the same.

I got out of my clothes. My suit was beyond salvage; I emptied the pockets and stripped the belt from the slacks and stuffed them and the jacket into the wastebasket. My shirt was ripped and my tie was a mess. I tossed them both.

I drew a hot tub and soaked in it for a long time, let the water drain out and filled it up again. I sat there and soaked while I picked bits of glass and gravel out of the palms of my hands.

193

I don't know what time it was when I finally got to bed. I never did look at the clock.

I had swallowed some aspirin before I went to bed, and I took some more as soon as I got up, and another hot bath to draw some of the ache out of muscle and bones. I needed a shave but knew better than to scrape a blade over my face. I found the electric shaver my kids gave me a few Christmases back and did what I could with it.

There was blood in my urine. It's always a shock to see that, but I'd taken kidney punches before and knew what they did to you. It was unlikely he'd done me any lasting damage. My kidney ached where he'd poked me, and it would probably pain me for a while, but I figured I'd get over it.

I went out and had coffee and a roll and read *Newsday*. Breslin's column was all about the criminal-justice system, and he wasn't giving it any raves. Another columnist got slightly hysterical on the subject of a death penalty for major narcotics dealers, as if that would make them all weigh the consequences of their actions and turn their talents to investment banking instead.

If the previous day was up to the year's average to date, there had been seven homicides within the five boroughs in the course of its twenty-four hours. *Newsday* had four of them covered. None were in my neighborhood, and none of the victims had names I found familiar. I couldn't say for sure, but from what I read it didn't look as though any of my friends had been murdered yesterday.

I went over to Midtown North but Durkin wasn't around. I caught the noon meeting at the West Side Y on Sixty-third. The speaker was an actor who'd sobered up on the Coast, and his energy gave a California rah-rah quality to the hour. I

194

walked back to the station house, stopping on the way to get a slice of pizza and a Coke and eat on the street. When I got to Midtown North Durkin was back, holding the phone to his ear and juggling a cigarette and a cup of coffee. He motioned me to a chair and I sat down and waited while he did a lot of listening and not much talking.

He hung up, leaned forward to scribble something on a pad, then straightened up and looked at me. "You look like you walked into a fan," he said. "What happened?"

"I got in with bad company," I said. "Joe, I want that bastard picked up. I want to swear out a complaint."

"Against Motley?" I nodded. "He did that to you?"

"Most of what he did is where it doesn't show. I let myself get suckered into an alley on the Lower East Side late last night." I gave him a condensed version, and his dark eyes narrowed as he took it in.

He said, "So what do you want to charge him with?"

"I don't know. Assault, I suppose. Assault, coercion, menacing. I suppose assault's the most effective charge to bring."

"Any witnesses to the alleged assault?"

"Alleged?"

"You have any witnesses, Matt?"

"Of course not," I said. "We didn't meet in Macy's window, we were in an empty lot on Ridge Street."

"I thought you said it was an alley."

"What's the difference? It was a space between two buildings with a fence across it and a gap in the fence. If it was a passage to anything, I suppose you could call it an alley. I didn't get far enough into it to find out where it went."

"Uh-huh." He picked up a pencil, looked at it. "I thought you said Attorney Street before."

"That's right."

"Then a minute ago you said Ridge Street."

"Did I? I met the hooker on Ridge, in a toilet of a place called the Garden Grill. I don't know why they call it that.

There's no garden, and I don't think there's a grill, either." I shook my head at the memory. "Then she took me around the block to Attorney."

"She? I thought you said a transsexual."

"I've learned to use female pronouns for them."

"Uh-huh."

"I suppose she's a witness," I said, "but it might be a trick to find her, let alone get her to testify."

"I can see where it might. You get a name?"

"Candy. That would be a street name, of course, and it might have been made up for the occasion. Most of them have a lot of names."

"Tell me about it."

"What's the problem, Joe? He assaulted me and I have a bona fide complaint to file."

"You'd never make it stick."

"That's not the point. It's enough to get a warrant issued and pull the son of a bitch off the street."

"Uh-huh."

"Before he kills somebody else."

"Uh-huh. What time was it when you got in the alley with him?"

"I met her at midnight, so—"

"Candy, you mean. The transsexual."

"Right. So it was probably half an hour after that by the time the assault took place."

"Say twelve-thirty."

"Roughly."

"And then you went to a hospital?"

"No."

"Why not?"

"I didn't think it was necessary. He caused a lot of pain but I knew I didn't have any broken bones and I wasn't bleeding. I figured I'd be better off going straight home."

"So there's no hospital record."

"Of course not," I said. "I didn't go to a hospital, so how the hell could there be a hospital record?"

"I guess there couldn't."

"My cabdriver wanted to take me to a hospital," I said. "I must have looked as though I belonged there."

"It's a shame you didn't listen to him. You see what I'm getting at, don't you, Matt? If there was an emergency-room record, it would tend to confirm your story."

I didn't know what to say to that.

"How about this cabdriver?" he went on. "I don't suppose you got his hack license number?"

"No."

"Or his name? Or the number of his cab?"

"It never occurred to me."

"Because he could place you in the neighborhood and give evidence of your appearance and physical condition. As it is, all we've got is your statement."

I felt anger rising, and I made an effort to keep a lid on it. Evenly I said, "Well, isn't that worth something? Here's a guy who went away for aggravated assault on a police officer. After sentencing he threatened that officer in open court. He served twelve years, during which time he committed other acts of violence. Now, a few months after his release, you've got a sworn statement charging him with assault on that same police officer, and—"

"You're not a police officer now, Matt."

"No, but—"

"You haven't been a police officer for quite some time now." He lit a cigarette, shook the match out, went on shaking it after the flame had died. Without looking at me he said, "What you are, you want to get technical about it, you're an ex-cop with no visible means of support."

"What the hell is that supposed to mean?"

"Well, what else are you? You're a sort of half-assed private detective, but you don't carry a license and you get paid

197

off the books, so what do you think that looks like when you write it up?" He sighed, shook his head. "Late last night," he said. "Was that the first time you saw Motley yesterday?"

"It's the first time I saw him since his sentencing."

"You didn't go over to his hotel earlier?"

"What hotel?"

"Yes or no, Matt. Did you or didn't you?"

"Of course not. I don't even know where he's staying. I've been turning the city upside down looking for him. What's all this about?"

He rooted through papers on his desk, found what he was looking for. "This came through this morning," he said. "Late yesterday afternoon a lawyer named Seymour Goodrich turned up at the Sixth Precinct on West Tenth. He was representing one James Leo Motley, and he had with him a recently obtained order of protection on behalf of his client against you, and—"

"Against me?"

"—and he wanted a complaint on the record about your actions earlier that day."

"What actions?"

"According to Motley, you turned up at his lodgings at the Hotel Harding. You menaced him, threatened him, and laid hands on his physical person in a threatening and intim- idating manner, et cetera et cetera et cetera." He let go of the paper and it floated down onto the cluttered desktop. "You're saying it never happened. You never went to the Harding."

"Sure I went there. It's a flop at the corner of Barrow and West, I knew it well years ago when I was attached to the Six. We used to call it the Hard-on."

"So you did go there."

"Sure, but not yesterday. I went there when I was knock- ing on doors down there. Saturday night, it must have been. I showed his picture to the desk clerk."

"And?"

"And nothing. 'No, he don't look familiar, I never seen him before.'"

"And you never went back?"

"What for?"

He leaned forward, crushed out his cigarette. He pushed his chair back and leaned all the way back and fixed his gaze on the ceiling. "You can see how it looks," he said.

"Suppose you tell me."

"Guy comes in, swears out a complaint, he's got an order of protection, a lawyer, the whole bit. Says you shoved him around and got rough with him. Next day you come in looking like you fell down a flight of stairs and you're the one with a complaint this time, only it happened in the middle of the night somewhere in the asshole of Manhattan, Attorney Street for God's fucking sake, and there's no witnesses, no cabdriver, no hospital report, nothing."

"You could check trip sheets. You might find the cabbie that way."

"Yeah, I could check trip sheets. I could put twenty men on it, a high-priority thing like that."

I didn't say anything.

He said, "Going back twelve years, why'd he sound off in the courtroom? 'I'll get you for this,' all that crap. Why?"

"He's a psychopath. What does he need with a reason?"

"Yeah, right, but what was the reason he thought he had?"

"I was putting him in jail. That's as much of a reason as he needed."

"Putting him away for something he didn't do."

"Well, sure," I said. "They're all innocent, you know that."

"Yeah, nobody guilty ever goes away. He said you framed him, right? He never fired a gun, he never owned a gun. A frame-up all the way."

"According to him, he was innocent of all charges. It's a

199

funny stance to take when you're pleading guilty, but that's the way he told it."

"Uh-huh. Was it a frame?"

"What do you mean?"

"I just wondered," Durkin said.

"Of course not."

"Okay."

"It was a damn good case. The guy fired three shots at a police officer who was trying to collar him. He should have drawn a lot more than one-to-ten."

"Maybe," he said. "I'm just thinking about what it looks like now."

"And what's that?"

He avoided my eyes. "This Mardell," he said. "She was a snitch, is that right?"

"She was a source, yes."

"You make a lot of cases with the stuff she gave you?"

"She was a good source."

"Uh-huh. Cooperman a source, too?"

"I hardly knew Connie, I only met her a few times. She was a friend of Elaine's."

"And any friend of Elaine's was a friend of yours."

"What kind of—"

"Sit down, Matt. I'm not enjoying this, for Christ's sake."

"You think I am?"

"No, probably not. Did you take money from them?"

"Who?"

"Who do you think?"

"I just want to hear you say it."

"Cooperman and Mardell. Did you?"

"Sure, Joe. I wore a floppy purple hat, drove a pink Eldorado with leopard upholstery."

"Sit down."

"I don't want to sit down. I thought you were a friend of mine."

"I thought so, too. I still think so."

"Good for you."

"You were a good cop," he said. "I know that. You made detective early on and you had some damn good collars."

"What did you do, pull my file?"

"It's all in the computer, you just punch a few keys and it comes right up. I know about the letters of commendation you got. But you had a drinking problem, and maybe you got in over your head a little, and what good cop ever did everything by the book anyway, right?" He sighed. "I don't know," he said. "So far all you can show me is a domestic homicide in another state and a woman who takes a dive out a window five blocks from here. You say he did 'em both."

"*He* says so."

"Yeah, but nobody else heard him say it. Only you. Matt, maybe everything you're telling me is gospel, maybe he did those Venezuelans the other day, too. And maybe that was a hundred percent kosher bust twelve years ago, maybe you didn't sweeten it to make sure he got himself some jail time." He turned, and his eyes met mine. "But don't swear out a complaint against him and ask me to try and get a warrant. And for Christ's sake don't go looking for him, because the next thing you know somebody'll be arresting you for violating an order of protection. You know how that works. You're not allowed to go near him."

"That's a great system."

"It's the law. You want to get into a pissing contest with him, now's the wrong time to do it. Because you'd lose."

I started for the door, not trusting myself to speak. As I reached it he said, "You think I'm not your friend. Well, you're wrong. I'm your friend. Otherwise I wouldn't be saying all this shit to you. I'd let you find it out on your own."

FIFTEEN

"He's not at the Harding," I told Elaine. "He checked in the night before last and checked out the next day, right after I allegedly went over there and threatened him. I don't know that he ever actually occupied a room there. He registered under his own name, probably so he would have an address to use when his attorney applied for the order of protection."

"You went there looking for him?"

"After I left Durkin. I don't know that you can really say I was looking for Motley at the Harding, because I knew I wouldn't find him there." I thought for a moment. "I don't even know that I wanted to find him. I found him last night and I didn't come out of it too well."

"Poor baby," she said.

We were in her apartment, in the bedroom. I was stripped to my shorts and lying facedown on the bed. She had been giving me a massage, not working too deep, her hands gentle but insistent, working the muscles, taking some of the knots out, soothing some of the aches. She gave a lot of attention to my neck and shoulders, where much of the tension seemed to be centered. Her hands seemed to know just what to do.

"You're really good," I said. "What did you do, take a course?"

"You mean how did a nice girl like me get into this? No, I never studied. I've been getting massages once or twice a week for years. I just paid attention to what people did to me. I'd be better at it if I had more strength in my hands."

I thought of Motley, and the strength in his hands. "You're strong enough," I said. "And you've got a knack. You could do this professionally."

She started to laugh. I asked her what was so funny.

She said, "For God's sake don't tell anybody. If word gets out all my clients'll want this, and I'll never get laid anymore."

Later we were in the living room. I stood at the window with a cup of coffee, watching traffic on the Fifty-ninth Street Bridge. A couple of tugs sported on the river, maneuvering a barge around. She was on the couch, her feet tucked under her, eating a quartered orange.

I sat on a chair across from her and put my cup down on the coffee table. The flowers were gone. She had tossed them shortly after I'd left Sunday, not long after his phone call. It seemed to me, though, that I could still feel their presence in the room.

I said, "You won't leave town."

"No."

"You might be safer out of the country."

"Maybe. I don't want to go."

"If he can get into the building—"

"I told you, I spoke to them. They're keeping the service entrance bolted from inside. It's to be opened only when one of the porters or doormen is present, and it'll be refastened after each use."

That was fine, if they stuck to it. But you couldn't count on it, and there were just too many ways to get into an apartment building, even a well-staffed one like hers.

She said, "What about you, Matt?"

"What about me?"

"What are you going to do?"

"I don't know," I said. "I came pretty close to throwing a fit in Durkin's office. He as much as accused me of—well, I told you all that."

"Yes."

"I went there intending to accomplish two things. I was going to swear out a complaint against Motley. The son of a bitch worked me over pretty good last night. That's what you're supposed to do, isn't it? If you're a private citizen? Somebody assaults you, you're supposed to go to the police and report it."

"That's what they taught us in tenth-grade civics."

"They told me the same thing. They didn't tell me how pointless it would turn out to be."

I went to the bathroom and there was blood in my urine again, and my kidney throbbed as I returned to the living room. Something must have shown in my face, because she asked what was the matter.

"I was just thinking," I said. "The other thing I wanted from Durkin was for him to help me fill out an application for a pistol permit and rush it through. After the routine he gave me I didn't even bother mentioning it." I shrugged. "It probably wouldn't have done any good. They wouldn't issue me a carry permit, and I can't keep a loaded gun in my top dresser drawer and hope the bastard comes over for tea."

"You're afraid, aren't you?"

"I suppose so. I don't feel it but it has to be there. The fear."

"Uh-huh."

"I fear for other people's safety. You, Anita, Jan. It stands to reason that I'm at least as much afraid of getting killed

205

myself, but I'm not really aware of it. There's this book I've been trying to read, the private thoughts of a Roman emperor. One of the themes he keeps coming back to is that death is nothing to be afraid of. The point he makes is that since it's inevitable sooner or later, and since you're just as dead no matter how old you are when you die, then it doesn't really matter how long you live."

"What does matter?"

"How you live. How you face up to life—and to death, as far as that goes. That's what I'm really afraid of."

"What?"

"That I'll screw up. That I'll do what I shouldn't, or fail to do what I should. That one way or another I'll turn out to be a day late and a dollar short and not quite good enough."

The sun was down when I left her apartment, and the sky was darkening. I set out intending to walk back to my hotel, but I was breathing heavily before I'd covered two blocks. I walked over to the curb and held up a hand for a cab.

I hadn't eaten anything all day aside from a hard roll for breakfast and a slice of pizza for lunch. I walked into a deli to pick up something for dinner but walked out again before it was my turn to order. I didn't have any appetite and the smell of food turned my stomach. I went up to my room and got there just in time to throw up. I wouldn't have thought I'd have had enough in my stomach to manage it, but evidently I did.

The process was painful, involving muscles that were sore from the night before. When I was done heaving a wave of dizziness took me and I had to cling to the doorjamb for support. When it passed I walked to my bed, moving with the deliberate mincing steps of an old man walking the deck of a storm-tossed ship. I threw myself down on the bed, breathing like a beached whale, and I wasn't there for more than a minute or two before I had to get up and stagger back into the bathroom to pee. I stood there swaying and watched the bowl fill up with red.

Afraid he'd kill me? Jesus, he'd be doing me a favor.

The phone rang an hour or so later. It was Jan Keane.

"Hello," she said. "If I remember correctly, you don't want to know where I'm calling from."

"Just so it's out of town."

"It's that, all right. I almost didn't go."

"Oh?"

"It all seemed overly dramatic, can you understand that? When I drank I was always addicted to that kind of high drama. Jump up, grab a toothbrush, call a taxi, and grab the next plane to San Diego. That's not where I am, by the way."

"Good."

"I was in the cab, heading for the airport, and the whole thing seemed bizarre and out of proportion. I almost told the driver to turn the cab around."

"But you didn't."

"No."

"Good."

"It's not just drama, is it? It's real."

"I'm afraid so."

"Well, I needed a vacation anyway. I can always look at it that way. Are you all right?"

"I'm fine," I said.

"You sound, I don't know. Exhausted."

"It's been an exhausting day."

"Well, don't push yourself too hard, all right? I'll call every few days, if that's all right."

"That's fine."

"Is around now a good time to call? I thought I could have a good chance of finding you in before you left to go to a meeting."

"It's usually a good time," I said. "Of course my schedule's a little erratic right now."

"I can imagine."

Could she? "But call every few days," I said, "and I'll let you know if things clear up."

"You mean *when* they clear up, don't you?"

"That must be what I mean," I said.

I didn't get to a meeting. I thought about it, but when I stood up I realized I didn't want to go anywhere. I got back into bed and closed my eyes.

I opened them a little while later to the sound of sirens outside my window. It was the Rescue Squad, and I watched idly as they hauled someone out of the building across the street on a stretcher and loaded him into the ambulance. They sped off, heading for Roosevelt or St. Clare's, running with the throttle and the siren both wide open.

If they'd been readers of Marcus Aurelius they might have relaxed and taken it easy, knowing that it didn't make any real difference if they got there on time or not. After all, the poor clown on the stretcher was going to die sooner or later, and everything always happened just the way it was supposed to, so why knock yourself out?

I got into bed again and dozed off. I think I may have been running a fever, because this time I slept fitfully and came awake drenched in sweat, clawing my way out of some shapeless nightmare. I got up and drew a tub of water, as hot as I could stand it, and I lay gratefully in it, feeling it draw the misery out of me.

I was in the tub when the phone rang, and I let it ring. When I got out I called down to the desk to see if the caller had left a message, but he hadn't, and the genius on duty couldn't remember if it had been a man or a woman.

I suppose it must have been him, but I'll never know for sure. I didn't notice what time it was. It could have been anybody, really. I'd passed out my business cards all over town, and any of a thousand people could have been moved to call me.

And if it was him, and if I'd been there to take the call, it wouldn't have changed a thing.

When the phone rang again I was already awake. The sky was light outside my window and I'd opened my eyes ten or fifteen minutes ago. Any minute now I'd get up and go to the bathroom and find out what color urine I was producing today.

I picked up the phone and he said, "Good morning, Scudder," and it was chalk on a blackboard again, and an arctic chill that went right through me.

I don't remember what I said. I must have said something, but maybe not. Maybe I just sat there holding the goddamned phone.

He said, "I had a busy night. I suppose you've already read about it."

"What are you talking about?"

"I'm talking about blood."

"I don't understand."

"No, evidently you don't. Blood, Scudder. Not the kind you spill, although I'm afraid that did happen. But there's no sense crying over spilled blood, is there?"

My grip tightened on the telephone. I felt the anger and impatience rising in me, but I kept a lid on it, refusing to give him the response he seemed to want. I made myself take a breath, and I didn't say anything.

"Blood as in blood ties," he said. "You lost someone near and dear to you. My sympathies."

"What do you—"

"Read the paper," he said shortly, and he broke the connection.

*   *   *

I called Anita. While the phone rang I felt as though an iron band were tightening around my chest, but when I heard her voice on the other end of the line I couldn't think of a thing to say to her. I just sat there as wordless as a heavy breather until she got tired of saying *"hello?"* and hung up on me.

A blood tie, someone near and dear to me. Elaine? Did he know that she was my honorary cousin Frances? It didn't make sense but I called anyway. The line was busy. I decided he must have killed her and left her phone off the hook, and I got an operator to check and make sure. She did, and reported that the phone was in use. I'd identified myself as a police officer, so she cooperatively offered to break into the call if it was an emergency. I told her not to bother. It might or might not be an emergency, but I didn't want to talk to Elaine any more than I'd wanted to talk to Anita. I just wanted to assure myself that she was alive.

My sons?

I was looking in my book for phone numbers before the unlikelihood of that struck me. Even if he'd managed to find one of them and chase across the country after him, how could it have made today's paper? And why didn't I quit wasting time and go out and buy the paper and read about it, whatever it was?

I threw some clothes on, went downstairs and picked up the *News* and the *Post*. They both had the same story headlined on the front page. The Venezuelan family, it turned out, had been killed by mistake. They weren't drug dealers after all. The Colombians across the street were drug dealers, and the killers had evidently gone to the wrong house.

Nice.

I went to the Flame and sat at the counter and ordered coffee. I opened one of the papers and started going through it without knowing what I was looking for.

I found it right away. It would have been hard to miss. It was spread all over page 3.

A young woman had been killed in a particularly brutal fashion by a killer or killers who had invaded her home early the previous evening. She was a financial analyst employed by an investment-management corporation headquartered on Wall Street, and she had lived just below Gramercy Park on Irving Place, where she'd occupied the fourth floor of a brownstone.

Two photos ran with the article. One showed an attractive girl with a long face and a high forehead, her expression serious, her gaze level. The other showed the entrance to her building, with police personnel carrying her out in a body bag. The accompanying text stated that the well-appointed apartment had been ransacked by the killer or killers, and that the woman had been subjected to repeated sexual assault and unspecified sadistic mistreatment. The police were withholding details, as was customary in such cases, but the news story did mention that the victim had been decapitated, and one sensed that this was not the only surgery that had been performed.

Bugs Moran, intended victim of the St. Valentine's Day Massacre, knew right away who'd machine-gunned his men in a Chicago garage. "Only Capone kills that way," he said.

You couldn't say that here. All too many people kill in all too many ways, and Motley's murders didn't run to type, not as far as I could see.

All the same, this was one of his. That was obvious right away. I didn't have to look at the murder scene or interview the victim's friends and fellow workers.

All I needed to know was her name. Elizabeth Scudder.

SIXTEEN

Back in my room I flipped through the Manhattan White Pages to my own last name. There were eighteen listings, three of them businesses. I wasn't there, but Elizabeth was, listed as Scudder E J, with an address on Irving Place.

I picked up the phone and started to call Durkin but stopped with the number half-dialed. I sat there, thinking it through, and put the receiver back in its cradle.

The phone rang a few minutes later. It was Elaine. She'd had a call from him herself, and once again he'd begun by demanding that she turn off the answering machine and pick up the phone, and once again she'd done it. At that point he stopped whispering and began talking in his normal tone of voice, whereupon she reached over and flicked a switch on the answering machine so that it would record the conversation.

"But it didn't," she said. "Can you believe it? The fucking machine malfunctioned. Maybe I positioned the switch wrong, I don't know, I can't figure it out. The tape advanced as if it were recording, but when I played it back there was nothing on it."

"Don't worry about it."

"He told me all about killing a woman last night. I would have had it on tape, they could have checked it for voice-prints or whatever it is you do. And I screwed it up."

"It doesn't matter."

"Really? I thought I was being brilliant when I switched the tape on. I thought he'd incriminate himself and we'd have something on him."

"We would, but I don't think it would help. I don't think this whole thing's going to resolve itself on the basis of some piece of evidence that comes to light. The whole idea of an investigation seems pretty pointless to me. I can spend forever groping around in the dark while he goes on doing what he did last night."

"What *did* he do last night? He wasn't that specific, so maybe it wouldn't have helped to have a recording of the conversation. I gather he killed somebody."

"That's what he does."

"He told me to look in the newspaper but I didn't have one to look at. I put the all-news station on but they didn't have anything, or if they did I must have missed it. What happened?"

I filled her in, and she gasped predictably enough when she heard the victim's name.

"It's no relation," I told her. "I'm the only son of an only son, so I don't have any relatives named Scudder."

"Did your grandfather have any brothers?"

"My father's father? I don't know, he may have. He died before I was born, and I didn't have any Scudder great-uncles that I was aware of. The Scudders came from England originally. At least that's what I was told. I don't know much about that side of the family."

"So you and Elizabeth could have been distantly related."

"I suppose so. I suppose all the Scudders are related if you go back far enough. Unless one of my ancestors changed his name, or unless one of hers did."

"Even so, we all go back to Adam and Eve."

"Right, and we're all children of God. Thanks for pointing that out."

"I'm sorry. I may be taking this lightly because I'm not letting it register. It's so awful that I don't want to have to take it seriously. He must have thought she was a relative of yours."

"Maybe," I said. "Maybe not. There's something you have to remember about Motley. It's true that he's cunning and clever and resourceful, but that doesn't change the fact that he's nuts."

The phone book was still open on the bed. I looked at the list of my namesakes. It occurred to me that perhaps I ought to call the rest of them and warn them. "Change your name," I could say, "or face the consequences."

Was that what he was going to do next? Would he actually try working his way through the list? Then he could move on to the other four boroughs, and after that there were always the suburbs.

Of course if he killed enough people with the same last name, sooner or later some brilliant cop would spot a pattern. One of the listings was for the Scudder group of mutual funds; he could travel all over the country, knocking off all their shareholders.

I closed the phone book. I couldn't call the Scudders, but was there any point in calling Durkin? It wasn't his case, it was a long ways from his precinct, but he could find out who was in charge and get through to him. Elizabeth Scudder's murder would generate a lot of heat. The killing had been bloody and fierce, there was a sex angle, and the victim was young, white, upscale and photogenic.

What good was a tip from me? For a change there was no danger the case would get written off as a suicide, or a family squabble. A full lab crew would have long since labored over the scene, and every shred of physical evidence would have been measured and photographed and bagged and bottled. If he'd left prints, they'd have them, and by now they'd know who'd left them there. If he'd left anything, they'd have it.

Semen? Skin under her nails? Some part of his physical being that would do for a DNA match?

It wasn't like fingerprint evidence, where you could run a computer check and see what you had in your files. To get a DNA match you had to have a suspect in custody. If he'd left sperm or skin behind, they'd need someone to tell them whose it was. Then, after they'd picked him up, forensic techniques could put the rope around his neck.

The rope was figurative, of course. The state doesn't hang killers. It doesn't fry them, either, which is what it used to do. It does put them away, occasionally for life. Sometimes a life sentence translates into seven years or less, but in Motley's case I figured they'd want to hang on to him a little longer. The last time, he went away for one-to-ten and served twelve; if he was true to form the second time around, they'd bury him inside the walls.

Assuming he got there in the first place. DNA matching and similar sophisticated forensics added up to good corroborative evidence, but you couldn't expect to build a whole case out of it. Juries didn't know what the hell you were talking about, especially after the defense had brought in their hired experts to argue that the prosecution's hired experts were full of crap. If the accused was the victim's boyfriend and if they picked him up in her bedroom with her blood on his hands, then a DNA match on his semen would ice his cupcake nicely. If, on the other hand, the accused had no connection to the victim beyond the fact that she had the same last name as the cop who'd arrested him over a decade ago—well, under those circumstances it might not carry much weight.

I did give Durkin a call, finally. I don't know what I might have said to him. He wasn't in.

I didn't give my name, or leave a message.

*   *   *

I left the hotel around eleven-thirty intending to go to the
noon meeting at Fireside. That's the name of the group that
meets at the Y on West Sixty-third.

I didn't get there.

Walking wasn't as much of an effort as it had been the
day before. I was still stiff, and my body was holding on to a
considerable amount of pain, but my muscles weren't as tight
and I didn't tire as quickly. And it was warmer today, with
less of a breeze blowing and not so much dampness in the
air. Good football weather, I suppose you'd call it. A little
too warm for the raccoon coat, but brisk enough to make
you appreciate the flask on your hip, or the flat pint of rye in
your overcoat pocket.

I ambled over to Eighth Avenue and turned south instead
of north. I walked downtown as far as Toni Cleary's building
and stood looking at her landing site, then up at the window
he'd thrown her out of. A voice in my head kept telling me it
was my fault she was dead.

It seemed to me the voice was right.

I circled the block and wound up right back where I'd
started, which seemed to be my current role in life. I gazed
up at Toni's window again and wondered if she'd had a clue
what was happening to her, or why. Maybe he'd told her that
she was being punished for being one of my women. If so,
he'd very likely referred to me by my last name. That was
what he called me.

Had she even known my last name? I hadn't known hers.
She'd been killed because of her association with me, and she
might well have died without knowing who her killer was
talking about.

Not that it mattered. She'd have been in the twin grip of
pain and terror, and an understanding of her killer's motiva-
tions would have been fairly far down on her list of emotional priorities.

217

And Elizabeth Scudder? Had she died wondering about her long-lost cousin Matthew? I might have gone over and stared at her building if it hadn't been a mile and a half to the south of me and clear across town. Her building couldn't have told me anything, but Toni's wasn't giving me much, either.

I looked at my watch and saw that I'd missed the meeting. It was still going on but it would be all but over by the time I got there. That was fine, I decided, because I didn't really want to go anyway.

I bought a hot dog from one street vendor and a knish from another and ate about half of each. I got a cardboard container of coffee from a deli and stood on the corner with it, blowing on it between sips, finishing most of it before I got impatient and spilled the rest in the gutter. I held on to the cup until I got to a trash basket. They're sometimes hard to find. Suburbanites steal them, and they wind up in back-yards in Westchester. They make efficient and durable trash burners, enabling their new owners to contribute what they can to air pollution in their local communities.

But I was public-spirited, your ideal solid citizen. I wouldn't litter, or pollute the air, or do anything to lower the quality of life for my fellow New Yorkers. I'd just go through life a day at a time while the bodies piled up around me.

Great.

I never set out to look for a liquor store. But here I was, standing in front of one. They had their Thanksgiving window display installed, with cardboard figures of a Pilgrim and a turkey, and a lot of autumn leaves and Indian corn placed appropriately.

And a few decanters, seasonal and otherwise. And a lot of bottles.

I stood there looking at the bottles.

This had happened before. I'd be walking along with

nothing much in mind, certainly not thinking about drinking, and I'd come out of some sort of reverie and find myself looking at the bottles in a liquor-store window, admiring their shapes, nodding at various wines and deciding what foods they'd go with. It was what I'd heard people call a drink signal, a message from my unconscious that something was troubling me, that I was not at that particular moment quite as comfortable with my sobriety as I might think.

A drink signal wasn't necessarily cause for alarm. You didn't have to rush to a meeting or call your sponsor or read a chapter of the Big Book, although it might not hurt. It was mostly just something to pay attention to, a blinking yellow light on sobriety's happy highway.

Go home, I told myself.

I opened the door and went in.

No alarms went off, no sirens sounded. The balding clerk who glanced my way looked me over as he might have looked at any prospective customer, his chief concern being that I wasn't about to show him a gun and demand that he empty the till. Nothing in his eyes suggested any suspicion on his part that I had no business in his store.

I found the bourbon section and looked at the bottles. Jim Beam, J. W. Dant, Old Taylor, Old Forester, Old Fitzgerald. Maker's Mark. Wild Turkey.

Each name rang a bell. I can walk past saloons all over town and remember what I drank there. I may be less clear on what brought me there or whom I drank with, but I'll recall what was in my glass, and what bottle it came from.

Antique Age. Old Grand Dad. Old Crow. Early Times.

I liked the names, and especially that last. *Early Times.* It sounded like a toast. "Well, here's to crime." "Absent friends." "Early Times."

Early Times indeed. They got better the more of a distance you looked back at them from. But what didn't?

"Help you?"

"Early Times," I said.

"A fifth?"

"A pint'll be enough," I said.

He slipped the bottle into a brown paper bag, twisted the top, handed it over the counter to me. I dropped it into a pocket of my topcoat and dug a bill out of my wallet. He rang the sale, counted out change.

One drink's too many, they say, and a thousand's not enough. But a pint would do. For starters, anyway.

SEVENTEEN

There's a liquor store right across the street from my hotel, and I couldn't guess how many times I went in and out of it during the drinking years. This store, though, was a few blocks away on Eighth Avenue, and the walk back to the Northwestern seemed endless. I felt as though people were staring at me on the street. Maybe they were. Maybe the expression on my face was the sort to draw stares.

I went straight up to my room and bolted the door once I was inside it. I took the pint of bourbon from my coat pocket and laid it down on the top of my dresser. I hung my coat in the closet, draped my suit jacket over the back of a chair. I went over to the dresser and picked up the bottle and felt its familiar shape through the brown paper wrapping, and weighed it in my hands. I put it back down, still unwrapped, and went over to look out the window. Downstairs, across Fifty-seventh Street, a man in a topcoat like mine was entering the liquor store. Maybe he'd come out with a pint of Early Times and take it back to his room, and look out his window.

I didn't have to unwrap the damn thing. I could open the

window and pitch it out. Maybe I could take aim, and try to drop it on someone who looked as though he just got out of church.

Jesus.

I put the TV on, looked at it without seeing it, turned it off. I walked over to the dresser and took the bottle out of the paper bag. I put it back on the dresser but I stood it upright this time, then crumpled the paper bag and dropped it in the wastebasket. I returned to my chair and sat down again. From where I was sitting I couldn't see the bottle on top of the dresser.

Back when I was first getting sober I'd made Jan a promise. "Promise me you won't take that first drink without calling me," she said, and I'd promised.

Funny the things you think of.

Well, I couldn't call her now. She was out of town, and I'd ordered her not to tell anyone where she'd gone. Not even me.

Unless she hadn't left. I'd had a call from her the day before, but what did that prove? The connection, now that I thought about it, had been crystal clear. She might have been in the next room from the sound of it.

Failing that, she could have been on Lispenard Street.

Would she do that? Convinced that the danger was largely in my mind, would she have stayed in her loft and lied to me about it?

No, I decided, she wouldn't do that. Still, there was no reason I could think of not to call her.

I dialed, got her machine. Was there anyone left in the world who didn't have one of those damned things? I listened to the same message she'd had on there for years, and when it ended I said, "Jan, it's Matt. Pick up if you're there, will you?" I waited a moment while the machine went on taping the silence, and then I said, "It's important."

No answer, and I hung up. Well, of course she hadn't answered. She was miles away. She wouldn't have played it dishonest. If she'd decided to stay in the city, she'd have told me so.

Anyway, I'd kept my promise. I'd made the call. Not my fault there was nobody home, was it?

Except that it was. My fault, that is. It was my warning that got her in a cab to the airport, and it was my actions years ago, long before I met her, that made the trip necessary. My fault. Jesus, was there one thing in the fucking world that *wasn't* my fault?

I turned, and the pint of Early Times was on the dresser, with light from the overhead fixture glinting off its shoulder. I went over and picked up the bottle and read its label. It was eighty proof. All of the popular-priced bourbons had been eighty-six proof for years, and then some marketing genius had come up with the idea of cutting the proof to eighty and leaving the price unchanged. Since the federal excise tax is based on alcohol content, and since alcohol costs the manufacturer more than plain water, the distiller increased his profit while slightly boosting the demand at the same time, since dedicated drinkers had to swill down more of the product in order to get the same effect.

Of course the bonded bourbons were still a hundred proof. And some of the brands came in at odd figures. Jack Daniel's was ninety proof. Wild Turkey was 101.

Funny what sticks in your mind.

Maybe I should have picked up a fifth, or even a quart.

I put the bottle down and walked over to the window again. I felt curiously calm, and at the same time I was all hyped up. I looked out across the street, then turned and looked at the bottle again. I switched on the TV and clicked the dial from channel to channel, not even noticing what I was looking at. I went around the dial two or three times and turned the set off.

The phone rang. I stood there for a moment, looking at it as though I couldn't figure out what it was, or what to do

223

about it. It rang again. I let it ring a third time before I picked it up and said hello.

"Matt, this is Tom Havlicek." It took me a moment to place the name, and I got it just as he added, "In Massillon. Beautiful downtown Massillon, isn't that what they say?"

Did they? I didn't know how to respond to that, but fortunately I didn't have to. He said, "I just thought I'd give you a call, find out what kind of progress you were making."

Great progress, I thought. Every couple of days he kills somebody. The NYPD doesn't have a clue what's going on, and I stand around with my thumb up my ass.

What I said was, "Well, you know how it goes. It's a slow process."

"You don't have to tell me. I guess that's one thing's the same the whole world over. You put the puzzle together a piece at a time." He cleared his throat. "Why I called, I might have a piece of the puzzle. There's a night clerk at a motel on Railway Avenue who recognized your sketch."

"How did he happen to see it?"

"She. Little bitty woman, looks like your grandmother and has a mouth on her would shame a sailor. She took one look at him and knew him right away. Only problem was matching him to the right registration card, but she found him. He didn't call himself Motley. No surprise there."

"No."

"Robert Cole is what he put down. That's not far from the alias you said he used in New York. You had it written down on the sketch but I don't have it handy. Ronald something."

"Ronald Copeland."

"That's right. For address he put a post-office box, and he put down Iowa City, Iowa. He had a car, and he put down the plate number, and the motor vehicles people in Des Moines tell me there's no such plate been issued. They say they couldn't issue such a plate because it doesn't jibe with their numbering system."

"That's interesting."

"I thought so," he said. "Now my thinking is either he just made up the plate number or he used the one on the car he was driving, but it wasn't an Iowa tag in the first place."

"Or both."

"Well, sure. To take it the rest of the way, if he drove from New York he most likely had New York plates, and he might want to put down the correct plate number just in case some sharp-eyed clerk compared his car with the card he filled out. So if you were to check motor vehicles there at your end—"

"Good idea," I said. He gave me the plate number and I copied it down, along with the name Robert Cole. "He used an Iowa address at a local hotel here," I remembered. "Mason City, though. Not Iowa City. I wonder why he's fixated on Iowa."

"Maybe he's from there originally."

"I don't think so. He sounds like a New Yorker. Maybe he locked with somebody from Iowa in Dannemora. Tom, how did the motel clerk get to see the sketch?"

"How did she get to see it? I showed it to her."

"I thought the case wasn't going to be reopened."

"It wasn't," he said. "Still hasn't been." He was silent for a moment. Then he said, "What I do on my free time's pretty much up to me."

"You ran all over town on your own?"

He cleared his throat again. "Matter of fact," he said, "I found a couple of the fellows to help out. I was the one who showed the sketch to that woman, but that was just the luck of the draw."

"I see."

"I don't know what good all of this is, Matt, but I thought you ought to know what showed up so far. I don't know where we go from here, if anywheres, but you'll hear from me if anything else turns up."

I hung up and went over to the window again. On the

street a couple of uniforms were in conversation with a street vendor, a black man who'd set up shop a few weeks ago in front of the florist's, selling scarves and belts and purses, and cheap umbrellas when it rained. They come over from Dakar on Air Afrique, stay five and six to a room in the Broadway hotels, and fly back to Senegal every few months with presents for the kids. They learn quick over here, and evidently their curriculum includes low-level bribery, because the two blues left this one to tend his open-air store.

Nice of Havlicek, I thought. Decent of him, putting in his own time on a case his chief wouldn't reopen, even getting some other cops to work some of their off-hours.

For all the good it would do.

I looked over at the bottle and let it draw me across the room to the dresser. The federal tax stamp ran from one shoulder to the other, so arranged that you'd tear it when you twisted the cap. I teased the edges of the stamp with the ball of my thumb. I picked up the bottle and held it to the light, looking at the overhead bulb through the amber liquid the way you're supposed to view an eclipse through a piece of smoked glass. That was what whiskey was, I'd sometimes thought. The filter through which you can safely look upon a reality that's otherwise too vivid for the naked eye.

I put the bottle down, made a phone call. A gruff bass voice said, "Faber Printing, this is Jim."

"This is Matt," I said. "How's it going?"

"Not so bad. And you?"

"Oh, I can't complain. Say, I didn't catch you at a bad time, did I?"

"No, it's a slow day. What I'm doing right now is running carry-out menus for a Chinese restaurant. They buy thousands of them at a time and their deliverymen leave stacks of them in every vestibule and hallway they can find."

"So you're printing litter."

"That's exactly what I'm doing," he said cheerfully. "Contributing what I can to the solid-waste disposal problem. And you?"

"Oh, nothing much. It's a slow day."

"Uh-huh. There's a memorial service for Toni. Did you hear about that?"

"No."

"What's today, Thursday? It's sometime Saturday afternoon. Her family's holding a funeral somewhere in Brooklyn. Is there a section called Dyker Heights?"

"Near Bay Ridge."

"Well, that's where the family lives, and they'll be having a wake out there, and a service with a requiem mass. Some of Toni's friends in the program wanted a chance to remember her, so somebody arranged the use of an assembly room at Roosevelt. There'll be an announcement at the meeting tonight."

"I'll probably be there."

We talked for a few more minutes, and then he said, "Was there anything else? Or can I go run the rest of these menus?"

"Go to it."

I hung up and sat down in my chair again. I must have sat there for twenty minutes.

Then I stood up and got the bottle from the dresser. I walked into the bathroom, and when I got there I gave the cap a twist, breaking the seal and tearing the tax stamp. In one motion I removed the cap with my right hand and tilted the bottle in my left, letting its contents spill into the sink. The smell of good bourbon came rushing up from the porcelain basin, even as the booze spiraled down the drain. I stared down at it until the bottle was empty, then raised my eyes to regard myself in the mirror. I don't know what I saw there, or what I'd expected to see.

I held the bottle inverted over the sink until every drop was out of it, capped it, dropped it in the wastebasket. I

227

turned on both taps and let the water run for a full minute. When I turned it off I could still smell the booze. I ran more water and splashed it up against the sides of the basin until I was satisfied that I'd washed it all away. The smell of it still rose from the drain, but there was nothing I could do about that.

I called Jim again, and when he answered I said, "This is Matt. I just poured a pint of Early Times down the sink."

He was silent for a moment. Then he said, "There's something new available that you ought to know about. It's called Drano."

"I think I may have heard of it."

"It's better for the drains, it's cheaper, and it's not a whole lot worse for you if you should happen to drink it by mistake. Early Times. What's that, bourbon?"

"That's right."

"I was more a scotch drinker myself. Bourbon always tasted like varnish to me."

"Scotch tasted medicinal."

"Uh-huh. They both did the job though, didn't they?" He paused for a moment, and when he spoke again his voice was serious. "Interesting pastime, pouring whiskey down the sink. You did this once before."

"A couple of times."

"Just once that I recall. You were about three months sober. No, not quite that, you were just coming up on your ninety days. You say there was another time?"

"Around Christmas last year. Things had fallen apart with Jan, and I was feeling sorry for myself."

"I remember. You didn't call me that time."

"I called you. I just didn't happen to mention the bourbon."

"I guess it slipped your mind."

I didn't say anything. Neither did he for a moment. Outside, someone hit his brakes hard and they squealed long and loud. I waited for the crash, but evidently he stopped in time.

Jim said, "What do you suppose you're trying to do?"

"I don't know."

"Is it limit-testing? You want to see how close you can come?"

"Maybe."

"Staying sober's hard enough when you do all the right things. If you go and sabotage yourself, the odds get longer and longer against you."

"I know that."

"You had a lot of chances along the way to do the right thing. You didn't have to go into the store, you didn't have to buy the bottle, you didn't have to take it home with you. I'm not telling you anything you don't know."

"No."

"How do you feel now?"

"Like a damn fool."

"Well, you earned it. Aside from that, how do you feel?"

"Better."

"You're not going to drink, are you?"

"Not today."

"Good."

"A pint a day's my limit."

"Well, that's plenty for a fellow your age. Will I see you at St. Paul's tonight?"

"I'll be there."

"Good," he said. "I think that's probably a good idea."

But it was still only the middle of the afternoon. I put on my jacket and got my topcoat from the closet. I was halfway out the door when I remembered the empty bottle in the wastebasket. I fished it out, wrapped it in the brown bag it had come in, and returned it to my coat pocket.

I told myself I just didn't want it in my room, but maybe I didn't want the maid to find it during her weekly visit. It probably wouldn't mean anything to her, she hadn't been working at the hotel all that long, she very likely didn't know that I used to drink or that I'd stopped. Still, something made me carry the thing in my coat pocket for a couple of blocks and then slip it almost surreptitiously into a trash basket, like a pickpocket ditching an empty wallet.

I walked around some. Thinking about things, and not thinking about things.

I had told Jim I felt better, but I wasn't sure that was the truth. It was true that I had been very close to drinking, and it was true that I was no longer in any real danger of taking a drink. That crisis had passed, leaving in its wake a curious residue, a mixture of relief and disappointment.

Of course that wasn't all I felt.

I was on a bench in Central Park a little ways west of the Sheep Meadow. I'd been thinking of Tom Havlicek and trying to figure out if there was any point in calling the DMV and trying to run that license plate. I couldn't see what good it would do. If the plate led anywhere, it would probably be to a stolen vehicle. So what? He wasn't going to go away for auto theft.

I went on sorting things out, deep in my own thoughts, and the kid with the radio was pretty close before I was aware of him. He and the radio were both oversize. It was as large a ghetto blaster as I'd ever seen, all gleaming chrome and shiny black plastic, and you'd have had to check it on an airplane. It was too big for carry-on.

He'd have been a small man on a basketball court, but nowhere else. He was six-six easy, and built proportionately, with wide shoulders and thighs that bulged the legs of his jeans. His jeans were black denim, ragged at the cuffs, and he had high-top basketball sneakers on his feet, their laces untied. The hood of a gray sweatshirt hung over the collar of his warm-up jacket.

On the other side of the asphalt path from me was a

bench occupied solely by a heavyset middle-aged woman. Her ankles were badly swollen, and there was an air of great weariness about her. She was reading a hardcover book, a best-seller about extraterrestrial aliens in our midst. She looked up from it when he approached, his radio blaring.

The music was heavy-metal rock. I think that's what it's called. It was senselessly loud, of course, and it didn't sound like music to me, it sounded like noise. Every generation says that of the next generation's music—and, it seems to me, always with increasing justification. As loud as it was you still couldn't make out the words, but the underlying rage was evident in every note.

He sat down at one end of the bench. The woman looked at him, a pained expression on her round face. Then she stirred herself and heaved her bulk over to the other end of the bench. He didn't seem aware of her presence, or indeed of anything but himself and his music, but as soon as she'd moved he swung the radio up onto the spot she'd vacated. It sat there, blaring across at me. Its owner stuck his long legs out into the path, crossing one over the other at the ankle. The untied shoes, I noted, were Converse All-Stars.

My eyes went to the woman. She did not look happy. You could see her weighing alternatives in her mind. At length she turned and said something to the kid, but if he heard her he gave no indication. I don't see how he could have heard her over the wall of noise rising between them.

Something was rising within me, too, as angry as the music he liked. I breathed into the feeling and felt it building in my body, warming me.

I told myself to get the hell out of there and take a hike, or find another bench. There was an ordinance against loud radio playing, but nobody was paying me to enforce it. Nor did some code of chivalry demand that I come to this woman's aid. She could haul ass and go elsewhere if the noise bothered her. And so could I.

Instead I leaned forward and called out. "Hey," I said.

231

No response, but I was fairly certain he'd heard me. He just didn't want to let on.

I stood up and moved a couple of yards toward him, covering maybe half the width of the path. Louder I said, "Hey, you! *Hey!*"

His head swung around slowly and his eyes moved to fix on me. He had a big head, a square face with a thin-lipped mouth and an upturned porcine nose. He lacked definition around the jawline, and he'd be jowly in a few years. A flat-top haircut accented the squareness of the face. I wondered how old he was, and how much weight he was carrying.

I pointed at the radio. "Want to turn that down?"

He gave me a long look, then let his whole face relax into a smile. He said something but I couldn't get it by lip-reading or make it out over the roar of the radio. Then he reached out very deliberately and turned the volume control, not lowering but raising the sound level. It didn't seem possible that more noise could come out of that box, but it got discernibly louder.

He smiled wider. Go ahead, his eyes said. Do something about it.

I felt a tightness in my upper arms and in the backs of my thighs. That inner voice was chattering away, telling me to cool it, but I didn't want to hear it. I stood there for a moment, my eyes locked with his, then heaved a sigh and shrugged theatrically and walked away from him. It seemed to me that his laughter followed me, but I don't see how that could be the case. He couldn't have laughed loud enough for me to hear him over the radio.

I kept on walking for twenty or thirty yards before turning to see if he was watching me. He wasn't. He sat as before, legs out, arms draped over the bench, head tilted back.

Let it alone, I thought.

My blood was racing. I left the path and doubled back behind the row of benches. The ground was thick with fallen leaves, but the last thing I had to worry about was their rustling underfoot. With all that cacophony filling his ears he wouldn't have heard a fire engine.

I came right up behind him and got close enough to smell him. *"Hey!"* I yelled, loud, and before he could react I dropped an arm down in front of his face and pulled back, the crook of my elbow under his chin, my arm drawn tight against his throat. I hauled up and back, bracing my hip against the rear of the bench and putting some muscle into it, keeping my arm tight around his thick neck, hauling him right off the edge of the bench.

He was struggling, trying to duck his chin, trying to twist loose from my grasp. I bulled my way onto the path and dragged him along after me. He was trying to cry out but the sound got trapped in his throat and all he could manage was a gurgle. I felt it more than I heard it, felt his voice box vibrating against my arm.

His legs twitched and his feet scrabbled at the ground. One of his untied sneakers slipped off. I tightened my grip and his body twitched convulsively, and I dropped him and left him flopping on the ground. I went back for the radio, snatched it up in both hands, raised it high overhead and dashed it down onto the asphalt. Dials and bits of plastic went flying but the damned thing continued to play. I picked it up again, eager for the kill now, and I whirled around and smashed the thing against the concrete base of the bench. The case broke into fragments and the music stopped abruptly, leaving a cavernous silence.

He lay where I'd dropped him. He'd managed to reach a sitting position, one hand behind him for support, the other raised to rub his throat. His mouth was open and he was trying to say something but he couldn't get words out, not after the way I'd throttled him.

Here he was, mute in a suddenly silent world. While he puzzled over this I ran at him and kicked him in the side, just below the ribs. He went sprawling. I let him get up onto his

233

hands and knees and then I kicked him again, under the right shoulder, and he fell down and stayed down.

I wanted to kill him. I wanted to pound his face into the pavement, I wanted to flatten his nose and smash his teeth. The wanting was physical, in my arms, in my legs. I stood over him, daring him to move, and he managed to raise himself a few inches and turn his face toward me. I looked at his face and drew my foot back to kick it in.

And stopped myself.

I don't know where I found the strength, but I wrapped one hand around his belt and bunched the other in the protruding hood of his sweatshirt and yanked him to his feet. "Now get out of here," I said, "or I'll kill you. I swear I'll fucking kill you."

I gave him a shove. He swayed and almost fell but got his balance and managed to stay on his feet. He took a few shuffling steps in the direction I had him pointed, turned his head, looked at me, turned again and kept on going. He wasn't running, but neither was he taking his sweet time.

I watched him around the bend in the path, then turned back toward the scene of the crime. His magnificent radio lay in pieces over several square yards of Central Park. Earlier I'd carried a cardboard coffee container for blocks to avoid littering, and now look what a mess I'd made.

The woman was still on the bench. Our eyes met, and hers went very wide. She looked at me as though I were far more of a danger than the creature I'd just rousted. When I took a step in her direction she swung the book up in front of her, as if it were a cross and I a vampire. On its cover, an alien with a triangular head gazed at me with almond-shaped eyes.

I smiled ferociously at her. "It's nothing to worry about," I told her. "That's the way we handle things on Mars."

EIGHTEEN

Jesus, it felt great. I got all the way to Columbus Circle, carried along on adrenaline, riding the wave with my blood singing in my veins.

Then the rush wore off and I felt like an asshole.

And a lucky one at that. Fate had smiled at me, handing me the perfect adversary, someone bigger and younger and even more of a lout than I. It had filled me with righteous anger, always the best kind, and it had even furnished a maiden whose honor I could defend.

Wonderful. I'd almost killed the kid. I'd beaten him up good, launching what the courts would have rightly called an unprovoked assault. I might very well have done some real damage to him, and I'd run the risk of killing him. I could have crushed his windpipe, or ruptured internal organs when I kicked him. If a cop had witnessed the incident I'd be on my way downtown now. I'd wind up in jail, and I'd deserve to be there.

I still couldn't work up much sympathy for the kid with the flattop. He was by all objective standards a first-rate son of a bitch, and if he came out of this with a sore throat and a bruised liver he wasn't getting a whole lot more than he had coming. But who appointed me the avenging angel? His behavior was none of my business, and neither was his punishment.

Our Lady of the Swollen Ankles hadn't needed me to defend her. If she'd had enough of an aversion to heavy metal she could have bestirred herself and waddled away. And so could I.

Face it—I'd done a number on him because I couldn't get anyplace with Motley. I couldn't stop his taunting, so I silenced the kid's radio instead. I couldn't win when I was face-to-face with him on Attorney Street, so I evened things up by putting the boot to the kid. I was powerless over what mattered, so I made up for it by demonstrating power over what didn't matter.

Worst of all, I'd known better. The rage that had empowered me had not been quite strong enough to shut out the little voice in my head that told me to cut the shit and act like a grown-up. I'd heard the voice, just as I'd heard it before when it counseled against buying the booze. There are people who never hear their own inner voices, and maybe they can't honestly help the things they do in life, but I'd heard it loud and clear and told it to shut the fuck up.

I'd caught myself just in time. I hadn't taken the drink, and I hadn't kicked the kid's head in, but if those were victories they struck me as small ones.

I didn't feel very proud of myself.

I called Elaine from the hotel. She had nothing to report and neither did I, and we didn't stay on the phone long. I went into the bathroom to shave. My face had recovered enough so that I felt I could use a disposable razor instead of the electric thing. I shaved carefully and didn't nick myself.

Throughout it I was aware of the smell of alcohol wafting

up from the drain. I don't think it was real, I don't see how it could have been, but I smelled it all the same.

I was patting my face dry when the phone rang. It was Danny Boy Bell.

"There's somebody you ought to talk to," he said. "You free around twelve, one o'clock?"

"I can be."

"Come up to Mother Goose, Matthew. You know where that is?"

"Amsterdam, I think you said."

"Amsterdam Avenue and Eighty-first Street. Three doors up from the corner, east side of the avenue. Some nice soft music, do you good to listen to it."

"No heavy metal?"

"What a nasty thought. Shall we say twelve-thirty? Ask for my table."

"All right."

"And Matthew? You'll want to bring money."

I stayed in my room and watched the news, then went out for dinner. I had the urge for hot food, and it was the first real appetite I'd felt since the ambush on Attorney Street, so I wanted to indulge it. I was halfway to the Thai place when I changed my mind and walked over to Armstrong's. I had a big plate of their black-bean chili, adding a lot of crushed red pepper to the already potent mixture the waitress brought me. It left me feeling almost as good as smashing that radio in the park, and I was considerably less likely to regret it afterward.

I used the john while I was there, and there was blood in my urine again but it wasn't as bad as it had been, and my kidney hadn't been bothering me lately. I went back to my table and drank some more coffee. I had Marcus Aurelius along for company but I didn't make much headway. Here's the passage I read:

237

Never surpass the sense of your original impressions. Perhaps they tell you that a certain person speaks ill of you. That was their sole message; they did not go on to say you have been harmed by him. Perhaps I see my child suffers illness; my eyes tell me so but do not tell me his life is in danger. Always keep to your original impressions; add no interpretation of your own and you remain safe. Or at the most add a recognition of the great world order by means of which all things come to pass.

That seemed to hold some advice for a detective, but I wasn't sure if I agreed with it. Keep your eyes and ears open, I thought, but don't try to make any sense out of what you see and hear. Or was that what he was saying? I played with the idea for a while, then gave up and put the book away and enjoyed the coffee and the music. I don't know what it was, something classical with a full orchestra. I enjoyed it, and didn't feel driven to smash the machine that was playing it.

I got to the meeting a few minutes early. Jim was there, and we chatted for a few minutes by the coffee urn without either of us referring to our earlier conversation. I talked to a few other people, too, and then it was time to take a seat.

The speaker was from the Bronx, an Irishman from the Fordham Road section. He was a big florid-faced fellow, still working the same job as the butcher in a neighborhood supermarket, still married to the same woman, still living in the same house. Alcoholism had left him visibly unscarred until it put him in a detox three years ago with nerve and liver damage.

"I was a good Catholic all my life," he said, "but I never said a real prayer until I got sober. Now I say two prayers a day. I say please in the morning and thank you every night. And I don't take that drink."

During the discussion an older fellow named Frank, sober since the Flood, said there was one prayer that had served him well over the years. "I say, 'God, thank you for everything just the way it is,'" he said. "I don't know what good it does Him to hear it, but it does me good to say it."

I raised my hand and said I'd come close to a drink that afternoon, as close as I'd ever come since I got sober. I shied away from going into detail, but said I'd done every possible thing wrong except take the drink. Someone else responded to that, saying that not taking the drink was the only thing any of us absolutely had to get right.

Toward the end there was an announcement of Toni's memorial service, to be held in one of the big rooms at Roosevelt Hospital at three Saturday afternoon. Several people had mentioned Toni during the sharing, speculating on what might have caused her suicide and relating it to their own lives.

There was more speculation along those lines afterward at the Flame. It made me uncomfortable. I knew something they didn't know and wasn't willing to fill them in. It felt curiously disloyal to Toni to let her death pass as a suicide, but I didn't know how to set matters straight without causing more of a stir than I wanted and making myself too much the center of attention in the process. When the conversation stayed on that subject I thought about leaving, but then someone switched to another topic and I relaxed.

The meeting broke at ten, and I spent about an hour drinking coffee at the Flame. I stopped at my hotel to check for messages, then walked back out to the street without going upstairs.

I was early for my meeting with Danny Boy. I walked uptown, taking my time about it, stopping to look in store windows, waiting for lights to change even in the absence of oncoming traffic. Even so I reached the corner of Eighty-first and Amsterdam ahead of schedule. I walked a block past the place on the avenue, crossed the street, and planted myself in a doorway across from Mother Goose. I stayed there in the shadows and watched people go in and out of the place, keeping an eye on other activity on the street at the same time. On the southeast corner of the intersection, three people were standing around, heroin addicts waiting for the man. I couldn't see that they had any connection with Mother Goose, or with me.

At 12:28 I crossed the room and entered the club. I stepped into a dark narrow room with a bar along the left-hand wall and a coat room on the right near the door. I handed my coat to a girl who looked to be half black and half Asian, took the numbered plastic disc she gave me in return, and walked the length of the bar. At its end the room opened up to twice its width. The walls were brick, with sconces providing muted indirect lighting. The floor was tile in a pattern of red and black checkerboard squares. On a little stage, three black men played piano, bass and drums. They had short hair and neatly trimmed beards and they all wore dark suits and white shirts and striped ties. They looked like the old Modern Jazz Quartet, with Milt Jackson gone around the corner for a quart of milk.

I stood a few feet from the end of the bar, scanning the room, and a headwaiter glided over. He looked as though he could have been a fourth member of the group onstage. I couldn't see Danny Boy, my eyes hadn't adjusted to the lighting, but I asked for Mr. Bell's table and he led me to it. The tables were set close together, so it was a narrow serpentine path he led me on.

Danny Boy's table was at ringside. There was an ice bucket on the table, a bottle of Stolichnaya resting in it. Danny Boy wore a vest boldly patterned in vertical stripes of yellow and black; otherwise his attire matched the band and the headwaiter. He had a tumbler of vodka in front of him and a girl at his right. She was a blonde, her hair cut in an extreme punk style, long on one side, cropped close to the skull on the other. Her dress was black, and cut to show a lot of cleavage. She had one of those greedy little hill-country fox faces, the kind you get growing up in a house with three or four broken cars permanently installed on the front lawn.

I looked at her, then at Danny Boy. He shook his head, glanced at his watch, nodded to a chair. I sat down, having been informed that the girl was not the person I'd come to meet, that the person in question would be along in a little while.

The set lasted another twenty minutes, during which time no one at our table said a word, nor was there any audible conversation at the surrounding tables. From where I sat the crowd looked to be about half black and half white. I saw one man I recognized. He'd been a pimp when I first knew him, and since then he'd gone through what you could call a mid-life crisis, I suppose, and reemerged as a dealer in African art and antiquities, with a shop on upper Madison Avenue. I'd heard he was doing well, and I could believe it. He'd always done superbly as a pimp.

When the trio left the stage, a waitress came over with a fresh drink for Danny Boy's companion, something in a tall glass with fruit and a paper parasol in it. I asked if they had coffee. "Just instant," she said apologetically. I told her that would be fine and she went off to fetch it.

Danny Boy said, "Matt, this is Crystal. Crystal, say hello to Matthew."

We said hello to each other, and Crystal assured me it was a pleasure to meet me. Danny Boy asked me what I thought of the group and I said they were fine.

"Piano player's special," he said. "Sounds a little bit like Randy Weston, a little like Cedar Walton. You can hear it especially when the other two sit out and he plays solo. He played one whole set solo the other night. Very special, very tasteful."

I waited.

"Our friend'll be along in about five minutes," he said. "I

241

thought you might like to come early and catch a set. Nice place, wouldn't you say?"

"Very nice."

"They treat me right. And you know me, Matthew. Creature of habit, when I like a place I'm there all the time. Every night, or pretty near."

The coffee came. The waitress set it down and hurried off with drinks for somebody else. They didn't serve during the set, so they made up for it by working feverishly during the breaks. A lot of the customers ordered two or three drinks at a time. Some, like Danny Boy, had a bottle on the table. That used to be illegal, and very likely still is, but it was never a hanging offense.

Danny Boy poured more vodka into his glass while I stirred my coffee. I asked what he knew about the person we were waiting for.

"Meet him first," he said. "Look him over, hear him out."

At one o'clock I saw the headwaiter coming our way with a man in tow. I knew he was the fellow we were waiting for because he was all wrong for the club. He was a thin white man wearing a houndstooth sport jacket over a navy-blue corduroy shirt, and he looked out of place in a room full of black men dressed like bank vice presidents. He appeared to feel out of place, too, and he stood awkwardly with one hand on the back of his chair. Danny Boy had to tell him to sit down a second time before he pulled the chair back and sat on it.

As he sat down, Crystal got to her feet. It must have been her cue. She smiled all around and threaded her way among the tables. Our waitress came over right away. I said I'd have more coffee, and the new arrival ordered a beer. They had six brands on hand and the waitress named them all. He looked irritated by the need to make a decision. "Red Stripe," he said. "What's that?" She told him it was Jamaican. "That's fine," he said. "Bring me one of those."

Danny Boy introduced us, first names only. His was

Brian. He put his forearms on the table and looked down at his hands, as if to make sure that his nails were clean. He was about thirty-two, with a lumpy round face that looked to have taken its share of punches over the years. His hair, a dark blond, was going thin in front.

You could see he'd done time. I can't always tell, but some guys might as well be wearing a sign.

His beer came, and my coffee. He picked up the longneck bottle and read the label, frowning as he did so. Then, ignoring the glass the waitress had provided, he took a drink from the bottle and wiped his mouth with the back of his hand.

"Jamaican," he said. Danny Boy asked him how it was. "It's all right," he said. "All beer's the same." He put the bottle down and looked at me. "You're looking for Motley," he said.

"You know where he is?"

He nodded. "I seen him."

"Where do you know him from?"

"Where else? The joint. We were both on E-block. Then he went in the hole for thirty days, and when he got out they switched him somewhere else."

"Why did they put him in solitary?"

"A guy got killed."

Danny Boy said, "That's the punishment for murder? Thirty days' solitary confinement?"

"They couldn't prove it, they didn't have no witnesses, but everybody knew who done it." His eyes touched mine, then slid to the side. "I know who you are," he said. "He used to talk about you."

"I hope he said nice things."

"Said he was going to kill you."

"When did you get out, Brian?"

"Two years ago. Two years and a month."

"What have you been doing since then?"

"This and that. You know."

"Sure."

243

"What I gotta do. I started usin' again when I got outta the joint, but now I'm in a methadone program. I get day work out of the state employment, or I'll turn a buck. You know how it is."

"I know. When did you see Motley?"

"Must of been a month ago. Maybe a little more."

"You talk to him?"

"What for? No. I seen him on the street. He was comin' down the steps of this house. Then I seen him a few days later and he's goin' into the house. Same house."

"And that was over a month ago?"

"Say a month."

"And you haven't seen him since?"

"Sure I did. A couple of times, on the street in the neighborhood. Then I got the word, somebody's lookin' for the guy, so I hung around a little. Stood on the corner where I could keep an eye on the house. Had coffee next door to it so I could see who's goin' in and out. He's still there." He showed me a bashful smile. "I asked some questions, you know? There's a broad he's living with, it's her apartment. I found out, you know, which apartment it is."

"What's the address?"

He shot a look at Danny Boy, who nodded. He took another pull from his bottle of Red Stripe. "He better not know where this came from."

I didn't say anything.

"All right," he said. "Two eighty-eight East Twenty-fifth, that's near the corner of Second. There's a coffee shop on that corner serves you a good meal reasonable. Good Polish food."

"Which apartment?"

"Fourth floor in the back. Name on the bell is Lepcourt. I don't know if that's the broad's name or what."

I wrote all this down, closed my notebook. I told Brian that I wouldn't want Motley to know about our conversation.

He said, "No fuckin' way, man. I ain't talked to him since they switched him outta E-block. I ain't gonna talk to him now."

"You haven't said a word to him?"

"What for? I seen him, you know, an' I reckanized him right off. He's got this funny-shaped head, kind of a long face. If you seen him once you'd never miss him. Me, I got a face your eyes'll slide right over. He looked at me the other day, Motley, looked at me on the street. His eyes never even slowed down. He didn't reckanize me." Another shy smile. "A week from today you won't reckanize me."

He seemed proud of this. I looked at Danny Boy, who flashed two fingers at me. I got out my wallet and took out four $50 bills. I folded them, palmed them, and reached across the table to slip them into Brian's hand. He took the money and dropped his hand into his lap, holding the money out of sight while he had a look at it. When he looked up the smile was back. "That's decent," he said. "That's real decent."

"One question."

"Shoot."

"Why rat him out?"

He looked at me. "Why not? We was never friends. A guy's gotta turn a buck, you know that."

"Sure."

"Anyway," he said, "he's a real bad fucker. You know that, don't you? Shit, you gotta know it."

"I know it."

"That woman he's living with? I bet he kills her, man. Maybe he killed her already."

"Why?"

"I guess he likes it or something. I heard him talkin' about it one time. He said women didn't last, they got used up quick. After a while you had to kill 'em and get a new one. I never forgot that, not just what he said but how he said it. You hear all kinds of shit, but I never heard nothing like that." He took another pull on his beer and put the bot-

245

tle down. "I gotta go," he said. "I owe for the beer or are you taking care of that?"

"It's taken care of," Danny Boy said.

"I only drank half of it. It's okay, though. Anybody wants the rest of it, feel free." He got to his feet. "I hope you get him," he said. "A guy like that don't belong on the street."

"No, he doesn't."

"The thing is," he said, "he don't belong in the joint, either."

I said, "What do you think?"

"What do I think, Matthew? I think he's one of Nature's noblemen. Generous, too. I don't suppose you'd care to finish his bottle of beer."

"Not just now."

"I think I'll stay with Stoly myself. What do I think? I don't think he told you any lies. Your friend may not still be on Twenty-fifth Street, but it won't be because Brian tipped him off."

"I think he's scared of him."

"So do I."

"But somebody else gave a very convincing performance of fear the other night, and then she led me right into a trap." I ran down what had happened on Attorney Street. He thought about it while he refilled his glass.

"You walked right into it," he said.

"I know."

"This doesn't have that kind of feel to it," he said. "Then again, our Brian didn't show up with character references. Still, you'll want to exercise caution."

"For a change."

"Quite. If it's not a setup, I don't think he'll sell you out. I don't think he'd want to get that close to Motley." He drank. "Besides, you paid him well."

"A deuce was more than he expected to get."

"I know. There's an advantage, I've found, in giving people more than they expect to get."

That wasn't a cue, but it reminded me. I opened my wallet in my lap and found a pair of hundreds. I passed them to him and he smiled.

"As Brian would say, that's real decent. But there's no need to pay me now. Why not wait until you find out if his information is valid? Because you don't owe me anything if it's not."

"You hang on to it," I suggested. "I can always ask for it back if it's old news."

"True, but—"

"And if it's straight," I said, "I might not be around to pay you. So you'd better take the money now."

"I won't dignify that with an answer," he said.

"But you'll keep the money."

"I doubt I'll keep it long. Crystal's an expensive toy. Do you want to stay for another set, Matthew? If not, would you stop at the bar and tell the little darling it's safe to return? And put your money away, I'll pay for your coffee. My God, you're as bad as Brian."

"I only drank half of that last cup," I told him. "It's not bad for instant, though. You're welcome to the rest of it."

"That's decent of you," he said. "That's real decent."

NINETEEN

The cabbie had it all figured out. The only way to handle the crack problem was to cut off the supply. You couldn't lessen the demand because everybody who tried the stuff got addicted to it, and you couldn't seal the borders, and you couldn't control production in Latin America because the dealers were more powerful than the governments.

"So you gotta *be* the government," he said. "What we do, we annex the fuckers. Take 'em over. Make 'em territories at first, until they shape up and they're ready for statehood. Right away you dry up your drugs at the source. And you got no more wetbacks, because how can people sneak into a country when they're already there? Any place where you got your insurgents, your rebels up in the hills, you declare 'em citizens and draft their asses into the U.S. Army. Next thing you know they got three hots and a cot, they got clean uniforms and GI haircuts and they're shopping at the PX. You do this right, you solve all your problems at once."

He let me out at the ideal place for solving all my problems at once. Tenth and Fiftieth. Grogan's Open House, Michael J. Ballou, proprietor.

249

I walked in the door and the beer smell reached out to embrace me. The crowd was light and the room was quiet. The jukebox was silent, and nobody was playing darts at the back. Burke was behind the bar with a cigarette in his mouth, trying to make his lighter produce a flame. As I came in he gave me a tiny nod, put down the lighter and lit the cigarette with a match.

I didn't see his lips move but he must have said something because Mick turned at my approach. He was wearing his butcher's apron, more a coat than an apron. It buttoned up to the neck and covered him to the knees. It was gleaming white except where it showed reddish-brown stains. Some of them had faded over the years, and some had not.

"Scudder," he said. "Good man. What will you drink?"

I said a Coke would be fine. Burke filled a glass and slid it across the bar to me. I picked it up, and Mick raised his own glass to me. He was drinking JJ&S, the twelve-year-old Irish that the Jameson people turn out in small quantities. Billy Keegan, who'd worked behind the stick at Armstrong's some years back, used to drink it, and I'd tried it on a few occasions. I could still remember what it tasted like.

"It's a late hour for you," Mick said.

"I was afraid you might be closed."

"When did we ever close at this hour? It's not two yet. We're open till four, as often as not. I bought this bar to have a place for late drinking. Sometimes a man has need of a late night." His eyes narrowed. "Are you all right, man?"

"Why?"

"You look like a man who's been in a fight."

I had to smile. "This afternoon," I said, "but it didn't put a mark on me. A few nights ago it was a different story."

"Oh?"

"Maybe we should sit down."

"Maybe we should," he agreed. He snatched up the whiskey bottle and led the way to a table. I brought my Coke and followed him. As we sat down, someone at the far end of the room played the jukebox and Liam Clancy declared himself to be a freeborn man of the traveling people. The volume was low and the music didn't get in your way, and neither of us said anything until the song had ended.

Then I said, "I need a gun."

"What sort of gun?"

"A handgun. An automatic or a revolver, it doesn't matter. Something small enough to conceal and carry around but heavy enough to have some stopping power."

His glass was still a third full, but he drew the cork stopper from the JJ&S bottle and topped it up, then picked up the glass and looked into it. I wondered what he was seeing.

He drank off some of the whiskey and put the glass down. "Come on," he said.

He stood up, pushed his chair back. I followed him to the back of the room. There was a door to the left of the dart board. Press-on letters announced that it was private, and a lock guaranteed privacy. Mick opened it with a key and ushered me into his office.

It was a surprise. There was a big desk, its top completely clear. A Mosler safe as tall as I was stood off to one side, flanked by a pair of green metal filing cabinets. A brass coatrack held a raincoat and a couple of jackets. There were two groups of hand-colored engravings on the walls, some of Ireland, the others of France. He'd told me once that his mother's people came from County Sligo, his father from a fishing village near Marseilles. Behind the desk there was a much larger picture, a black-and-white photograph with a white mat and a narrow black frame. It showed a white frame farmhouse shaded by tall trees, with hills in the distance and clouds in the sky.

"That's the farm," he said. "You've never been."

"No."

"We'll go one day. It's up near Ellenville. We should have snow soon. That's when I like it the most, when all those hills have snow on them."

"It must be beautiful."

"It is." He went to the safe, worked the combination lock, opened the door. I went over and examined one of the French engravings. It showed sailing boats in a small and well-protected harbor. I couldn't read the caption.

I went on looking at it until I heard the door of the safe swing shut. I turned. He had a revolver in one hand and half a dozen shells in the palm of the other. I went over and he handed me the gun.

"It's a Smith," he said. "Thirty-eight caliber, and the shells are hollow-point, so you won't lack for stopping power. As for accuracy, that's another matter. Someone's cut the barrel down to an inch, and of course that did for the front sight. The rear sight's been filed down, and so's the hammer, so you can't cock it, you have to fire it double-action. It'll go in your pocket and come free without snagging on the lining, but you won't win a turkey shoot with it. You can't really aim it, I don't think. You can only point it."

"That's all right."

"Will it do you, then?"

"It'll do fine," I said. I turned the gun over in my hands, getting the feel of it, smelling the gun oil. There was no powder smell, so it had most likely been cleaned since its last firing.

"It's not loaded," he said. "I've only the six shells. I can make a phone call and get more."

I shook my head. "If I miss him six times," I said, "I can forget the whole thing. He's not going to give me time to reload." I swung the cylinder out and began filling the chambers. You can make a case for leaving one chamber empty so you won't have a live shell under the hammer, but I figured I'd rather have one more bullet in the gun. Besides, with the hammer filed down the possibility of an accidental discharge was slight.

I asked Mick what I owed him.

He shook his head. "I'm not in the business of selling guns," he said.

"Even so."

"I've no money in it," he said. "And no need to see money out of it. Bring it back if you don't use it. Failing that, forget about it."

"It's unregistered?"

"As far as I know. Someone picked it up in a burglary. I couldn't tell you who owned it, but I doubt he registered it. The serial number's gone. A man who licenses his gun rarely files down the number. You're sure it'll do you?"

"I'm sure."

We went back to the other room and he locked the office door. The same Liam Clancy record was playing as we returned to our table. The television set behind the bar was tuned to a western movie, and the sound was too low to carry past the three men watching it. I drank some Coke and Mick drank some Irish.

He said, "What I said before, that I'm not in the gun business. I've been in and out of that business in my day. Did you ever happen to hear the story of the three cases of Kalashnikovs?"

"No."

"Now this was some years ago. It might be long enough that I could tell it in court. It's seven years, isn't it? The statute of limitations?"

"On most felonies. There's no statute of limitations on tax evasion or murder."

"Don't I know it." He picked up his glass and looked at it. "Here's how it was. There were these three cases of Kalashnikovs. AK-47s, you know. Assault rifles. They were in a storage bin in Maspeth, just off Grand Avenue. Big crates they were, with more than thirty rifles in each, so you had close to a hundred in all."

"Whose were they?"

253

"Ours, once we blew the lock on that storage shed. The crates were too large for the van we had. We broke them open and loaded the rifles into the back of the van. I don't know whose guns they were, but he couldn't own them legally, and he couldn't go to the police about it, could he?" He took a drink. "We already had a buyer for them. You wouldn't steal something like that if you didn't."

"Who was your buyer?"

"Some lads who looked like Hitler's next of kin. Their heads this close to shaved, and the three I saw were dressed alike. Blue shirts with designs on the pocket and khaki trousers. They said they had a training camp in the Adirondacks, up around Tupper Lake. They wanted the guns, and they paid more than they had to, I'll say that for them."

"So you sold them."

"So I did. And two nights later I'm having a drink at Morrissey's, and Tim Pat himself calls me aside. You remember Tim Pat Morrissey."

"Of course."

"'I hear you've a few extra rifles,' he says. 'Wherever did you hear that?' I say. Well, the whole of it is that he wants the lot of them for some friends of his in the north of Ireland. You knew they were involved in all of that, the brothers. Didn't you?"

"I'd certainly heard as much."

"Well, nothing would do but he must have these rifles. He won't believe I've already sold them. He's sure I couldn't have moved them so quick, you see. 'You don't want them in this country,' he says. 'Think what your man may do with them.' Why, I said, he and his friend will go and play toy soldier with them, or at worst they'll go and shoot a few niggers. 'You don't know that,' he says. 'Maybe they'll start a revolution and storm the governor's mansion. Maybe they'll give the guns to the niggers. Sell them to me and you'll know where they're going.'"

He sighed. "So we stole them back and sold them to Tim

Pat. He wouldn't pay the price the little Nazis paid, either. What a bargainer he was! 'You're doing this for Holy Ireland,' he said, driving the price down. Still, when you collect twice for the same fucking guns, any price is a good price."

"Did the original buyers come back at you?"

"Ah," he said. "Now there's the part the statute of limitations doesn't cover. You might say they were in no position to retaliate."

"I see."

"I made good money on those guns," he said. "But once they were out of the country, well, that was an end to it. I was out of guns, and so I was out of the gun business."

I went to the bar and got another Coke. This time I had Burke cut me a wedge of lemon to cut the sweetness. When I got back to the table Mick said, "Now what made me tell you that story? The gun business, that's what put me in mind of it, but why go on and tell it?"

"I don't know."

"When we sit together, you and I, the stories roll."

I sipped my Coke. The lemon helped. I said, "You never asked me what I needed with a gun."

"Not my business, is it?"

"Maybe not."

"You happen to need a gun and I happen to have one. I don't think you'll shoot me, or hold up the bar with it."

"It's not likely."

"So you owe me no explanation."

"No," I said. "But it makes a good story."

"Well," he said, "now that's another thing entirely."

I sat there and told him the whole thing. Somewhere along the way he held up a hand and drew a short horizontal line in the air, and Burke chased the last few customers and started shutting down the bar. When he started putting the chairs up on the tables Ballou told him to let it go, that he'd see to the rest of it. Burke turned off the lights over the bar and the ceiling lights and let himself out, drawing the sliding gates across but not engaging the padlock. Mick locked the door from inside and cracked the seal on a fresh bottle of whiskey, and I went right on with my story.

When I got to the end he looked again at the sketch of Motley. "He's a bad bastard," he said. "You can see it in his eyes."

"The man who drew the picture never even saw him."

"No matter. He put it in the picture whether he saw him or not." He folded the sketch and gave it back to me. "The woman you brought in the other night."

"Elaine."

"I thought so. I didn't recall her name, but I thought it must be the same one. I liked her."

"She's a good woman."

"You've been friends a long time then."

"Years and years."

He nodded. "When it all started," he said. "Your man said you framed him. Is he still saying it now?"

"Yes."

"Did you?"

I'd left that part out, but I couldn't see any reason to hold it back. "Yes, I did," I said. "I got a lucky shot in and he went out cold. He had a glass jaw. You wouldn't remember a boxer named Bob Satterfield, would you?"

"Wouldn't I though? His fights looked fixed. The ones he lost, that is. He'd be way ahead, and then he'd get tapped on the jaw and go down like a felled steer. Of course you'd never fix a fight that way, but the average man's reasoning powers don't reach that far. Bob Satterfield, now his is a name I've not heard in years."

"Well, Motley had Satterfield's jaw. While he was out I stuck a gun in his hand and squeezed off a few rounds. It wasn't a complete frame. I just made the charges more serious so that he'd draw a little jail time."

"And you trusted her to back you?"

"I figured she'd stand up."

"You thought that well of her."

"I still do."

"And rightly so, if she did stand up. Did she?"

"Like a little soldier. She thought it was his gun. I had a throw-down with me, an unregistered pint-size automatic I used to carry around just in case. I palmed it and pretended to find it when I frisked him, so she had no reason not to believe it was his gun. But she was there to see me wrap his fingers around it and shoot holes in her plaster, and she still went in and swore he'd done the shooting and he'd been trying to kill me when he did it. She put it in her statement and signed it when they typed it up and handed it to her. And she would have sworn to it all over again in court."

"There's not many you could count on like that."

"I know."

"And it worked. He went to prison."

"He went to prison. But I'm not sure it worked."

"Why do you say that?"

"Since he got out he's killed eight people that I know of. Three here, five in Ohio."

"He'd have killed more than that if he'd spent the past twelve years a free man."

"Maybe. Maybe not. But I gave him a reason to select certain people as his targets. I broke some rules, I pissed into the wind, and now it's blowing back in my face."

"What else could you do?"

"I don't know. I didn't take a lot of time to think it through when it happened. It was the next thing to instinctive on my part. I figured he belonged inside and I'd do what it took to put him there. Now, though, I don't think I'd do it that way."

"Why? All because you gave up the drink and found God?"

I laughed. "I don't know that I've found Him yet," I said.

"I thought that was what your lot did at those meetings." Deliberately he uncorked the bottle and filled his glass. "I thought you all learned to call Him by His first name."

"We call each other by our first names. And I suppose some people develop some kind of a working relationship with whatever God means to them."

"But not you?"

I shook my head. "I don't know much about God," I said. "I'm not even sure if I believe in Him. That seems to change from one day to the next."

"Ah."

"But I'm not as quick to play God as I used to be."

"Sometimes a man has to."

"Maybe. I'm not sure. I don't seem to feel the need as often as I used to. Whether or not there's a God, it's beginning to dawn on me that I'm not Him."

He thought that over, working on the whiskey in his glass. If it was having any effect on him, I couldn't see it. Nor was it affecting me. The incident in my hotel room that afternoon had been some sort of watershed, and the threat of picking up a drink had lifted for the time being once the bourbon was done splashing in the sink basin. There were times when it was dangerous for me to be in a saloon, sipping Coke among the whiskey drinkers, but this was not one of those times.

He said, "You came here. When you needed a gun, you came here for it."

"I thought you might have one."

"You didn't go to the cops, you didn't go to your sober friends. You came to me."

"There's nobody on the force who'd bend the rules for me, not at this point. And my sober friends don't pack a lot of heat."

"You didn't just come here for the gun, Matt."

"No, I don't suppose I did."

"You had a story to tell. Is there anybody else who's heard the whole of it?"

"No."

"You came here to tell it. You wanted to tell it here and you wanted to tell it to me. Why?"

"I don't know."

"It had nothing to do with the gun. What if I'd had no gun for you?" His eyes, cool and green as his mother's homeland, took my measure. "We'd be here just the same," he said. "Saying these words."

"Why did you let me have the gun?"

"Why not? It was doing me no good locked in the safe. I have other guns I can lay my hands on, if I feel the sudden need to shoot somebody. Why not give it to you?"

"Suppose you hadn't had one. You know what you'd have done? You'd have called around and gone out and found one."

"Why would I do that?"

"I don't know," I said, "but it's what you would have done. I don't know why."

He sat there thinking about it. I went to the men's room and stood at a urinal full of cigarette butts. My urine had a slight pink cast to it, but it was a lot less alarming than it had been lately. My kidney seemed to be mending.

On the way back I went behind the bar and helped myself to a glass of club soda. When I got back to the table Ballou was on his feet. "Come on," he said. "Grab your coat, we'll get some air."

He kept his car in a twenty-four-hour lot on Eleventh Avenue. It was a big silver Cadillac with tinted glass all around. The attendant treated it and its owner with respect.

The city was still, the streets next to empty. We cruised

across town, turned right at Second Avenue. As we crossed Thirty-fourth Street he said, "You ought to look at the house he's staying in. As much as you paid for the address, you'll want to know it's not an empty lot."

"That's not a bad idea. The last empty lot I went into didn't turn out so well for me."

He parked in a bus stop and I checked my notebook and walked around the corner to the address Brian had given me. The building was a six-story tenement, its ground floor now occupied by a tailor. A sign, hand-lettered, promised reasonable alterations and fast service. I went into the vestibule and checked the names. There were four apartments to a floor, and the tenant in 4-C was Lepcourt.

"The right name's on the bell," I told Mick. "That doesn't mean Motley's living here, but if my guy was making up a story at least he wove a little truth into it."

"Ring the bell," Mick said. "See if he's home."

"No, I don't want to do that. Watch the street, would you? I want to look around."

He stood at the street door while I got the lobby door open, slipping the lock with a credit card. I walked the length of a narrow hallway, past the staircase, and between the doors of the two rear apartments. One-C was the right rear apartment. All the way at the back was a fire door leading to the rear courtyard. I pressed the panic bar and pushed it open, then wedged a toothpick into the locking mechanism to avoid locking myself out.

My presence in the courtyard alarmed a couple of rats and sent them scuttling for cover. I made my way to the back of the tiny area and counted windows to determine which was 4-C. My view was imperfect, largely obscured by the fire escape, but I would have been able to tell if there was a light on in the Lepcourt apartment. There wasn't. Not in the room with the rear window, anyway.

If you moved one of the garbage cans and stood on it you could reach the fire escape and either lower the ladder or swing up onto the metal stairs. I actually considered this for a moment before ruling it out as too much risk with too little point. I went back into the building, leaving my toothpick in the lock in case I felt the need to get into the building from the back at some later time. I climbed the stairs to the fourth floor and looked at the keyhole, and under the door. No light showed through. I put my ear to the door and couldn't hear anything.

I put a hand in my pocket and touched the little Smith, working it with my fingers like a worry stone while I tried to figure out what to do next. He was either in there or he wasn't. If I knew he was home I could force the door and try to take him by surprise. If I knew the apartment was empty I could try to gain entrance by stealth. I couldn't do either unless I knew if he was there, and I couldn't find that out without running the risk of alerting him. And that was too great a risk. My one edge at this point was that he didn't know I had his address. It wasn't much of an advantage, but I couldn't afford to give it away.

When I got downstairs the entryway was empty. Ballou was outside, leaning against a streetlamp, his butcher's apron a vivid white. We went to his car and he said he was hungry and that he knew a place I'd like. "And they'll pour you a drink without checking the clock first," he said. "That's if they know you."

"I ought to get to sleep," I said.

"You're not even tired."

He was right. I wasn't. I don't know how he knew it, because I must have looked tired, but the whole evening had somehow energized me. He drove downtown and west and parked at a fire hydrant in front of an old-fashioned diner across from the river a few blocks south of the entrance to the Holland Tunnel. A white-haired waitress brought us menus. He ordered steak and eggs, the steak rare, the eggs

261

over easy. They had Philadelphia-style scrapple on the menu, and I ordered that with scrambled eggs. And coffee, I said.

"Did you want the special coffee?"

I asked what it was. She looked uncomfortable, and Ballou told her I'd have plain black coffee, but that he'd like the special coffee. At that point I caught on, and I wasn't surprised when the special coffee turned out to be straight scotch served in a coffee mug.

He said, "You can give the police his address."

"I could. I don't know what they'd do with it. I tried to press charges against him and Durkin wouldn't even listen to me."

"There's more," he said. "You have to do this alone."

"Do I?"

"I think you do. It's between the two of you, and that's how it has to be settled."

"That's how it feels to me, too," I admitted. "But it doesn't make sense. It's not as though he's a worthy foe and I have to meet him as an equal. He's a murderous psychopathic son of a bitch and I'd love it if he got hit by a bus crossing the street."

"I'd buy the driver a drink."

"I'd buy him a new bus. But I can't wait for a bus to get him, and there's as much chance of that as the cops bagging him. I got a call earlier from the police lieutenant in Ohio. He did some work on his own, found a motel clerk who ID'd Motley. But nothing like that is going to make a difference in this case. I have to face him myself and I wish I knew why."

"Your business with him is personal."

"Is it? I'm not even in a rage. I was before, God knows, but I used it all up on that big stupid kid in the park. It ran away from me, Mick. I could have killed him."

"Small loss."

"A big loss to me if I went away for it. Anyway, my rage went away somewhere after that. I must be carrying a lot of anger, but I swear to God I can't feel it. I must hate the bastard, but I don't feel that, either. I just feel—"

"What?"

"Driven."

"Ah."

"He's my problem and I have to solve him. Maybe it's because I set him up twelve years ago. I didn't play according to the rules, and everything that's happened since has to be charged to my account. Or maybe it's simpler than that. It's personal to him, and maybe there's no way to avoid buying into his perception of it. Either way, I have to do something about him. He's the boulder in front of my door. If I don't shove him out of the way I'll never leave the house again." I drank the rest of my coffee. The grounds were like sludge on the bottom of the cup. "Except he's an invisible boulder," I said. "I've got a sketch of him based on a pair of twelve-year-old memories. I never get to see him. I keep looking over my shoulder and he's never quite there."

"He was there the other night. In the empty lot."

"Was he? I think back on it and it might as well have happened in a dream. I never quite got to see him. He was behind me almost all the time. The one time I took a swing at him I couldn't really see what I was doing. It was dark as a coal mine in there, all I saw was a shape. Then I was face-down in the dirt, and then I was unconscious, and then I was all by myself. I suppose I should be grateful for the aches and bruises. They were proof the whole thing really happened. Every time I pissed blood I knew I hadn't made it all up."

He nodded, and ran his right forefinger over a scar on the back of his left hand. "Sometimes pain's a great comfort," he said.

"I want to take him down and bring him in," I said. "In a funny way I have a better shot than the cops do. I'm a private citizen, so none of the Supreme Court rulings get in my way. I don't need probable cause to search his dwelling, and I can

263

enter the premises illegally without disqualifying any evidence I turn up. I don't have to read him his rights. If I get a confession out of him, they can't disallow it on the grounds that he didn't get to consult an attorney. I can record anything he says without getting a court order first, and I don't even have to tell him I'm doing it."

The waitress brought me more coffee. I said, "I want him in cuffs and leg irons, Mick. I want to see him sent away and know he won't be coming out again. And I think you're right. I think I have to bring him in myself."

"You may not be able to. You may have to use the gun."

"I'll use it if I have to."

"I'd use it first chance. I'd shoot him in the back."

Maybe I would, too. I couldn't really say what I'd do, or when I might get to do it. Chasing after him was like pursuing mist once the sun came up. So far all I had was an address and an apartment number, and I didn't even know if he really lived there.

When I was a working cop there had been restaurants where I didn't get a check. The owners liked having us around, and I guess they thought our presence was worth the occasional free meal. Evidently some establishments feel similarly about career criminals, because there was no check for us at the diner. We each left five dollars for the waitress, and Mick stopped at the counter to pick up a couple of containers of coffee.

The Cadillac had a ticket on the windshield. He folded it and tucked it in a pocket without comment. The sky was growing light, the morning still and fresh around us. He drove up along the river and over the George Washington Bridge to the Jersey side, then headed north on the Palisades Parkway, pulling off at an overlook high above the Hudson. He parked with the big car's nose against the guardrail and we sat and watched the dawn come up over the city. I don't think either of us had said more than a dozen words since we left the diner, and we didn't speak now.

After a while he got our coffees out of the paper sack and handed one to me. He reached across me to open the glove compartment and removed a half-pint silver flask. He uncapped it and added an ounce or two of whiskey to his coffee. I must have reacted visibly because he turned and raised his brows at me.

"I used to drink coffee that way," I said.

"With twelve-year-old Irish?"

"With any kind of whiskey. Bourbon, mostly."

He capped the flask, took a long pull of the sweetened coffee. "Sometimes," he said, "I wish to God you'd take a drink."

"So you've said."

"But do you know something? If you reached for the flask right now I'd break your arm."

"You just don't want me drinking up your whiskey."

"I don't want you drinking any man's whiskey. And I couldn't tell you why. Have you been up here before?"

"Not in years. And never at this hour."

"It's the best time. In a little while we'll go to mass."

"Oh?"

"The eight o'clock at St. Bernard's. The butchers' mass. You went with me once before. What's so funny?"

"I spend half my life in church basements, and you're the only person I know who goes to church."

"Your sober friends don't go?"

"I suppose some of them must, but if so I haven't heard them talk about it. What do you want to drag me to mass for, Mick? I'm not even a Catholic."

"Weren't you raised one?"

I shook my head. "I was brought up sort of half-assed Protestant. Nobody in the family went regularly."

"Ah. Well, what difference does it make? You don't have to be a fucking Catholic to go to the fucking mass, do you?"

"I don't know."

"I don't go for God. I don't go for the fucking church. I go because my father went every morning of his life." He took a short pull straight from the flask. "God, that's good. It's too good to put in coffee. I don't know why the old man went and I don't know why I go. Sometimes it's where I want to be after a long night, and it's a good night we've just had. Come to mass with me."

"All right."

He drove back into town and left the car on West Fourteenth in front of Twomey's funeral parlor. The eight o'clock mass was held in a small chapel off the main sanctuary at St. Bernard's. There were less than two dozen people in attendance, perhaps half of them dressed like Mick in white butcher's aprons. When the mass ended they would go to work in the meat markets just south and west of the old church.

I took my cues from the others, standing or sitting or kneeling when they did. When they handed out the communion wafers I stayed where I was. So did Mick, along with three or four of the others.

Back at the car he said, "Where now? Your hotel?"

I nodded. "I ought to get some sleep."

"Wouldn't you sleep better in a place unknown to him? I've an apartment you could use."

"Maybe later," I said. "I'm safe enough for now. He's saving me for last."

TWENTY

In front of the Northwestern he shifted the car into park but left the engine running. He said, "You've got the gun."

"In my pocket."

"If you need more shells—"

"If I need more shells I'm in deep trouble."

"Well, if there's anything you need."

"Thanks, Mick."

"Sometimes I wish you drank," he said, "and then I'm glad you don't." He looked at me. "Why is that?"

"I don't know, but I think I understand. Sometimes I wish you didn't drink, and sometimes I'm glad you do."

"I never have nights like this with anybody else."

"Neither do I."

"The mass was all right, wasn't it?"

"It was fine."

He fixed his eyes on me. "Do you ever pray?" he demanded.

"Sometimes I talk to myself. Inside my head, I mean."

"I know what you mean."

267

"Maybe that's praying. I don't know. Maybe I do it in the hope that something is listening."

"Ah."

"I heard a new prayer the other day. A fellow said it was the most useful one he knew. 'Thank you for everything just as it is.'"

His eyes narrowed and he mouthed the words silently. Then his lips curled into a slow smile. "Oh, that's grand," he said. "Wherever did you hear that one?"

"At a meeting."

"That's the sort of thing you hear at those meetings, is it?" He chuckled, and for a moment I thought he was going to say something else. Then he straightened up in his seat. "Well, I won't keep you," he said. "You'll want to get some sleep."

In my room I shucked off my topcoat and hung it up, then drew the gun out of my jacket pocket. I swung the cylinder out, dumped the shells into the palm of my hand. They were hollow points, designed to expand upon impact. That made them do more damage than standard rounds, but it also lessened the likelihood of a dangerous ricochet, because the slug would shatter into fragments upon impact with a solid surface instead of ricocheting intact.

If I'd had hollow points in my gun some years ago I might not have caused the death of that child in Washington Heights, and who could say what a difference that might have made in all our lives? There was a time when I could drink away hours on end running that one through my mind.

Now I reloaded the gun and aimed at objects in the room, getting the feel of the weapon. I took off my jacket and tried to find a convenient and comfortable way to tuck the gun under my belt. A shoulder holster might be best, I decided, and I made a note to go get one later in the day. There were other things I could use, too. Handcuffs, certainly, so that I could immobilize Motley while I questioned him, and neutralize the unnatural strength in those hands of his. I could pick up a set of cuffs at a store specializing in police items. There was at least one such store downtown near One Police Plaza, and I seemed to remember another in the East Twenties, near the Academy. I could stop there on my way to the Lepcourt apartment, and they could very likely supply a shoulder holster as well. Some of their goods were available only to working cops, but most were unrestricted, for sale to anyone who wanted them, and handcuffs were certainly in that category.

You could buy body armor there, too, and I wondered if a Kevlar vest might be a wise purchase. I didn't think he'd be shooting at me, and the mesh won't do much to stop a knife thrust, but would it be likely to afford me any protection against his fingers? I didn't know, and I couldn't quite see myself trying to pry that information from a clerk. "Will this protect me if somebody pokes me in the ribs?" "What's the matter, sir, you ticklish or something?"

A small tape recorder would be good. One of those pocket-size models that take the microcassettes. They had them at the Reliable office, and maybe they'd let me check one out for a couple of days. Or maybe it would be simpler if I went to Radio Shack and bought my own. I didn't need state-of-the-art equipment, so how much could it cost me?

I set the gun on top of the dresser and got undressed. I went into the bathroom to run a tub of hot water, and while it filled I came back and switched on the television set and scanned the dial. I caught a newscast on one of the independent channels. The lead item was something about a crisis in the savings-and-loan industry, and then a cheerful girl reporter with a Pepsodent smile came on to tell me that police believed there might be a connection between last night's bizarre murder of an Auxiliary Police officer in the West Village and this morning's pre-dawn assault in exclusive Turtle Bay.

269

I'd missed hearing about the AP officer earlier, so I paid attention. I was hooked in tighter when she went on to say that police were speculating further about the possibility of a connection between both crimes and the brutal rape and murder of Elizabeth Scudder earlier in the week at her home on Irving Place. The victim in this morning's assault, an unmarried woman residing at 345 East Fifty-first Street, had been rushed to New York Hospital with multiple stab wounds and other unspecified injuries.

The screen filled with a shot of the building entrance, with paramedics rushing a stretcher out to a waiting ambulance. I tried to make out the face of the woman on the stretcher but I couldn't see anything.

Then the reporter was back, showing what was probably supposed to be a serious smile. The victim, she chirped, was currently undergoing emergency surgery, and a police-department spokesman rated her survival chances as slim. Her identification was being withheld pending notification of next of kin.

I hadn't been able to see her face, but I'd seen the building entrance. Anyway, I'd recognized the address. And I think I'd have known anyway. I think I knew from the moment the item began.

It couldn't have taken me more than five minutes to get dressed and out the door. As it closed behind me the phone started ringing. I let it ring.

TWENTY-ONE

Here's how it must have happened:

At ten o'clock Thursday night, around the time we were closing the meeting at St. Paul's, Andrew Echevarria and Gerald Wilhelm finished their tour of duty and reported back to their commanding officer at the Sixth Precinct on West Tenth Street. Since six that evening the two men had comprised one of five Auxiliary Police patrols walking assigned beats in the precinct, carrying nightsticks and walkie-talkies, and serving as the eyes and ears of the regular police while providing a visible police presence on the streets of the city.

Gerald Wilhelm left his uniform in a locker and went home in civilian clothes. Andrew Echevarria wore his uniform to and from his weekly service, as was his right. He left the station house around twenty minutes after ten and walked north and west toward a converted warehouse on Horatio Street between Washington and West, where he shared a one-bedroom apartment with his lover, a textile designer named Clarence Freudenthal.

Maybe Motley started tailing him early in the evening. Maybe he picked him up for the first time shortly after he left the station house. Then again, maybe the whole thing was a matter of impulse. Motley was certainly a frequent habitué of the western edge of the Village, and God knows he was capable of spur-of-the-moment indecency.

What's evident is that he lured Echevarria into a darkened passage between two buildings, probably by asking for help. Echevarria, still in uniform, would expect to be asked for assistance. Then, before the young airlines ticket agent could guess what was happening, Motley immobilized him and very likely rendered him unconscious by manually constricting his throat.

That's not how he killed him, though. For that he used a long narrow-bladed knife, but he didn't do this until he'd removed the young man's jacket and shirt. Then he killed Echevarria with a single thrust to the heart.

He stripped the corpse of everything but the underwear and socks. He took the shoes off in order to remove the trousers, but either they were the wrong size or he preferred his own, because he left them behind. (Surprisingly enough, they were still there when the body was discovered. If a street person had been first on the scene, those shoes probably would have walked.)

He left Echevarria in the alley, dressed in socks and underwear and quite dead. The undershorts were down around the victim's thighs and some sort of indignity had been performed upon him, but a subsequent examination did not reveal the presence of semen in the dead man's anus. He had been penetrated anally, but either the assailant failed to ejaculate or the agent of penetration was Echevarria's own hardwood nightstick.

In any event, Motley took the nightstick away with him, along with his other gear—handcuffs and key, notebook, walkie-talkie, AP shield, and, of course, shirt and jacket and pants and cap. He probably wore his own clothing and carried these articles, and he may have had some sort of shopping bag with him to facilitate this task. (If so, that would support the conjecture that he planned the attack on Echevarria, that he deliberately picked out a uniformed officer similar to himself in height and build and then stalked him.)

Echevarria's death evidently took place between 10:30 and 10:45, and his killer was probably out of the passageway and off into the night before eleven o'clock. It was another hour before police from the Sixth Precinct, responding to an anonymous phone tip, discovered the body where the killer had left it. One of the officers on the scene happened to recognize the victim, having seen him just a couple of hours earlier; but for this bit of luck, he might not have been identified, or known to have been an auxiliary cop, for a considerable time.

At this point James Leo Motley was a full hour away from the murder scene, with few clues left behind to point to him. He probably went directly to the Lepcourt apartment on East Twenty-fifth, where he stowed his street clothes and dressed in Echevarria's uniform. Did he look at himself in his new uniform? Did he stride to and fro across the floor, slapping his nightstick against the palm of his hand? Did he, like every rookie cop since Teddy Roosevelt was commissioner, try twirling his nightstick?

One can only imagine. Just what he did is uncertain, as is the time he arrived at the Twenty-fifth Street apartment and the time he left it. He may have been there while I stood in the courtyard behind the building, peering up through the fire escape at his window and listening to the rats scuttling among the garbage cans. He may have been on the other side of the apartment door while I was in front of it, looking for light under the door, listening for sounds within. I doubt it myself. I don't think he stayed in the apartment for very much longer than the time it took him to change his clothes for his victim's, but there's no way to know.

At four-thirty, while Mick Ballou and I were having an early breakfast at the diner, he was entering the lobby at 345 East Fifty-first.

273

*　　*　　*

He found the easy way to get through all those locks. He got her to open them for him.

First he presented himself to the doorman. He showed up in full police regalia and announced that he'd come to talk with one of the building's tenants, a woman named—and here he flipped his notebook's black leather cover and read the name off—a woman named Elaine Mardell.

The doormen were never supposed to let anyone in unannounced, and they'd received special instructions recently as far as visitors for Miss Mardell were concerned. Even so, the doorman might not have called on the intercom if Motley had cautioned him against it. A blue uniform cuts through a lot of rules and regulations.

Any NYPD officer looking at him would have seen an Auxiliary Police uniform. If you knew what to look for it wasn't hard to spot the difference. His badge was a seven-pointed star instead of a shield, his shoulder patch was different, and of course he wasn't wearing a holstered firearm. But everything else was right, and there are so many different kinds of cops in the city, Transit Police and Housing Police and all, that he looked good enough to get by.

In any event, he asked the doorman to use the intercom. The attendant had to ring a few times—she was sound asleep at the time—but eventually she came to the phone and the doorman told her that a police officer was asking to speak to her. And handed the phone to Motley.

He probably changed the pitch of his voice. This wouldn't have been necessary. Her intercom distorted voices all by itself, but he might not have known that. Anyway, except for a couple of phone calls she hadn't heard his voice in twelve years, and her doorman had just announced that the caller was a cop, and she was fresh out of bed and barely had her eyes open.

He told her he had to ask her some questions regarding

an urgent matter. She asked for more details, and he let out that there had been a homicide earlier that evening, and that the victim was someone presumably known to her. She asked him who it was. He said it was a man named Matthew Scudder.

She told him to come up. The doorman pointed him to the elevator.

When she looked through the peephole she saw a cop. His brimmed cap concealed the shape of the top of his head. He was wearing a pair of drugstore glasses, and he had the notebook in front of him so that the shape of his chin was concealed. That was probably unnecessary, because she was expecting a cop, she'd just talked to him, for God's sake, and here he was in uniform. And she was in a state anyway because somebody was trying to kill her and the man she'd been counting on for protection was dead.

So she unlocked all her locks and let him in.

He was in her apartment for over two hours. He had the knife with which he'd killed Andy Echevarria, a spring-powered stiletto with a five-inch blade. He had Echevarria's nightstick. And of course he had his own two hands, with their long strong fingers.

He used them all on Elaine.

I haven't wanted to think too much about what he did, or the order in which he did it. I suspect there must have been intervals during which she was unconscious, and I'm sure he spent a fair part of the time talking to her, telling her just how strong and brilliant and resourceful he was. Maybe he quoted Nietzsche, or some other genius from the prison library.

When he walked out of there he left her sprawled on her living-room floor with her blood soaking into the white rug. It's possible he thought she was already dead. She would have been in shock, with her breathing imperceptibly shallow

275

and all her vital signs muted. She was still breathing, though, and her heart was still beating, but she would have died there on the floor if it hadn't been for the doorman.

He was a Brazilian, tall and heavyset, with a headful of glossy black hair and a belly that strained the buttons of his uniform. His name was Emilio Lopes. Something began bothering Lopes an hour or so after he showed Motley to the elevator. Finally he picked up the intercom and called up-stairs to make sure everything was all right.

He rang a few times and no one picked up. The ringing of the intercom may have prompted Motley to hurry his work and get out of there. When he did leave, striding hur-riedly through the lobby around seven o'clock, something in his manner set off Lopes's internal alarm. He rang through on the intercom again, and of course there was no answer. Then he remembered the sketch he'd been shown, the por-trait of the one man who most emphatically was not to be given access to Miss Mardell's apartment, and it struck him that the police uniform might have covered that very man. The more he thought about it, the surer he was.

He abandoned his post and went upstairs. He rang the bell and pounded on the door. He tried the door, and it was locked; Motley had pulled it shut. The police locks were un-engaged, as was the deadbolt, but the spring lock was enough to secure the door and it engaged automatically when you closed the door.

He turned away, intending to go back downstairs and root around for a passkey. Failing to find one, perhaps he would phone the local precinct. But then something made him turn back again and do what not one doorman in twenty would have done.

He drew back his foot and kicked the door. He kicked a second time, hard, and he was a big man and his legs were strong from carrying his bulk around all day long. They'd always been strong; when he was younger and lighter his legs had been strong from soccer.

The spring lock gave and the door flew open. He saw her on the rug and ran across the room to kneel at her side. Then he got up and crossed himself and picked up the phone and called 911. He knew it was too late but he did it anyway.

And that's what must have happened while I was drinking coffee at the Flame and walking uptown to Mother Goose, while I sat there listening to quiet jazz, while I paid out money to Brian and to Danny Boy. While I traded stories with Mick Ballou, and scared the rats away from their garbage feast, and breakfasted on scrapple in view of the Hudson. While I sat in a car on the other side of that river and watched the sun come up over the city.

I may have some of the details wrong, and I'm sure there are things that happened that I don't know about, and never will. But I think that's pretty close to the way it went down. In any case, I'm sure of one thing. It happened just the way it was supposed to happen. Andy Echevarria might argue the point, and so might Elaine, but just check with Marcus Aurelius. He'll explain the whole thing to you.

TWENTY-TWO

New York Hospital is at York and Sixty-eighth. My cab dropped me at the emergency-room entrance and the woman behind the desk determined that Elaine Mardell had come down from surgery and was in the intensive-care unit. She pointed to a floor plan of the building and showed me how to get to the ICU.

A nurse there told me they only allowed immediate family in the ICU. I said the patient didn't have any family, that I was probably as close to family as she had. She asked the nature of our relationship, and I said we were friends. She asked if we were intimate friends. Yes, I said. Intimate friends. She wrote my name on a card, and made a notation.

She showed me to a waiting room. There were several other people there, smoking, reading magazines, waiting for their loved ones to die. I leafed through a copy of *Sports Illustrated,* but none of the words registered. Every once in a while I turned the page out of force of habit.

After a while a doctor came into the waiting room and looked around and asked for me by name. I stood up and he

279

motioned me into the hallway. He had a very young face and a head of hair already thickly shot with gray.

He said, "This is a rough one. I don't know what to tell you."

"Is she going to live?"

"She was in surgery for almost four hours. I forget how many units of blood we gave her. She'd lost a lot of blood by the time we got her and there was a lot of internal bleeding. She's still bleeding now and still receiving transfusions." He had his hands clasped in front of his lab coat, and he was wringing them together. I don't think he was aware that he was doing it.

He said, "We had to remove her spleen. You can live without a spleen, there are thousands of people who manage. But she sustained considerable trauma to her entire system. Her renal function's off, her liver's damaged—"

He went on, cataloguing her injuries. I only caught about half of what he said and only understood a fraction of that. "She's intubated," he said, "and we've got her on a respirator. Her lungs failed. That happens sometimes, it's what they call Adult Respiratory Distress Syndrome. You see it sometimes in accident victims. Traffic accidents, I mean. The lungs quit."

There was more, too technical for me to understand. I asked how bad it was.

"Well, it's bad," he said, and he told me all the things that could go wrong.

I asked if I could see her.

"For a few minutes," he said. "She's completely sedated, and as I said we've got her hooked up to a respirator. It's doing the breathing for her." He led me toward a door at the far side of the ICU. "It may be a shock for you to see her like this," he said.

There were machines everywhere, and tubes strung all over the place. Dials flashed numbers, machines beeped and whirred, needles jumped. In the midst of it all she lay still as death, her skin waxy, her color awful.

I asked my first question again. "Is she going to live?"

He didn't answer, and when I looked up he was gone and I was alone with her. I wanted to reach out and touch her hand but I didn't know if that was allowed. I went on standing there, and a nurse came into the room and began doing something to one of the machines. She told me I could stay for a few more minutes. "You can talk to her," she said.

"Can she hear me?"

"I think there's a part of them that hears everything, even when they're deep in coma."

She went out, and I stayed for five or ten minutes. I talked some. I don't remember what I said.

The same nurse came in a second time to tell me she'd have to ask me to leave. I could wait in the waiting room and they would call me if there was any change in the patient's condition.

I asked what kind of change she expected.

She didn't answer either, not exactly. "There are just so many things that can go wrong," she said. "In a case like this. He hurt her so badly in so many ways. I'm telling you, this city we live in—"

It wasn't the city. The city didn't do it to her. It was one man, and he could have turned up anywhere.

Joe Durkin was in the waiting room. He got to his feet when I walked in. He hadn't shaved that morning, and he looked as though he'd slept in his clothes.

He asked how she was.

"Not good," I said.

"She say anything?"

"She's out cold and she's got tubes up her nose and down her throat. It limits her conversation."

281

"That's what they told me but I wanted to check. Be nice if she said it was Motley, but we don't need her to ID him. The doorman confirmed it was him."

He told me a little about what had happened. Echevarria's murder, and how Motley had gained access to the building on East Fifty-first.

He said, "We got an all-points out, we're using your sketch, putting it out all over the city. He killed an auxiliary cop. That damn well ought to turn the heat up."

Most cops think the auxiliaries are a joke, a bunch of starry-eyed buffs who come around once a week to play Dress-up. Then every once in a while one of them gets killed and is instantly inducted into that glorious band of blue-coated martyrs. There's nothing like death for lowering the barriers and opening the doors.

"He's killed nine people, minimum," I said. "Ten, if you count Elaine."

"Is she going to die?"

"Nobody's quite coming out and saying that yet. I think it's against their religion to speak that plainly. But if this were Las Vegas they'd take the game off the boards. That's how much of a chance they seem to think she has."

"I'm sorry, Matt."

I thought of a couple of things to say and left them unsaid. He cleared his throat and asked me if I had any kind of line on Motley's possible whereabouts.

"How would I know?"

"I thought you might have scouted something up."

"Me?" I looked at him. "How could I do that, Joe? He got an order of protection against me, remember? If I went looking for him and found him, somebody like you would have to show up and arrest me."

"Matt—"

"I'm sorry," I said. "Elaine's good people and I've known her a lot of years. I think it probably got to me, seeing her like that."

"Of course it did."

"And I'm running on empty. I was up all night, in fact I was just getting ready for bed when I caught a newscast."

"Where were you? Out looking for Motley?"

I shook my head. "Just sitting up all night telling old stories with Mickey Ballou."

"Why him, for Christ's sake?"

"He's a friend of mine."

"Funny friend for you to have."

"Oh, I don't know," I said. "When you think about it, all I am is a guy who used to be a cop a long time ago. And what I am now is a sort of a shady character with no visible means of support, so—"

"Cut it out."

I didn't say anything.

"I'm sorry, all right? I played it the way it looked as though it had to be played. You were on the job long enough to know how it works."

"Oh, I know how it works, all right."

"Well," he said. "If you think of anything, you'll let me know, right?"

"If I think of anything."

"Meantime, why don't you go home and get some sleep? You can't do her any good here. Go get some rest."

"Sure," I said.

We walked out of there together. They were paging some doctor on the intercom. I tried to remember the name of the one I'd talked to. He'd been wearing one of those plastic badges with his name on it, but it hadn't registered.

Outside the sun was shining, the air a little warmer than it had been lately. Durkin said he had a car parked around the corner and offered me a ride downtown. I said I'd take a cab, and he didn't press.

I didn't have to loid the door at 288 East Twenty-fifth. A woman was on her way out as I came in from the street. From the smile she gave me, I think she must have thought she recognized me. She held the door for me and I thanked her and went on in.

I walked the length of the hallway. The door to the rear courtyard was as I'd left it, with my toothpick wedged in place to keep it from locking. I pushed it shut behind me and stood at the back of the yard and looked up at his window.

I'd made two stops on the way downtown. As a result, I had a pair of standard-issue NYPD handcuffs in one of my topcoat pockets and a miniature tape recorder in the other. I found room in one of my pants pockets for the cuffs and put the recorder in a jacket pocket, where it shared space with Marcus Aurelius's *Meditations,* which I seemed as incapable of getting rid of as I was of reading. My other jacket pocket held the .38 Smith. I took off my topcoat, folded it, and set it down on top of one of the garbage cans. It was too bulky for what I had in mind.

No rats scuttled as I moved among the garbage cans. They were probably hidden away somewhere, sleeping off the effects of the long night. Maybe Motley was doing the same.

Making as little noise as possible, I positioned one garbage can beneath the fire escape and clambered on top of it. I straightened up and reached overhead to grasp the descending ladder. I pulled on it and nothing happened. I gave a yank and it creaked a little in protest, and there was a screech of metal scraping against metal as it lowered itself for my ascent.

I waited, but no heads emerged from the windows overlooking the courtyard. The noise was minimal, and most of the tenants were probably at work at that hour, while the night workers would be asleep.

Over on Second Avenue somebody leaned on a car horn, and another driver answered with a series of staccato beeps. I hauled myself upward, pulling myself hand over hand until I could get a foot onto the lowest rung. The Smith in my pocket clanged against the metal railing. I climbed onto the first horizontal walkway, leaned my weight against the brick wall of the building, and tried to catch my breath.

After a minute or two I was ready to go the rest of the way. I climbed up to the fourth floor and kept a low profile when I reached it, hunkering down on the metal parapet and peering over the windowsill.

The apartment was dark within. There were window gates to render the place burglar-proof, but they were unfastened, and the window itself was open a few inches at the bottom. I got up close to the window and looked in, first through the space at the bottom, then through the glass. I was looking into a small bedroom. There was an old-fashioned metal bedstead, a chest of drawers, a pair of milk crates set on end to serve as bedside tables. One of them held a phone, the other a digital clock-radio.

I sat perfectly still for what the clock-radio assured me was a full minute. The seconds ticked silently but visibly away, and not a sound issued from the apartment within. And the bed was empty, and unmade.

But it was the right apartment, and Brian's information was good. And he'd been back since his visit to Elaine's apartment.

A jacket with a New York Auxiliary Police shoulder patch hung from the knob of the closet door.

So he had been there. And he would be back. And I would be waiting for him.

Slowly, carefully, I gripped the window at the bottom and lifted. It went up readily and made hardly any sound at all. I turned to look around, on the chance that someone was watching all of this from a neighboring building. I could envision myself waiting in there for him, only to have to open the door to some cops dispatched by some public-spirited citizen.

But there was nobody paying any attention. I opened the window the rest of the way and stepped in over the sill.

Inside, the bedroom smelled like some animal's lair. It

was a woman's apartment, you could see that from the clothes in the closet and the clutter on the dresser top, but the scent was masculine and predatory. I couldn't tell how recently he'd been here but I could feel his presence in the room, and without even thinking about it I dipped into my jacket pocket and brought out the Smith. The butt was snug in my palm and my index finger found the trigger.

I walked over to the closet door and took Echevarria's jacket from the knob. I don't know what I expected to glean from it. I studied the shoulder patches, poked around in the pockets, put it back where I'd found it.

I moved to the dresser and looked at the articles on its top. Coins, subway tokens, earrings, ticket stubs, perfume bottles, cosmetics, lipstick tubes, hairpins. I wondered who Ms. Lepcourt might be, and how she'd gotten involved with James Leo Motley. And what the involvement might have cost her. I reached to open the top dresser drawer, then told myself to quit wasting time. I wasn't going to find her in there, or him either.

The apartment layout was typical for tenements of that sort, three small rooms in a row, with the doorways lined up. From the apartment's front door you could see straight through to the window I'd entered through, and for a moment I considered closing the window so that he wouldn't spot the change the minute he walked in. But that was silly, he wouldn't notice it, and as soon as he opened the door I'd be standing in front of him with a gun in my hand, so what possible difference could an open window make?

Even so, I took my time getting into position to wait for him. I passed through the middle room, and checked the little bathroom with its clawfooted tub. I hesitated at the archway leading to the front room. I stood there, holding the gun out in front of me like a torch, wishing it would cast a beam. Still, I could see well enough in the darkness. There was some light coming from the bedroom window behind me, and more light from windows in the living room that faced onto an airshaft between the building and the one next door.

I started into the room.

Something came out of nowhere and slammed down onto my arm a few inches above the wrist. My hand went dead and the .38 went flying.

Two hands fastened on my arm, one in the middle of the forearm, one near the shoulder. He heaved, and I went stumbling across the room as if launched by a catapult. I careened into a table, upending it, and my feet went out from under me. I reached out for support, grabbed at empty air, bounced off a wall and wound up on the floor.

He stood there and laughed at me.

"Come on," he said. "Get up."

He was wearing Echevarria's uniform, everything but the jacket. The shoes were wrong, though. The uniform code calls for plain black shoes with laces. He was wearing brown wing tips. He'd switched on a lamp; otherwise I wouldn't have noticed the color of his shoes.

I got to my feet. He just didn't look like a cop, I thought, and it wouldn't make any difference what shoes he wore. There are a lot of cops who don't look like cops either, not since they killed the height requirement and allowed facial hair, but he didn't look like any kind of cop, regular or auxiliary, old or new style.

He leaned in the doorway, flexing his fingers, looking at me with evident amusement. "So noisy," he said. "You're not much good at sneaking up on people, are you? Climbing on garbage cans and running up fire escapes at your age. I was worried about you, Scudder. I was afraid you might fall and break a bone."

I looked around, trying to track the Smith. I spotted it on the other side of the room, half-hidden under an armchair with a needlepoint back and seat. My eyes went from it to him, and his smile flashed.

"You dropped your gun," he said. He picked up Echevarria's nightstick and slapped his palm with it. My forearm was still numb where he'd struck it with the stick. It would hurt for days once the feeling returned.

If I lived that long.

"You could try to get it," he said, "but I don't think your odds are very good. I'm closer to it than you are, and I'm faster. I'd have you before you got the gun. All in all, I think you'd have a better chance of getting out the door."

He nodded toward the front door, and I obediently glanced over toward it. "It's unlocked," he said. "I had the chain on but I took it off when I heard you making a racket in the backyard. I was concerned that you might see the chain and know somebody was home. But I don't think you'd have noticed. Would you?"

"I don't know."

"I hung the jacket on the closet doorknob for your benefit, you know. Otherwise you might have gone into the apartment next door. You're such a buffoon, Scudder, that I've had to make things as easy for you as possible."

"You're making it all very easy," I said.

I looked within myself, scanning for fear, and I couldn't find any. I felt curiously calm. I wasn't afraid of him. I didn't have anything to be afraid of.

I shot a glance at the door, as if I was considering making a run for it. It was a ridiculous idea. It very likely wasn't unlocked, even if the chain was off, but even if it were he'd be on me before I could get the door open and myself through it.

Besides, I hadn't come here to run away from him. I'd come here to take him down.

"Go ahead," he said. "Let's see if you can get out the door."

"We'll go through it together, Motley. I'm taking you in."

He laughed at me. He raised the nightstick and pointed it at me and laughed again. "I think I'll stick this up your ass," he said. "Do you think you'll like it? Elaine liked it."

He was looking at me carefully, watching for a reaction. I didn't give him one.

"She's dead," he said. "She died hard, the poor darling. But I guess you know that."

"You're wrong about that one," I said.

"I was there, Scudder. I could report in detail, if I thought you could stand hearing it."

"You were there but you left early. The doorman got there in time and called an ambulance. She's in New York Hospital and doing fine. She already gave them a statement, and the doorman backed up her ID."

"You're lying."

I shook my head. "But I wouldn't worry about it," I said. "Remember what Nietzsche said. It'll just make you stronger."

"That's true."

"Unless it destroys you, of course."

"You're becoming tiresome, Scudder. I like you better when you're begging for mercy."

"Funny," I said. "I don't remember doing that."

"You'll be doing it soon."

"I don't think so. I think you've had your run and now you're finished. You were very careful early on. Lately you've been getting sloppy. You're ready for it to end, and you know how things always end for you. You wind up losing."

"I'll tape your mouth," he said, "so nobody can hear the screams."

"You're done," I said. "You lost the momentum when you left Elaine alive. You had her for two hours and you couldn't even manage to make sure she was dead when you left. Now all you can do is stand there and make threats, and threats don't mean much when the person you threaten isn't afraid of you. You have to back them up, and you can't do that anymore."

I turned away, as if to show contempt for him. He stood there, getting ready to do something about it, and I reached down for a bronze Chinese incense burner. It was about the size of a half-grapefruit and it had been on top of the table until I'd come crashing into it.

I picked it up and threw it at him, and I went in under it.

This time he didn't make the mistake of trying to catch what I tossed his way. He swung out a hand, knocking the incense burner aside, then moved forward to meet my charge. I feinted at his head, ducked in and hammered punches at his middle. There was no softness there, nothing but ridged muscles. He swung a fist that caught me on the side of the head. It was a glancing blow and it didn't do much. I ducked the next punch he threw, tucked my chin into my chest and hit him just below the navel, then swung a knee up at his crotch.

He pivoted, blocking with his hip. He grabbed at my shoulder and his fingers dug in. His grip was as strong as ever but he wasn't on a pressure point now and the pain was nothing I couldn't stand.

I hit him again in the gut. He tensed in response, and I bulled forward, shoving him back against the wall. He rained blows on my shoulders and the top of my head, but he was better at pressing and probing and squeezing than he was at infighting. I tried for his groin again, and when he moved to protect himself I stomped down on his instep. That hurt him, and I pressed the advantage and did it again, raking his shin with the heel of my shoe, stomping down hard on his foot, trying to break a couple of its small bones.

His hands moved, one settling on my upper arm, the other fastening on the back of my neck. He let his fingers look for hot spots now and he hadn't lost his touch. His thumb dug in behind my ear and the pain came in Technicolor.

But it was somehow different. It was there, God knows, and it could not have been more intense, but this time I was able to feel it without feeling it. I was aware of it but unaffected by it. Something enabled me to allow it to pass through me and leave me whole.

He shifted his grip, both of his hands on my neck now, the thumbs at the base of my ears, the fingers reaching to circle my throat. Maybe the pain wouldn't stop me, but if he shut off my air or blocked the flow of blood through the carotid I'd be just as dead as if I died in agony.

I went for his foot again. His grip loosened a little, and I crouched lower. He loomed over me, his hands finding their grip again, and I gathered my legs under me and thrust straight up, leading with the top of my head, using it as a battering ram.

Some things don't change. He still had fingers like eagle's talons, the strongest I'd ever encountered. And, thank God, he still had a glass jaw.

I butted him a couple of times, but I think the first one was all it took. When I let go of him and took a step back he slid down the wall like a dead man. His long jaw was slack and saliva trailed from one corner of his mouth.

I dragged him out into the middle of the room and cuffed him. I used the cuffs I'd just bought to fasten his hands behind his back, and I used Echevarria's set, hanging from his belt in their leather case, to shackle his ankles together. I got my little tape recorder out of my pocket and made sure it still worked, then cued a cassette so I could start recording when he came to.

Then I sat back and gave myself time to catch my breath. I started thinking about what would happen now. If Elaine lived, her testimony ought to be enough to ensure conviction. If she died—

I called New York Hospital and they put me through to the ICU. Her condition was critical, they told me. That was all I could get from them over the phone.

But she was still alive.

If she died, the doorman could identify Motley. And, once the department put its full resources into the case, any of a number of witnesses might turn up to put him on the scene when Echevarria got stabbed, when Elizabeth Scudder was butchered, when Toni Cleary went out the window. No end of physical evidence might come to light if enough trained personnel looked in the right places for it. And a full-scale investigation in New York would almost certainly tip the balance in Massillon, where Tom Havlicek's chief would okay reopening the Sturdevant case. And Ohio was a death penalty state, wasn't it?

Still, a confession would make a big difference. All I had to do was wait until he came to and get him talking. No question the bastard liked to talk.

He was lying facedown, his hands cuffed behind him. I rolled him over onto his back and lifted an eyelid with my thumb. His eye was rolled way back up into its socket, with only the white part showing. He was out cold, and looked as though he'd be out for a while.

I went and got the Smith. I looked at it and I looked at him. I thought of everything he'd done and I looked within myself, trying to summon up the hate I felt for him. But it didn't seem to be there. At least it wasn't anywhere that I could find it.

And that had been oddly true a few minutes ago, when he had been far removed from the inert bundle in the middle of the floor. I had been very literally fighting for my life, and all the same I'd been oddly calm, and fresh out of hate and anger. I hadn't hated him then. I didn't seem to hate him now.

I put the gun to his temple and let my finger test the

tension in the trigger. I withdrew my finger from the trigger and put the gun down on the floor.

I thought it all over. I must have spent several minutes running it through my mind. Then I took a breath deep enough to hurt my ribs, and then I let it all out, and then I picked up the Smith and broke it open.

I unloaded all six chambers. I got out my handkerchief and wiped off the bullets and the gun itself, cleaning every surface that might have held a print. Then I made sure he wasn't playing possum before removing the cuffs from his wrists. I took hold of his fingers and touched them to the bullets, then loaded them back into the gun.

I put the gun down and took hold of him under the arms. I dragged him a few yards, then hauled him onto his feet and dropped him in the needlepoint chair. He started to slide back onto the floor but I pulled him up into a seated position and balanced him there. I went back for the Smith, wiped it again with the handkerchief, and fitted it into his right hand. I slipped his finger inside the trigger guard. With my own left hand I worked his jaw to get his mouth open, and then I got the short barrel of the little revolver between his teeth.

I made sure I had the angle right. Cops eat their guns all the time, it's their favorite single method of committing suicide, and sometimes they miss, sometimes the bullet goes on through without doing mortal damage. I wanted to do this properly, and I was only going to get one chance. I wanted the bullet to go right up through the roof of the mouth and into the brain.

When I had the gun the way I wanted it, I just stayed in position for a moment. There was something I seemed to want to say, but whom was I going to say it to?

I thought, Say it to him. And I remembered what the ICU nurse had told me. According to her, patients in coma understood what was said to them.

I said, "I'm not sure this is a good idea. But suppose you got out again. Suppose your lawyer pulled off some kind of half-assed insanity defense. Or suppose you went away for life and escaped. How can I take that kind of chance?"

I paused for a moment, then shook my head. "I'm not even sure that's it. I just don't want you to be alive anymore.

"And I want to be the one who sees to it, and that's how all this shit started in the first place, isn't it? I had to play God and frame you for attempted murder. What would have happened if I'd just let things take their course back then? Would it have made a difference?"

I waited, as if he might answer. Then I said, "And here I am playing God again. I know better and I'm doing it anyway."

That was all I said. I stayed there at his side, down on one knee, the gun in his mouth, his finger on the trigger, my finger on his. I don't know how long I waited, or what I was waiting for.

Eventually his breathing changed slightly and he started to stir. My finger moved, and so did his, and that was that.

TWENTY-THREE

I set the stage before I left. I got Echevarria's cuffs loose from Motley's ankles and returned them to the case on his belt. I righted the table that had gotten upended earlier and straightened out other articles disturbed during our struggle. I went around the apartment, handkerchief in hand, and removed my prints from every surface where I might have left them.

While I was doing this, I picked up a lipstick tube from the dresser in the bedroom and used it to leave a last message on the living-room wall. In block caps three inches tall I printed, IT HAS TO END. I MAKE MY PEACE WITH GOD. SORRY I KILL SO MANY. You couldn't prove it was his writing, but I couldn't see how you could prove that it wasn't. Just to keep it neat I capped the lipstick tube, got his prints on it, and tucked it into his shirt pocket.

I fastened the chain lock on the apartment's front door and left the same way I'd come in, via the window. This time I drew it all the way shut after me. I went down the fire escape, lowered the ladder, descended it. Someone had moved the garbage can to its original position, so I had to drop the last few feet, but that was easy enough.

Someone had also removed my topcoat. I thought at first someone had walked off with it, but something made me lift the lid of one of the garbage cans and there it was, reposing under a layer of eggshells and orange peels. The person who'd put it there had evidently assumed it had been discarded, and decided further that it wasn't worth rescuing. It had been a perfectly respectable coat, or at least I'd thought so, but now I figured it was time to buy myself a new one.

I thought the same conscientious tenant who'd tossed my topcoat might have removed my toothpick from the lock, but it was still in place and all I had to do was draw the door open. I retrieved the toothpick and let the door lock behind me, went on out through the front of the building, and walked over to First Avenue where I caught a cab headed uptown. I got out at the hospital's main entrance and went directly to the ICU. The nurse said Elaine's condition was unchanged but wouldn't let me go in to see her. I sat down in the waiting room and tried to look at a magazine.

I would have liked to pray but I couldn't think how to go about it. AA meetings generally close with either the Lord's Prayer or the serenity prayer, but neither seemed especially appropriate at the moment, and giving thanks for everything just as it was felt like a joke, and not a very tasteful one. In the course of things I did say some prayers, even including that one, but I don't really think anyone was listening.

Every now and then I would go to the desk, only to be told that nothing had changed and that she couldn't have anyone in the room with her just yet. Then I'd go back to the waiting room and wait some more. I dozed off in my chair a couple of times but never got deeper than a sort of waking dream state.

Around five in the afternoon I got hungry, which wasn't too surprising given that I hadn't had anything since Mick and I ate breakfast. I got some change and bought coffee and sandwiches from machines in the lobby. I couldn't manage more than half a sandwich, but the coffee was good. It wasn't good coffee, not by any stretch of the imagination, but it was good to get it inside me.

Two hours after that a nurse came in with a grave expression on her pale face. "Maybe you'd better see her now," she said.

On the way I asked her what she meant by that. She said it looked as though they were losing her.

I went in and stood at her bedside. She didn't look any better or any worse than she had before. I picked up her hand and held it and waited for her to die.

"He's dead," I told her. There were nurses around but I don't think any of them could hear me. They were too busy to listen. Anyway, I didn't care what they heard. "I killed him," I told her. "You don't ever have to worry about him again."

I suppose you can believe people in comas hear what's said to them. You can believe God hears prayers, too, if that's what you want. Whatever makes you happy.

"Don't go anywhere," I told her. "Don't die, baby. Please don't die."

I must have been with her for half an hour before one of the nurses told me to return to the waiting room. A few hours after that another nurse came in and talked some about Elaine's medical condition. I don't remember what she said and didn't understand much of it at the time, but the gist of it was that she had passed a crisis, but that an infinite number of crises lay ahead of her. She could develop pneumonia, she could throw an embolism, she could go into liver or kidney failure—there were so many ways she could die that it seemed impossible for her to dodge them all.

"You might as well go home," she said. "There's nothing

you can do, and we have your number, we'll call you if anything happens."

I went home and slept. In the morning I called and was
told that her condition was about the same. I showered and
shaved and got dressed and went over there. I was there all
morning and part of the afternoon, and then I rode a
crosstown bus through the park and went to Toni's memorial
service at Roosevelt.

It was all right. It was like a meeting, really, except that
everybody who spoke said something about Toni. I talked
briefly about our trek out to Richmond Hill and back, and
mentioned some of the funny things Toni had said in her
talk.

It bothered me that everybody thought she'd killed herself, but I didn't know what to do about that. I would have
liked to tell her relatives in particular what the real circumstances had been. Her family was Catholic, and it might have
mattered to them. But I couldn't think how to handle it.

Afterward I went out for coffee with Jim Faber, and then
I went back to the hospital.

I was there a lot during the next week. A couple of times
I was on the verge of making an anonymous call to 911 to
tip them off about the dead body at 288 East Twenty-fifth
Street. As soon as Motley's corpse was discovered, I could
phone Anita and tell her she could stop worrying. I couldn't
reach Jan, but sooner or later she would reach me, and I
wanted to be able to say it was all right to come home. If I
said as much to either of them ahead of schedule, I might
someday be called upon to explain myself.

What kept me from calling 911 was the knowledge that
all such calls were taped, and that I could be identified as the
caller through voiceprint comparison. I didn't think anyone
would ever check, but why leave the possibility open? At first
I'd thought Ms. Lepcourt would come home to her apartment and discover the body, but when that didn't happen

over the weekend I had to consider the possibility that she'd never be coming home.

That just meant I had a couple more days to wait. On Tuesday afternoon a neighbor finally realized that the odor she was smelling was not a dead rat in the wall, and that it wasn't going to go away of its own accord. She called the police, they broke the door down, and that was that.

On Thursday, almost a week after Motley left her bleeding on her rug, a resident internist told me he thought Elaine was going to make it.

"I never thought she would," he said. "There were so many things that kept threatening to go wrong. The stress she underwent throughout was enormous. I was afraid her heart might fail, but it turns out she has a real good heart."

I could have told him that.

A little later, around the time she came home from the hospital, I had dinner with Joe Durkin at the Slate. He said it was on him and I didn't argue. He downed a couple of martinis to start, and he told me how neatly Motley's suicide had closed out a batch of files. They were hanging Andrew Echevarria and Elizabeth Scudder on him, and there was an unofficial understanding that he'd caused the deaths of Antoinette Cleary and Michael Fitzroy, the young man Toni'd landed on. They also figured him as the probable killer of one Suzanne Lepcourt, who'd floated to the surface of the East River earlier that week. It was hard to tell what had caused her death—as a matter of fact, without dental records it would have been next to impossible to tell who she was, let alone what had killed her. But there wasn't much doubt that she'd died as the result of foul play, or that the foul player was Motley.

"Decent of him to kill himself," Durkin said. "Since nobody seemed capable of doing it for him. He saved us a lot of aggravation."

"You had a good case against him."

"Oh, we would have put him away," he said. "I've got no doubts of that. Still, this makes it simpler all around. Did I tell you there was a note?"

"On the wall, you said. In lipstick."

"Right. I'm surprised he didn't use the mirror. I bet the landlord wishes he had. It's a lot easier scraping it off a mirror than covering it with paint. There's a mirror on the wall next to the door, too. You must have noticed it."

"I was never in the apartment, Joe."

"Oh, of course. I forgot." He gave me a knowing look. "Anyway," he said, "offing himself was the first decent thing the bastard ever did. You wouldn't figure a guy like him to do it, would you?"

"Oh, I don't know," I said. "Sometimes a man will have that one moment of clarity, when all the illusions fall away and he sees clearly for the first time."

"That moment of clarity, huh?"

"It happens."

"Well," he said, picking up his drink, "I don't know about you, but whenever I feel a moment of clarity coming on, I just reach out for one of these and let the clouds roll in."

"That's probably wise," I said.

Of course he was hoping I'd tell him what happened on Twenty-fifth Street. He had his suspicions and he wanted me to confirm them. If that's what he wants, he's going to have a long wait.

I've told two people. I told Elaine. In a sense I'd already told her in Intensive Care, but if a part of your mind really does hear what's said at such times, it doesn't tell the rest of your mind later on. I let her think Motley had killed himself until she was home from the hospital. Then, the same day I brought her her Christmas present, I told her what really happened.

"Good," she said. "Thank God. And thank you. And thank you for telling me."

"I don't see how I could not tell you. I don't know if I'm glad I did it, though."

"Why not?"

I told her how my framing him had set it all in motion in the first place, and how I'd done the same thing all over, playing God again.

"Honey," she said, "that's crap. He would have come back at us anyway. This way it took him twelve years instead of a couple of months. And killing the son of a bitch pretty much guarantees he won't cause any more trouble. Not in this world, anyway, and that's the only world I'm going to worry about right now."

Around the middle of January Mick and I had a long night together, but after we closed the bar we didn't go to the butchers' mass. It had snowed a few days earlier, and he wanted to show me how pretty his place upstate looked with snow covering the hills. We drove up there and I stayed over and rode back with him the following afternoon. It was peaceful up there, and as beautiful as he'd said it was.

On the way up I told him how Motley's life had ended. It didn't come as a surprise to him. After all, he knew I had the address, and he knew too that I'd had to handle my business with Motley on my own.

I called Tom Havlicek after Motley's body was discovered, but I didn't give him anything beyond the official version. At that point, of course, they reopened the case in Massillon—now that it didn't make any difference. It did clear Sturdevant's name, however, which I suppose was of value to his friends and relatives. At the same time it sullied Connie's, because the local paper came up with the fact that she'd been a hooker years back and shared this tidbit with their readers.

301

Tom said I ought to come out and he'd take me hunting, and I said that really sounded nice, but I think we both knew how unlikely I was to take him up on it. He called the other day when the Bengals got beaten in the Super Bowl and said he might be getting down to New York one of these days. I told him to make damn sure he gets in touch with me when he does, and he said I could count on it, that he'd make a point of it. And perhaps he will.

I haven't told Jim Faber yet.

We have dinner at least once a week, and I've come close to telling him a couple of times. I suppose I'll get around to it one of these days. I'm not sure what's stopped me so far. Maybe I'm afraid of his disapproval, or that he'll do what he so often does and put me face-to-face with my own conscience, a sleeping dog I let lie as much as I possibly can.

Oh, I'll get it off my chest sooner or later. After a particularly meaningful meeting, say, when I'm just overflowing with enough spirituality to drown a saint in.

But in the meantime the only people I've told are a career criminal and a call girl, and they seem to be the two people in the world to whom I'm closest. I don't doubt that says something about them, and I should think it would say even more about me.

It's been a cold winter, and they say we've got a lot more of the same coming. It's hard on the street people, and a couple of them died last week when it went down below zero. But for most of us it's not that bad. You just dress warm and walk through it, that's all.